The solicitor's words still rang in his ears: "You are not divorced, my lord."

How could it *be*? For six years, all the time he'd been abroad, he'd assumed she had become Lady Edmonds, he'd forced himself to think of his Priss as another man's wife...

And now this...

A low moan escaped from Captain Alec Tyrrell's handsome throat.

A REGENCY CHARADE
A Regency Love Story by
ELIZABETH MANSFIELD

Elizabeth Mansfield

A Regency Charade

A JOVE BOOK

A REGENCY CHARADE

A Jove Book / published by arrangement with
the author

PRINTING HISTORY
Berkley edition / March 1981
Jove edition / February 1987

ISBN: 0-515-08916-8

Jove Books are published by The Berkley Publishing Group,
200 Madison Avenue, New York, NY 10016.
The words "A JOVE BOOK" and the "J" with sunburst
are trademarks belonging to Jove Publications, Inc.

PRINTED IN THE UNITED STATES OF AMERICA

Prologue

Although the jubilation after Waterloo had long since subsided, and the sight of a returning soldier on the streets of London no longer caused a commotion among the passers-by, the appearance of the tall, imposing uniformed officer standing at the top of the stone steps before number 17, Chancery Lane, drew the eyes of the people on the street. Their attention was captured not by the splendor of the officer's dress uniform, with its scarlet, frogged coat and gilt epaulettes, nor by the strong features of the man himself under the impressive regimental shako, but by something in his stance which seemed out of keeping with the dignity of his appearance. He seemed bemused, perturbed, even muddled. His eyes peered down at the street in a blank, unseeing stare, and when he started down the stairs, his step was decidedly unsteady. " 'E's lushy," sneered one of the oglers to his companion. The other shook his head in disgusted agreement as they walked off.

The officer reached the bottom step, but, having taken no notice of the fact that he'd reached street level, stumbled and lost his balance, falling awkwardly against a passing gentleman who had been watching his unsteady descent. The gentleman, somewhat past middle age, was quite robust and sturdy, and he was able, by the quick extending of a supporting arm, to keep the soldier from falling on his face. Helping him to steady himself, the gentleman remarked with a wide grin, "Easy, old chap. Ye don't want the world to know ye've drunk London dry in one day!"

The officer blinked at him in embarrassed confusion. "I do beg your pardon, sir. I wasn't looking—"

"Still celebratin' the vict'ry, are ye?" the elderly gentleman inquired with an indulgent laugh.

"What? Oh . . . I see." A small smile lit the officer's face. "No, I'm not drunk," he assured the older man. "Just . . . absent-minded." His smile faded and his mouth set in a straight line. "Although I could use a dram of spirits quite well at this moment."

The older man eyed him shrewdly. There was nothing in the fellow's manner or speech which suggested an overindulgence in liquor. In fact, now that the officer had been shaken into attention, even his stance was sober and soldierly. The pallor that still remained in his cheeks and the confused look that still lingered at the back of his eyes now indicated to the perspicacious observer that the poor fellow had more likely been served a shocking blow than a large brandy. "Do ye truly crave a drink?" the older man asked sympathetically. "Well, Captain—you *are* a Captain, ain't ye?—it just happens that I'm on my way to wet my whistle. I'd be honored to have yer company."

The officer, who had been adjusting his shako to the proper angle, looked at his companion with another of his quick smiles. "It would be my pleasure, sir. Lead the way."

By the time the two arrived at the Grape and Barrel, they were arm-in-arm and addressing each other by name. Captain Alexander Tyrrell had revealed to Mr. Isaiah Hornbeck that he'd just returned from the continent and had indeed been a participant in the battle of Waterloo. Mr. Hornbeck, on his part, had told the Captain that he was the owner of a successful cotton mill located near Birmingham ("It wouldn't surprise me at all," he'd chortled proudly, "if ye wasn't wearin' some of my cotton on yer person at this very moment.") and had come to London on mill business.

But as he chattered on, Mr. Hornbeck was aware that

Captain Tyrrell's inner tension had not eased. The older man, despite his blunt manners, was gifted with an innate sensitivity and a keen intelligence, and he took note of the fact that the Captain's eyes had not lost their look of almost blind confusion. Keeping up a stream of inconsequential banter, he led the officer to an empty table and ordered a bottle of the best brandy the house could offer. Then, uttering a hearty "Cheers!" he handed a large glass to the troubled soldier, lapsed into silence and let the Captain think his own thoughts.

Captain Tyrrell's thoughts were in such an agonized muddle that one could hardly call the turmoil in his brain "thinking" at all. He took a quick, generous swig of the brandy, leaned back in his chair and closed his eyes. Perhaps the liquor, as it released its warmth into his blood, would ease the shock his solicitor had just dealt him, and he could begin to think sensibly.

His solicitor's words still rang in his ears: "We're sorry to have to tell you, my lord, that you are still married." The Captain shuddered. *Still married*? How could it *be*? For six years, all the while he'd been abroad, he had assumed that he was free, that the ties between him and his wife had been severed . . . that he would never again have to lay eyes on Priss. No, he mustn't think of her as Priss. He'd assumed that she had become Lady Edmonds; he'd trained himself to think of her that way. But his solicitor had referred to her repeatedly as Lady *Braeburn*. Good God, Lady Braeburn—she still used *his name*! She was still his wife! A little moan escaped from his throat.

"Are ye feelin' a bit out o' frame, Captain?" Mr. Hornbeck asked in concern.

Captain Tyrrell opened his eyes and tried to smile reassuringly. "No, not at all. I'm quite all right. I'm just . . . mulling over some news I learned from my solicitor."

"Oh, is that it?" Mr. Hornbeck nodded knowingly. "Solicitors do have a way o' dimmin' down the sunshine." He reached for the bottle. "Here, have another. Ye look as though ye need it."

The Captain tossed down a second drink and stared absently into the empty glass. Mr. Hornbeck was quite right, he thought morosely. His solicitor certainly *had* taken the sunshine out of his day. "We're sorry to have to tell you, my lord," Mr. Newkirk had said quite distinctly, "that you are still married." At least Newkirk had had the sense not to look him in the eye as he'd said it. He'd fussed over his papers as nervously as a hungry chicken pecking through the weeds for a crumb, muttering something about having "tried our best." (The damned fellow worked in his office without a single assistant, yet he always referred to himself as "we.") Tyrrell had felt his blood freeze in his veins at the words.

"What do you *mean*?" he'd demanded. "I left you with *strict instructions*—!"

"We know, my lord," the solicitor had muttered miserably. "But as we told you before you left, a divorce would be quite difficult and expensive to obtain—"

"And I told *you*, Newkirk, that I didn't give a *hang* about the expense!" he'd said furiously.

"Yes, we quite understood that. But as we explained to you at the time, the aftereffects would be most painful. A blot on your name . . . social ostracism for her ladyship . . . your future blighted . . ."

"Yes, yes, I remember. But didn't you say you'd apply for a decree of nullity or some such legal bibble-babble?"

Mr. Newkirk had nodded guiltily and lowered his eyes again. "Just so, my lord . . . a decree *a vinculo matrimonii*, which voids the marriage and permits both parties to remarry freely. But you see, it is very difficult to find acceptable grounds—"

The Captain had jumped to his feet impatiently. "But . . . you assured me that you'd manage it!" he cried.

Mr. Newkirk had bit his underlip unhappily. "Yes, my lord, but her ladyship . . ."

"What about her ladyship?"

"She begged us to . . . to postpone the action until she could speak to you."

Tyrrell had put his hand to his throbbing forehead in bewilderment. "See here, Newkirk, this makes no sense. You *knew* she'd have no opportunity to speak to me . . . that I'd left immediately for Spain. It was you, yourself, who'd procured my commission."

"Her ladyship knew you'd departed. She meant . . . after the war . . ." the lawyer had mumbled.

"*After the war*? Didn't you warn her it might take years? I thought . . . didn't she express to you her desire to wed Blake Edmonds?"

"No, my lord, she did not."

Tyrrell had stared at the solicitor in utter bafflement. Feeling distinctly like someone who's had the ground pulled from under him, he'd sunk into the nearest chair. "Then . . . she *didn't* marry him. But . . . *why*?"

"I'm sure we couldn't say, my lord."

Captain Tyrrell had brooded darkly for a long moment over the strange ways of women. Then he'd looked up at his solicitor angrily. "Then, hang it, Newkirk, why didn't you *tell* me?"

The color in Mr. Newkirk's cheeks heightened in a guilty flush. "Lady Braeburn urged us . . . quite persuasively . . . not to do so. She said she didn't want you to be disturbed while you were facing enemy bullets."

The Captain had jumped to his feet in renewed fury. "Well, damn it, Newkirk, I'm not facing enemy bullets now! So you can take yourself out from behind that desk and procure that decree! Do you hear me, man?"

"Yes, my lord," the solicitor had said with a troubled but steady gaze, "but it will be necessary to have a document stating that Lady Braeburn had entered into a valid pre-contract with Sir Blake Edmonds prior to your nuptials. Those are the only grounds on which we can base our case for nullity."

The Captain had glared at him and marched to the door. "Then go ahead and get it."

"You don't quite understand, my lord," the poor

solicitor had called after him. "She will not sign such a document at *our* request."

Tyrrell had turned back to him in surprise. "What—?"

"I'm very much afraid, my lord, that *you'll* have to get it from the lady *yourself*."

Yes, that was the very nub of the problem, the Captain thought with a deep sigh as he reached for another drink. Six long years had passed since he'd last laid eyes on her. Fortunately, time and the war had matured and hardened him. He was certain he had recovered from the wound she'd dealt him. But he had not counted on the necessity of facing her again, of talking with her about the very matters which had once caused him such bitter pain. He was not at all sure that the thin veneer with which he'd covered over the injury would be able to withstand such an encounter. He groaned again and reached for the bottle.

"Are ye certain, Captain, that ye're quite well?" Hornbeck asked solicitously.

Captain Tyrrell was beginning to feel the effects of the brandy and had difficulty in focusing on the kind gentleman who'd befriended him. "I'm 's fine 's a married man c'n be," he said thickly.

Hornbeck laughed. "Nothin' wrong with that. I was a married man myself 'til my Sarah died, and I never had no regrets."

"Ah, but you haven't been thinking of yourself 's a *bachelor* for six years," Captain Tyrrell said, wagging an unsteady finger in front of Hornbeck's nose.

"I don't see how ye can think o' yerself as a bachelor if ye're a married man," Hornbeck pointed out sensibly. "I think the brandy's beginnin' to muddle you."

"Not so muddled tha' I don't know I'm in a fix," Tyrrell insisted gloomily, reaching for the nearly empty bottle.

"Perhaps ye've had enough," Mr. Hornbeck suggested gently, a slightly worried frown appearing at the corners of his mouth.

"More 'n enough," Captain Tyrrell agreed with a

nod, "but I don' feel much better. May as well get foxed. No place t' go now. *She's* still livin' in m' house!"

"Well, of course she is. So why don't you go home to her? Kiss and make up. Ye'll feel much better fer it, I promise ye. I was married more 'n thirty years, so there's not much about marriage that I don't know."

The Captain gave a mirthless laugh. "Y' speak like a babe. An innocent babe. Do y' know John Donne?"

Mr. Hornbeck blinked. "No. Can't say I've met the gentleman. In the service with ye, was he?"

"A poet, Mr. Hornbeck. A true poet. An' do y' know what he said? Lis'n:

> *If thou beest born to strange sights,*
> *Things invisible to see,*
> *Ride ten thousand days and nights,*
> *Til age snow white hairs on thee.*
> *Thou, when thou return'st, wilt tell me*
> *All strange wonders that befell thee,*
> *And swear*
> *Nowhere*
> *Lives a woman true, and fair.*"

Mr. Hornbeck shook his head admiringly. "Very fine words, those. And ye declaim 'em like an orator, damn if ye don't. But it was a bitter man that wrote 'em. Ye can't believe—"

"But I do, Mr. Hornbeck, I do," the Captain insisted, emptying the last of the brandy into his glass.

"Nay, lad, it's not right. You young fellows always have yer heads in the clouds. Too idealistic by half. Bound to stub yer toes on a few realities before very long. But ye'll get over it in time, see if ye don't."

Tyrrell frowned at him in besotted earnestness. "Never. Never get over it, Mr. Hornbeck. But . . . I'm . . . too sleepy t' argue with . . ." The soldier's eyes closed waveringly, and his head fell forward on his arms.

Mr. Hornbeck looked at the Captain with indulgent

affection. "Come on, Captain, give us an arm. Over my shoulder like a good lad, eh? I'll call a hackney and get ye home."

"Not home," the soldier murmured dizzily. "Can't go there . . . *she's* there."

"O' course she is," Mr. Hornbeck said heartily, pulling the Captain to his feet and propelling him firmly toward the door. "Best thing in the world fer ye. Good night's sleep in yer own bed."

"No . . . *no!* M' hotel! Fenton's . . ."

"Yes, yes, old fellow. Just leave everything to me."

The Captain nodded drunkenly. "Good man, Hornbeck. Good old fellow. Verit-able port . . . in a storm. But who would ha' b'lieved . . .? Still *married!* What'm I to do, Hornbeck, eh? What 'm I to do?"

Chapter One

In 1809 Alexander Tyrrell, the grandson and heir of the
Earl of Braeburn, became twenty-one, received an advanced degree with honors from Oxford University and
wondered what on earth he was to do with the rest of his
life. It seemed to him that most of his days had been
spent in cloistered security behind the walls of the
university. The outside world was a vast unknown, and
although it seemed to hold out to him the promise of all
sorts of romantic adventures, he felt totally unprepared
to deal with the problem of how to go about seeking
them. A solid grounding in Greek aesthetics, Latin
verses and English philosophy, he realized, was not
proper preparation for making one's way in the real
world. Of course, one could always reject the "real
world" and live the life of a scholar, cloistered in the
university forever. Many of his friends had predicted
that this would be the course of his life. But Alec Tyrrell
had no intention of living a cloistered life.

On his last day at Oxford, he looked around his
familiar room with a sigh. All his personal possessions
were packed in one small portmanteau. Under his
academic robes, he was wearing a shabby coat and well-
worn breeches that had not been stylish even in their
better days. He studied his reflection in the faded
looking glass of his dressing room with a worried frown.
It occurred to him that, when he divested himself of his
academic robes, he would not cut a very impressive
figure. Tall, thin, bookish and painfully shy, he could

see nothing in his appearance to suggest that he was an heir to a wealthy earldom, or even that he was a person worthy of attention.

In this conclusion he was too self-deprecatory and quite mistaken. Although he was indeed youthfully lanky, his face had already taken on a look of strength and character. His abundant, dark hair fell over his forehead with what most young women would have considered a most attractive carelessness, his hazel eyes glinted with intelligence and humor, his mouth was kind and his chin firm. He had a circle of close friends who spoke of him in the most glowing of terms as a superior scholar, a quick wit, a modest but effective debater and a man of honor. His closest friend and classmate, Garvin Danforth, would have added that he was a loyal and affectionate friend and a fellow of deep and private feelings.

None of these traits, however, was noticeable in the reflection in the glass. Was there a young lady in all the world, he wondered, who would look twice at such a scarecrow? Like most young men, he had dreams of becoming a leader of men and a charmer of women. But those dreams seemed far from realization if that gawky, pale-faced stringbean of a fellow who looked back at him from the mirror was his true self.

Then and there he decided to seek out his grandfather. As always when he needed support and practical wisdom, he turned to the old Earl. As soon as the graduation ceremonies had been concluded and he'd escaped from the affectionate embraces of Garvin Danforth and the rest of his friends, he picked up his portmanteau and made his way home to Braeburn in Derbyshire. It was there that the aging Earl, his only living relative, spent his days.

The Earl had, over the years, lost everyone dear to him—his wife and both his sons. The only one left was his grandson, and the old man doted on the boy. For a few years after Alec's father had died, the Earl had taken up residence at Tyrrell House in London and tried to forget his grief by indulging in gambling. But he was not a gamester at heart, and, after a time, he'd returned to Braeburn, the only residue of his venture into gambling being a love for whist and a tendency to pepper his remarks with the expression "I'll lay odds on that."

Alec had known no other parent for so many years that he'd learned to make most of his decisions on his own. But when severely pressed, he found that his grandfather's advice was most helpful and comforting. If anyone in the world would be able to advise Alec about how to proceed with his life, that person was the old Earl.

But, as it turned out, Alec never managed to ask his grandfather the question about his future, for the Earl had an answer for him before he even asked. They had exchanged warm greetings and had just sat down to their first dinner together in many months when the Earl announced without preamble that he'd arranged for Alec to marry.

The news struck Alec with a blow. In all his many plans for the future, he had not thought of marriage. How could he *marry* anyone? He was not at all ready for it. "Grandfather, you can't mean it!" he objected, horrified. "I don't even know how to *speak* to a lady!"

The old Earl chuckled. "You'll have no trouble speaking to *this* one, I'll lay odds on that! You and she grew up together."

Alec whitened. "You don't mean . . . *Priss*!"

"Who else?"

"I . . . I don't believe you. This is some sort of . . . of joke. Priss wouldn't have me!"

The glee in the Earl's eyes faded, and his cheeks grew mottled with anger. "What do you *mean*, wouldn't have you? Of *course* she'll have you. You're going to be the Earl of Braeburn!"

"What has *that* to say to the matter? Do you expect me to *buy* her with the promise of a title?" Alec asked in disgust, pushing away his plate.

"You don't have to do anything. It's all arranged."

"*Arranged*? Who arranged it?"

"Who *always* arranges such matters? Her father and I arranged it, of course."

"Her father's been dead for . . . well, it must be more than *ten years*!"

"What does *that* signify? We arranged this matter just after Prissy was born. It was a sensible agreement then, and it's a sensible agreement now. I'd lay odds on it. Ask Lady Vickers. Ask *Prissy!*"

Alec felt as if he were strangling. "This is complete nonsense. Priss never even *liked* me."

"It's you who're talking nonsense. You played together all the time when you were children," the Earl said, glowering at the boy. "Of course she liked you."

"She detested me. She said I was scrawny and stupid, and she abused me all the time. I didn't run as fast as she, or climb a tree as quickly. She was always laughing at me. Why, once she pushed me off the high rock at the top of Welking Hill and didn't even wait to see if I'd been hurt. I rolled all the way to the bottom and lay there bruised and bleeding for over an hour, but she never came back."

The Earl gave a snorting laugh. "The little vixen. Well, she won't be pushing you down hills now, I'll lay odds on that."

"You'd lose your shirt! But I don't intend to let her have the opportunity," Alec muttered bitterly.

The Earl put down his fork, leaned forward and peered at his grandson's face. "You're not trying to tell me that you don't *like* our little Prissy, are you?"

"I don't like 'our little Prissy' one bit!" Alec said fervently. But he felt his color rise as he said the words, and he found that he couldn't meet his grandfather's eyes. Priscilla Vickers, who had grown up at Three Oaks, the house just beyond the home woods, was not someone he could honestly say he "liked." The truth was he adored her! She'd been a tow-headed little siren with golden skin and blue eyes, and she'd tantalized him for years. Even when she'd insulted and scorned him, he'd been her willing slave. And after he'd escaped from her spell by going off to school, he dreamed of her. He had been invited by her mother to attend her come-out in London a year ago, but he'd had to sit for examinations and had sent his regrets. He'd heard, however, that she had become a real beauty. He was not at all surprised—she had *always* seemed breathtakingly beautiful to him.

"*Ha*!" The old Earl could always read his grandson's thoughts. "Still taken with her, eh? I'd have laid odds on it. Well, finish up your dinner and get yourself into a presentable coat. I promised you'd wait on them this evening."

Alec almost choked. *This evening*? He didn't even know how to *dance* with a girl, much less *court* her! "Grandfather, this is preposterous," he said, agonized. "I'm not . . . ready for this sort of thing. I ought to see a bit more of the world before I—"

"And so you shall," the Earl agreed calmly. "But the world is a much more attractive place to explore if you have a wife beside you while you do it." And with that, he pushed himself from the table and walked to the door. "Do hurry, boy. It won't do to keep them waiting."

The only presentable coat the miserable lad could find to wear was one that had been cut for him two years before. It was too short in the sleeves and made him feel like a gawk. Nevertheless, his grandfather, who was waiting in the foyer to see him off, beamed at him approvingly and insisted that he take the laudalet rather than cross the fields and the wood on foot. "And don't forget, even though the matter is already a settled thing, you must *offer* for her. Do it nicely, mind."

"I will pay my respects, Grandfather, but I don't intend to do anything else. Are you listening to me, sir? I am *not* going to offer for her!" And he slammed out of the house.

Three Oaks, while certainly not comparable to Braeburn's impressive size and style, was an old and substantial residence. While Sir John Vickers was alive, every acre of the property had been cultivated and cared for. But this evening, as the laudalet pulled into the drive that curved around the oak trees which gave the property its name, it appeared to Alec that the place looked smaller and shabbier than he remembered. It dawned on him with some surprise that the widowed Lady Vickers must be in need of funds. No wonder she wished to honor an agreement made between her husband and the wealthy Earl of Braeburn so many years ago! Well, Alec would be happy to give them what financial assistance he could, but he'd be hanged if he'd permit himself and Priss to be pushed into a *mariage de covenance*.

The old butler, who remembered him from childhood, pumped his hand and led him into the foyer. Lady Vickers rushed down the stairs and greeted him as warmly as if he were her own son. She was a woman small of stature and large of bosom (although her lack of height in no way impaired the impression of imperiousness which emanated from every pore), and she had to stand on tiptoe to reach up and embrace him. He bent his head to permit her to kiss his cheek, and, as she uttered the expected remarks about how tall and handsome he'd grown, he caught over his shoulder his first glimpse in four years of his adored Priscilla.

She had come down to the foot of the stairs and was grinning at him with the same taunting smile that had mocked him throughout his youth. Her skin had the same glowing, golden color he remembered so vividly, and her eyes were still bewitchingly blue. Her hair, however, was a richer gold than he remembered and was pulled back from her face, the long, curly tendrils that used to frame her face tied tightly back into a charming knot at the back of her head. She was quite womanly, taller and slimmer than he remembered, and as she flashed her teasing smile at him, he felt his pulse begin to race. To have such a woman for his wife would be a dream come true.

Before he could steady himself, he was propelled by Lady Vickers into the sitting room and urged to sit down on the sofa. Priss followed and took a place right beside him. Lady Vickers, with a knowing smile, made a quite obvious remark about having to see the cook about the next day's dinner and left the room. A feeling of irritation welled up in Alec at the arrangement of this entire affair, and he made up his mind that he would not, under any circumstances, be manipulated into marriage in this fashion.

He turned to face Priss, determined to make an end of it right here. She was coolly appraising him with her eyes. "Mama is quite right," she remarked with casual unconcern. "You *have* grown . . . more than a foot since we last saw you, I'd say."

Her coolness angered him even more, and the anger loosened his tongue. "But I'm still a spindle shanked clunch, isn't that what you mean to say?"

His attack was met with a surprising giggle that bubbled out of her throat with a charming lack of affectation. "Is *that* what I used to call you—a spindle-shanked clunch? I *was* incorrigible, wasn't I?"

"Yes, you were. The terror of my youth."

Another laugh bubbled out of her. "How dreadful. I remember making you walk for miles to fetch some trifle I'd left behind. Or pushing you into the brook. Or coaxing you down from your horse and riding off madly while you had to follow on shanks' mare. And . . . oh, dear, do you remember Welking Hill?"

"How could I forget? I still bear the scars."

"Do you?" She looked at him without a trace of regret. "I was a shameful brat," she admitted cheerfully.

"You were indeed. But is this confessional designed to make me believe that you are quite changed? If you've grown so advanced in years and dignity as to refrain from calling me a spindle-shanked clunch, I shall be very much surprised," he said suspiciously.

"But of *course* I've changed," she declared, rising and pirouetting gaily before him. "Can't you see it? I'm the 'Compleat Lady,' am I not? And a *lady* would not call a gentleman a clunch."

He gazed up at her, entranced against his will. "And how about the spindle-shanked part?" he asked, teasing.

"A lady shouldn't take notice of a gentleman's legs at all, sir," she chastised mockingly. "Although now that you mention them, they are not so spindly as they used to be."

Alec felt himself blushing, but he grinned up at her and continued to banter. "I think, Miss Vickers, that you are not quite a lady yet.''

"How dare you, *Mr. Tyrrell*!" she exclaimed, raising her eyebrows in hauteur. "Or shall I call you *your lordship*? If that's what you think, you needn't offer for me after all!"

He blinked up at her stupidly as his stomach lurched in surprise. "Wh-*What*?"

"I said, sir, that you needn't bother to offer for me."

"Did you think I *was*?" he asked, startled.

She perched on the sofa beside him. "Well, weren't you?"

He stared at her for a moment and then looked down at his fingers which were nervously clutching his knees. "Grandfather did say . . . er . . . something about my . . . making an offer," he mumbled.

"Then you may as well proceed," she ordered, leaning back against the cushions like a royal princess.

He threw her a quick, apprehensive glance. "P-Proceed?"

"With your speech. You *did* prepare something for the occasion, I presume."

"Well, no. I mean . . . I thought . . . er . . . that is, I didn't think . . ."

"Are you trying to say, in that very lucid and coherent way, that you intend to make your offer *extemporaneously*?"

Her mockery and her seemingly unshakable self-possession infuriated him. "See here, Prissy," he exploded, "you're not going to sit there and pretend that you *want* me to offer for you!"

She folded her hands in her lap complacently. "It's not so much what I *want* as what is *expected*," she explained.

"Expected?"

"Yes. When two people are to be married, as we are, the gentleman is expected to make the offer. It would not be considered at all ladylike, you see, for the *female* to do it."

"Stop joking, for heaven's sake! You can't have agreed to get married just because your mother has need of—!"

"My *mother*?" Priss drew herself up stiffly. "My mother has nothing whatever to do with my decisions in these matters."

He gaped at her in disbelief. "Prissy! You can't mean . . .! Are you saying . . .? I mean . . . you cannot *wish* to marry me!"

She glanced at him from the corners of her eyes. "No? Why not?"

"Why *not*? Why *not*?" He pushed his fingers through his hair in a kind of desperate bewilderment. "We don't even *know* each other! We haven't laid eyes on one another for more than four years! And before that . . ."

"Yes? Before that?"

"Before that, you completely detested me."

"Did I? I thought it was *you* who detested *me*," she said, dropping her eyes to her hands, her lips curled in a coy smile.

"Detested you?" He jumped to his feet and, enraged, placed himself squarely before her. "What sort of game *is* this? I *adored* you, and you know it!"

She grinned up at him mischievously. "Good. *That* is something like. Now, please sit down here beside me and get on with the rest of it."

His head swam in confusion. "The *rest* of it?"

"The offer, you gudgeon, the offer. You do *want* me to marry you, don't you?"

His heart began to hammer in his chest, and he dropped down on the sofa, completely stunned. "I . . . I never dreamed . . .! I mean, you wouldn't *really* . . . *would* you . . .?"

She laughed merrily, reached over and patted his hand. "Yes. I would. And I thank you for your very eloquent and moving offer. I accept."

He could not believe what was happening. Did this beautiful, golden girl truly wish to become his wife? His *wife*? It was a miracle . . . a dream . . . a fabrication of a fevered, too-long-sequestered imagination. If he put out his hand to touch her, she would undoubtedly dissolve . . . or disappear into the mist. And he'd wake up and find himself back at his rooms at Oxford. "Prissy, I . . . I . . ." he stammered.

"I know. You don't have to tell me. You've forgotten what comes next."

"N-Next?"

"I think that tradition demands it, you know." She leaned toward him, her sapphire eyes laughing into his.

"Demands what?" he asked dizzily.

"That you kiss me, of course."

"Oh!" Very slowly and tentatively, he reached out for her. To his amazement, she did not disappear at his touch, but she seemed to melt against him. And when he felt his lips on hers, it was a sensation so sweet and stirring that he literally trembled. Could it be true that this was happening to the very same awkward stringbean of a fellow who had stared out at him from the mirror just a few days ago? His brain, which always seemed to invent problems at the most inconvenient of moments, suggested that Miss Priscilla Vickers might have motives for this extraordinary behavior that he did not suspect—motives that were selfish or mercenary and that had nothing to do with caring for him. But her lips were soft and delicious, and her fingers were gently brushing his tousled hair from his forehead, and he told his brain to cease and desist. He had suddenly become the happiest man on earth, and he would brook no interference from his brain while he floated in this euphoric bliss.

Much too soon, his betrothed removed her lips from his. He took a deep, wavering breath and waited for the room to stop swirling about him. "I say," he asked hopefully when he'd regained his balance, "is there a tradition that says I may do that again?"

Priss leaned forward with a giggle and placed her lips against his ear. "You clunch!" she murmured lovingly.

Chapter Two

And so they were married. It was a quiet ceremony held at Braeburn, with the local vicar presiding and only the immediate families and their most intimate friends in attendance. The sun shone, the bride was radiantly lovely, the mother of the bride and the grandfather of the groom exchanged self-satisfied glances, and the groom himself beamed foolishly at everyone and everything. (Garvin Danforth, who had come up from Sussex to stand up for his friend, had never before known Alec to become besotted over anything, and he was heard to remark several times during the festivities that he was "mightily amused at the change love can make in a fellow.") It was the merriest of occasions, heartily enjoyed by all the participants, and not even the merest wisp of a cloud appeared on the horizon to dim the brightness of the day. The rest of the world, with its problems, its strife, its jealousies, its tendency to becloud the happiest of ceremonies, was kept far away. By the time the announcement of the nuptials appeared in the London newspapers, the happy couple had left on their two-month wedding tour of Europe.

The first intimations of the unpleasant realities of life occurred to them as soon as the first few days of the wedding trip had passed. They did not realize how very innocent and inexperienced they were, but they *did* discover, to their very great surprise, that they didn't know each other at all well. The differences in their tastes and their habits shocked them. Alec, for example, tended to waken at the first light, cheerfully ready to start the day's activities; Priss preferred to sleep away half the morning. Alec eagerly headed for the famous buildings and places of architectural interest, the museums, the bookshops and the universities; Priss much perferred to visit the modistes and milliners, pay calls on distant relatives and persons whose names her mother had given her or spend the afternoons preparing herself for whatever parties or balls they were invited to attend in the evenings. And at the parties, Alec gravitated toward those groups whose conversations were serious and philosophical; Priss much preferred teasing and flirting and laughing at nonsense. Alec was always direct and painfully honest in whatever he said; Priss enjoyed being enigmatic, evasive and even told little white lies when it was expedient to do so.

It was too much to expect, therefore, that their relationship would be smooth. A few mild disagreements were easily passed over at first, but by the time they reached Paris they had their first serious quarrel. They had received two separate invitations to dine for the same evening, and Alec, after determining which one had been received first, forthrightly sent an acceptance to the more prompt host. To his satisfaction, he learned shortly afterwards that a French diplomat whom he longed to meet would be a guest. Priss, however, preferred to attend the *other* dinner, and, without consulting her husband, she sent a letter to the host of the first in which she fabricated a tale about being indisposed and asked that they both be excused from attending. When Alec learned what she'd done, he lost his temper and accused her of brazen dishonesty. A loud and spirited argument followed, ending with a flood of very penitent tears from Priss and an agreement from Alec to attend the dinner which Priss preferred.

Quarrels thereafter were frequent and violent, but since they were quickly made up with tears and kisses, they did not greatly impair the pleasure of the trip and the enjoyment the couple found in travelling together.

However, another difficulty began to loom like a cloud on their bright horizon, and this one threatened to become more troublesome with time. It was their relationship in the bedroom. Priss, who had been less inhibited than Alec during their brief courtship, became unexpectedly shy during intimate moments after their marriage. When Alec approached her at night, she seemed to draw into herself in fright. Alec, himself a complete innocent in matters of conjugal love, did not press her but retreated to his own bedroom as soon as he sensed her reluctance.

Neither one spoke of the matter, and they both pretended to themselves that the problem was not of very great importance. But Alec was quite aware that sooner or later the subject would have to be faced. In the meantime, he pushed the problem aside and let himself bask in the considerable pleasure of seeing the grand sights of Europe with money in his pocket and a beautiful woman at his side.

Paris turned rainy, and the pair left for Italy, arriving in warm and welcoming sunshine. The very air of the country made them feel excitedly festive. They were both enchanted by the color and charm of the Italian cities. They were fascinated by the Roman antiquities, the magnificent churches, the beautiful paintings and sculpture, the dazzling fountains, the lavish meals and the jovial people. It was hard to worry about the undercurrents of their marriage in such surroundings.

They were out strolling, one sunny afternoon in Rome, when an accident occurred which was to change the entire nature of their relationship. The day was warm, and Priss had dressed in a filmy gown of white lawn with a full, graceful skirt and a wide lavender sash. On her head she'd tied a wide-brimmed hat of natural straw, trimmed at the crown with a row of lavender flowers. Alec thought he'd never seen her look more lovely. They made their way to the top of the famous Spanish Steps, a wide stone stairway which led to the street below. As they stood at the top, admiring the noble proportions of the steps and the impressive design of the balustrades, a gust of wind lifted the hat from Priss's head and carried it right down to the street below.

With a laugh, Alec ran down the steps four at a time and managed to snatch the headpiece before the mischievous wind could make off with it again. As he was about to climb up to his bride and restore her headpiece to her, he caught sight of a flower vendor selling her wares. One of the bouquets the woman had arranged was dotted with flowers of the very same sort that decorated Priss's hat. He gave the woman a coin, picked up the bouquet and waved it in the air. "Prissy, look!" he called.

Priss, looking down at him from the top, was a vision —a subject worthy of a master painter. The sun lit her hair, the wind made her skirt billow gracefully about her, and her skin seemed to glow with an inner light. He gazed up at her almost hungrily as she shielded her eyes to see what he held. "Oh, Alec! How *lovely* they are!" she shouted down eagerly and ran down the steps to meet him. About halfway down, however, she tripped on her skirt and fell, rolling helplessly toward the bottom.

Alec stood rooted in horror for a heart-stopping moment. Then, dropping the hat and flowers, he raced up to her and caught her in his arms. "Oh, my *God*!" he cried, looking at her in terror. Her head lolled alarmingly and her arms hung limply down as he gently lifted her head to rest on his shoulder. A cold wave of despair chilled him to the marrow of his bones. "Prissy, please!" he whispered urgently. "Please, open your eyes! Say something!"

A tap on his shoulder made him look round. The flower vendor, her face tense with sympathetic concern, handed him a metal dipper filled with water. "*Acqua*," she urged, pressing the dipper into his hand. "*Acqua per la signora*."

He took the dipper and held it to Priss's lips, letting the water seep into her mouth. She choked, and her eyelids fluttered open. "Oh . . . Alec . . ." she mur-

mured as her eyes lit up with recognition and memory.
"I . . . *fell*!" She smiled, a faint and somewhat embarrassed little smile.

"Yes, love. But it's all right. You'll be all right." He
pressed her to him and shut his eyes, praying silently for
his words to be true.

"My head hurts," she said with a tremulous giggle.
"I'll wager there'll be a lump. And . . . oh . . . my *elbow*
. . ."

"It will pass, dearest. Let me carry you back to our
rooms."

"Carry me? No, no. There's no need at all for such
heroics. I can walk," she insisted. But he lifted her in his
arms and carried her back to the hotel despite her
protests and the curious glances of the passers-by.

He brought her directly to her bedroom and set her
gently down against the pillows. "There. Now rest for
an hour or two, and then we'll see if you're well enough
to go out for dinner." He took a light comforter from
the foot of the bed and spread it over her.

"Alec, don't fuss," she said tenderly. "I'm fine,
really. Only a little headache and a couple of bruises. Sit
down, dear. No, here beside me on the bed." She
reached up and brushed his cheek with the back of her
hand. "There's no need to look so . . . stricken."

He felt a painful tightening in his throat, and he
grasped her hand and pressed it to his lips. "Oh, God,
Priss," he blurted out, his voice choked and indistinct,
"I thought I'd . . . lost you! I don't know what I'd *do*
if . . ."

She lifted her other hand, just to smooth away the
worried lines on his forehead, but suddenly he found
her in his arms, and he was kissing her in a way he never
had before. It was urgent and desperate, and he was
almost frightened of his own passion until he realized
that she was clinging to him, trembling and tearful and
responsive. And he knew, with a rush of dizzying joy,
that she was his, completely his, at last.

They didn't bother about dinner that night, and the
next day, over breakfast, Priss blushed and smiled and

hardly ever dared to meet his eyes. That afternoon, instead of paying a call on a distant cousin, she insisted on joining him in climbing about inside the Catacombs (despite his warning that it was a dank and dismal place). And that night, she told him—in a very shy little voice—that she didn't like the idea of separate bedrooms.

It was a very happy Alec who returned with his bride to London to set up housekeeping in the family townhouse in Hanover Square. Although the Earl had hoped they would settle in the country—he'd have been delighted to have them live with him at Braeburn—they had decided to live in town so that Alec could explore the possibilities of a career in politics. Their first three days in London were as happy as their honeymoon. Every day Alec would go off to meet with acquaintances in government service or in Parliament, and when he returned in the evening, an eager young wife would greet him with the exciting news that she'd rearranged the furniture in the upstairs sitting room, that she'd met an old friend at the Pantheon or that she'd bought him a gold fob for his watchchain. Life was indeed idyllic for the fortunate pair.

On the fourth day, however, Alec returned home to a very different scene. When the butler admitted him to the house, he noticed a man's beaver hat on the table near the front door. He turned to question the butler, but before the man could answer, he heard the sound of a distressed voice coming from the drawing room. Puzzled, he strode to the door and threw it open. To his horror, he found his wife weeping in the arms of a stranger. "Priss! What on *earth*—?" he exclaimed.

She looked up at him, her eyes wide with surprise and glittering with tears. "Oh, Alec! Thank *goodness* you—!"

But Alec scarcely heard her. His attentions were rivetted on the stranger, a well-built, almost stocky fellow who, because of his air of worldly sophistication, appeared to be a few years older than Alec. His dress and hairstyle proclaimed him a member of that breed of men with whom Alec had had little contact in his years at school—the Corinthians. Alec and his friends at the university had often spoken of the Corinthian set with the utmost scorn, but in truth they had all felt, in their secret hearts, a grudging admiration for that group of gentlemen who so admirably excelled in every sport, who could win a lady's love at the snap of a finger, who could depress the pretensions of a fop with a look, and who could devastate an opponent as easily with an epigram as with a dueling-pistol. This was a typical specimen of the species, and Alec disliked him on sight.

To make matters even more disturbing, the fellow was holding *his* Prissy in an embrace whose intimacy was beyond the respectable. He had one arm about her waist, holding her much too closely to be casual, and his other hand was cupped under her chin, tilting her tear-stained face up to his. Alec had the distinct impression that the bounder had been about to kiss her when he'd interrupted them.

The Corinthian turned toward the door and studied Alec with an expression of disdain. "So . . . *you're* Tyrrell," he sneered.

"Yes, I am," Alec said tightly, feeling a strange churning, like a presentiment of disaster, in the pit of his stomach, "but before you bother to tell me *your* name, I'd be much obliged if you'd unhand my wife."

"Don't care to oblige you, old man," the fellow responded coolly. "I had a prior claim on her, you see."

"Blake, *please*!" Priss said, wriggling out of his embrace. "I think you'd better go."

Something in the way she said his name and in their apparent familiarity made Alec's blood freeze. "What is this all about?" he asked, trying to keep his voice calm.

"It's about *you*, Tyrrell," the fellow said, stepping forward belligerently. "You, and what you've done to us."

"*Blake*!" Priss said sharply. "I told you to—"

"*Done* to you?" Alec repeated, turning quite pale.

"Yes. You, your blasted grandfather and Priss's mother. Taking advantage of a poor, helpless female just because her mother has let their finances go all to pieces—!"

"Blake, *stop*!" Priss interrupted impatiently. "I've *told* you that wasn't the—"

"Don't try to apologize for your mother—or for him!" the Corinthian ordered her. "Let him hear the truth for once!"

"But it *isn't*—" Priss protested.

Alec held up an unsteady hand. "Let him talk, Priss. What *is* this truth, Mr.—?"

"Edmonds. *Sir* Blake Edmonds. Only a baronet, and not nearly so plump in the pocket as the grandson and heir of the Earl of Braeburn, but mine is not a name to be ashamed of. At your service." And he made a mocking little bow.

"I'm afraid I don't see what your title and the plumpness of your pockets have to do with us," Alec said coldly.

"It has *everything* to do with you. If it weren't for my rank and my impecunious position, it would be *I* who'd be Priss's husband, not you."

Alec was beginning to feel quite sick, but he didn't understand why. None of this was making any sense. If he could only be rid of the fellow, have a chance to talk to his wife, and to *think*, perhaps he could understand. "Whatever the might-have-beens, sir," he said stiffly, "the fact remains that I *am* her husband, and this is my house. I must ask you to leave at once."

"Not until I've had my say," Edmonds insisted mulishly.

"Blake, do as he asks. Please leave," Priss urged.

"No, I'm going to say what has to be said," he muttered to her, "for I know *you* won't." He turned to Alec angrily. "She's too tenderhearted to tell you the truth. But you may as well know. We love each other. Have done for a long time. You and your grandfather have ruined two lives."

Priss made an exasperated gesture with her arm, but

Alec was staring at the fellow in complete revulsion. "I can't believe a *word* of this," he said, aghast.

"Can't you? Then ask her! Ask *Priss* if you don't believe me. Ask her if she didn't declare her love for me just three months ago! Said she'd love me all her life! Go on. *Ask* her."

Alec felt the blood drain from his face. He turned to face his wife, but everything seemed to swim before his eyes, and he couldn't focus properly. "Is this *true*?" he managed to croak, keeping his fists tightly clenched to try to steady his voice.

Priss ran to him. "Alec, don't *listen* to him! It was all so long ago—"

Three months, long ago? he wanted to cry out. He wanted to thrash someone, to shake himself out of this nightmare he seemed to have stumbled into. He had the strangest sensation that if he stood still, the entire world would begin to tremble and would soon come tumbling down about his head. He moved toward her blindly and grasped her by the arms. "*Is* it true?" he asked again, his voice sounding hollow and strange to his ears.

"Well, yes, in a *way*, but—"

"Of course its true!" Edmonds declared, coming up and pulling her from Alec's grasp. "She never would have had to marry you if she'd listened to me and stayed in London a little while longer. But no, her mother wanted her in Derbyshire. My uncle in Scotland was dying, and I had to go to see him. I *told* her I'd come back with an inheritance in my pocket. But her mother and your grandfather arranged things very cleverly. By the time I'd returned and read the announcement in the *Times*, you'd already been sent abroad on your honeymoon, and it was too late for me to stop it."

Priss rounded on Blake and spoke some angry words, but Alec didn't hear them. He stood rooted to the spot, feeling the world crash about his ears. What a simpleton he'd been! She'd never loved him. Never. His brain had tried to warn him the night he'd offered for her, but he loved her so much he'd blinded himself to the truth. And why *should* she have cared for him? He was

nothing but a dull scholar . . . no, a *schoolboy*! He had
none of the accomplishments of a Corinthian . . . no
social graces, no experience. It was only *logical* that a
girl like Priss should have been attracted to a more exciting man than he. There was no doubt that Edmonds
was, from a young lady's point of view, an exciting
man. Handsome, manly, he probably had all the sporting prowess, the *savoir faire*, the skill with horses and
women that all his set possessed. It had probably been
easy for him to sweep Priss off her feet. Alec couldn't
blame her for falling in love with him.

But he *did* blame her for her falseness. For *that* she
was unforgivably to blame. Priss, who pretended to care
for him, who had tempted him into marriage for the
basest of reasons, who had lain in his arms in Italy and
pretended—! Oh, God, the mere *thought* of it so
wrenched his insides that he feared he would be physically ill. The girl had deceived him in every way
possible! There was a roaring in his ears as the full
realization of the sham his marriage had been spread
through his being. If only he could leave this room . . .
this house . . . get away as fast as possible from this
shambles his life had become . . . !

Priss and Blake Edmonds were speaking together in
angry voices, and the sounds struck Alec's frayed nerves
like little hammers. "*Stop* it!" he ordered hoarsely.
"There's no need for more of this scene."

"But Alec—" Priss began.

"You can have him," Alec muttered.

"What?" Edmonds asked, puzzled.

"Take her! I'll free her somehow. It can't be . . . too
late . . ."

"Alec! What are you *saying*?" Priss cried.

He turned to her unsteadily and tried to focus clearly
on her face. "I should never have believed . . . ! I didn't
think, at first . . . that you really wanted me. But you
should have told me. You shouldn't have *lied* . . . !"

She grasped his shoulders violently, her eyes shocked
and frightened. "Alec! You don't think that *I* . . . ! You
can't believe that Blake is speaking for *me*!"

"No more lies," he said brokenly, shaking himself free of her. "I can't bear to hear any more of your lies!" And he turned and stumbled out of the door.

"Alec, wait!" she gasped, but he shut the door in her face and ran from the house.

As he made his way down the darkening street, he could hear voices calling his name, but he didn't turn back. He walked through the streets all night, sick and miserable and bewildered. But by morning he had decided what to do. He paid a visit to his solicitor. The next few days (he was in such a fog of numbness he never could be sure how many) were filled with the chores of signing papers, settling his affairs, being fitted for uniforms and packing. By the time his head cleared, he was on a ship bound for Spain.

Chapter Three

Priscilla Tyrrell, Lady Braeburn, stood morosely at the window of her dressing room in the London townhouse and watched the rain course down the pane. *Where can he be*? she asked herself for the thousandth time. The war had ended in June. Here it was, almost September, and she had not heard a word of him. He *must* have returned from abroad by this time. Was it possible that even after six years he still wished to avoid the sight of her? The thought made her wince, and she turned from the window in utter dispair.

She knew she should distract herself from her self-pity by occupying her mind with some useful or edifying pursuit, but she felt too listlessly miserable to summon up the energy. She wandered aimlessly across the room toward the chaise in the corner. Perhaps she should try to nap, as her mother was doing in the bedroom down the hall. But she knew she would not sleep. On other occasions when she'd tried in that way to make the days pass more quickly, the *nights* became unbearably long and sleepless. She turned back to the window, but her eye fell on a little miniature hanging on the wall. She had not noticed it for a long time. She took it down from its hook and looked at it closely.

It was a charming painting, done by a Derbyshire artist on the occasion of her fifteenth birthday. There had been a costume party for her, and she'd been dressed as a fairy-tale princess. Her mother had combed her long

hair loosely over her shoulders and had placed a little
papier-mâché crown on the top of her head. Her gown
had been of silk brocade with sleeves that were enor-
mously wide at the wrists so that they hung to the floor,
medieval style. The artist had said the costume suited
her and asked her to pose in it.

She took the tiny portrait to the window and stared at
it. How happy she looked! She had almost *felt* like a
princess then . . . fortunate, pretty, untroubled . . .
fated to live happily ever after. She gave an ironic laugh.
Happily ever after, ha! Her life may have *started out* as
a fairy story, but . . .

She smiled bitterly. *Once upon a time,* she thought,
composing the fairy story of her life in her mind, *there
lived a beautiful princess.* Well, perhaps not quite a
princess and not quite beautiful, but close enough. *She
had been, as all princesses, very indulgently reared. Her
mother, having been widowed before the girl was five,
had devoted herself exclusively to the well-being and
education of her only daughter. It was only natural,
therefore, for the child to expect the entire world to
revolve around her. As she grew, her prettiness and innate high spirits brought her a great deal of praise for
even the most minor of accomplishments and a great
deal of affectionate forgiveness for her misdeeds—even
when that forgiveness was not at all deserved.*

*She was rarely made to account for her offenses or to
make up for them. Her improprieties were usually the
result of thoughtlessness or youthful impetuosity,
but—minor though they were—no one ever made her
suffer remorse for committing them. She was such a
pretty, happy child—who would have been so hard-
hearted as to wish to cloud those clear eyes with tears? It
is no great wonder, then, that the girl grew up expecting
such cosseting and pampering to go on forever.*

*But the princesses of fairy tales are wont to be stalked
by evil witches, like the Thirteenth Guest at Sleeping
Beauty's birth. The Thirteenth Guest, whose name can
be Fate or Providence or Fortune, does not permit
anyone—not even fairy-tale princesses—to be indulged*

forever. Sooner or later Providence deals her blow. And it was Princess Priscilla's misfortune that the Thirteenth Guest caught up with her at the happiest time of her life.

Priss felt the sharp sting of tears under her eyelids and leaned her forehead against the window glass. What was the use of blaming Providence for what had happened to her? She had none but herself to blame. It had been *she*, all by herself, who had planted the seeds of her incipient tragedy. She'd planted them at the time of her come-out. It had seemed a completely innocuous act at the time. Who could have suspected how dearly she would have to pay?

She had wanted a come-out ball with all her heart, and her presentation to the elite society of London had been one of the indulgences her mother so enjoyed bestowing. There had been no earthly need for Priss to be presented—she was already as good as betrothed to the Earl-to-be of Braeburn, Alec Tyrrell. *Princess Priscilla's hand had been promised to Prince Alec at the time of her birth.* As in so many fairy stories, the arrangements had been made by her father and the old Earl years ago. It was their dearest wish that the two families be united in this way. Priss, for her part, had had no great objection to the plan. Alec had never seemed to her to be quite a Prince, but he was an old friend with whom she was very comfortable. He was cheerful, companiable, very rich and quite good-natured. He obviously adored her and would undoubtedly make a complaisant husband. *The Princess, who had only the most vague notions about matrimony and the responsibilities it entailed, could see nothing wrong in such a desirable arrangement.*

But the Princess didn't see why she should be prevented from having a London presentation just because her nuptials had already been arranged. Why shouldn't she have the opportunity—as all the other Princesses in her social set would have—to be expensively gowned, lavishly entertained and widely admired? The entire procedure was quite appealing to her. Her mother was equally eager, and when the old Earl, like a fairy godfather, offered to help defray the expenses with a generous gift, Princess Priscilla was granted her wish.

Priss stared out through the raindrops at the walled garden below. Why was it that, even in fairy stories, when wishes are granted they turn out to be more costly than their worth?

Everyone who knew the Princess predicted that her come-out would be a huge success. And so it proved to be, for the Princess, not having to worry about making a "suitable match," was quite relaxed, congenial and uncompetitive with the other Princesses who were making their bows that season. The world-weary dowagers who sat on the fringes of every presentation ball and usually made disparaging remarks behind their fans were unanimous in their praise of her. The young ladies she met were eager to become her friends. And a number of young Princes—those who were not hanging out for wealthier girls—quite overwhelmed her with admiration and offers of marriage.

Fortunately for the family "plan," Princess Priscilla found her suitors quite unexceptional, and she felt not the slightest inclination to accept any of them. Everything was proceeding in true fairy-tale style. Until she met Blake Edmonds.

Priss groaned. She could remember with absolute clarity her first sight of Blake. It had been at a ball given by her aunt, the Marchioness of Lavenham. *Edmonds had come into the ballroom at a shockingly late hour and had leaned against a pillar in a posture of utter boredom. Princess Priscilla had been engaged in a lively country dance with one of her admirers and, in the midst of a merry laugh, had chanced to look up and meet his eye. "Now there is a Prince," the Princess thought, "if ever I've seen one!" The electricity was immediate. She stopped in mid-turn to stare at him, while he jumped to an erect position as suddenly as if he'd been stung. In ten minutes he'd managed an introduction and had her in his arms on the dance floor.*

The Princess quickly became infatuated. Sir Blake, with his close-cropped hair, his elegant coats, his magnificently fitting breeches and gleaming Hessians, was the very model of a dashing Prince. A bit older and more knowing than her other admirers, he made her head swim with the flattery of his marked attentions. The experience thrilled her. It was exhilarating to ride with him in the park, to go to the opera under his escort, to meet his eye across a crowded ballroom and to steal kisses on a darkened balcony.

Priss hated to remember how foolish she'd been. She had believed herself to be truly in love, and it had lasted for *three weeks*! Her mother had been wiser. At first, her mother had probably wanted to bundle her daughter up and carry her home to Three Oaks. But she'd soon had the measure of the man. Blake was a fellow with a romantic surface but not much substance, and she cleverly decided to give her daughter enough latitude to discover that fact for herself. *In the meantime, the Princess was permitted to indulge herself, without opposition, in the luxury of her first romance.*

The Princess's mother had not been mistaken. Princess Priscilla soon found that the romance was beginning to cloy. Blake's frequent and effusive compliments began to lose their zest, and his declarations of undying affection began to bore her. Their activities together became too predictable, and their conversations seemed to lack variety. She decided that he was not her Prince after all.

Here was the point at which the story changed from fairy tale (where the Thirteenth Guest would prick Sleeping Beauty's finger) to something quite different. No evil spirit caused her to behave as she did. It had been her own lack of character.

She remembered the day she'd admitted to her mother that she was tired of Blake and was attempting to find a way to break her ties to him.

"What ties?" her mother had inquired worriedly. "Have you made him any promises?"

"Well, no, Mama, not exactly. Only expressions of . . . of affection."

"Do you mean that you told him you *care* for him?"

Priss had blushed in embarrassment. "I . . . suppose so."

Her mother had looked at her reprovingly—a look as severe as any she'd ever given. "Well, my dear, that was very foolish of you, wasn't it? Now you must be sure to make it quite clear to him that your feelings are not any stronger than they would be for a mere friend. It will not do to let him have false hopes."

"Yes, Mama," she'd promised.

But she had underestimated the depth of passion which Blake Edmonds was capable of summoning up, and she'd overestimated her ability to deal with it. The more she'd tried to show that her feelings had cooled, the warmer his became. If she failed to see him for one whole day, he would be quite dramatically miserable. If she said anything which he judged to be the least bit unkind, he would become quite painfully wounded. He played on her sympathies with great skill, and she'd found herself unable to admit to him her true feelings. *Princess Priscilla began to experience her first pangs of remorse and guilt.*

It was painful to remember all this, but Priss could not keep herself from reliving the story. She was like the Ancient Mariner in that strange and haunting poem by Mr. Coleridge—forced to tell and retell the saga of her guilt, if not to every passing stranger, at least to herself. As she watched the raindrops wind their way down the windowpane, she could see before her eyes the scene, in the sitting room of the small London house her mother had rented for her London season, when she'd tried to say goodbye to Blake.

It had become clear that Blake had had no intention of surrendering his hold on her, and her mother had suggested that the time had come for them to retreat to Derbyshire. Priss had been only too willing to do so—a retreat had seemed to her the easiest way to escape from her responsibility to Blake. But he'd dropped in to call and had found the front hallway full of trunks and boxes. When she'd admitted that she was leaving, he'd been horror-struck. He'd followed her into the sitting room. "Your mother is *forcing* you to do this, isn't she?" he'd accused.

"No, of course not. Mama doesn't coerce me," Priss had said honestly.

"If you're not being coerced, then why are you going?"

"Because I *want* to, silly. Derbyshire is my home. I love it there."

"Oh, I see." He'd taken an angry turn about the room. "You no longer enjoy my company, is that it?"

"Really, Blake, you needn't be petulant. You know I've enjoyed your company. A great deal."

He'd taken a seat beside her, caught both her hands in his and looked at her compellingly. "I thought you were willing to make *London* your home. I thought you loved it *here* . . . with *me!*"

"I did. Truly I did. But I've tried to tell you that there can be no future for us. It's best to part now, before it becomes too painful," she'd answered gently.

He'd dropped her hands and turned away in manly restraint. "It's too painful already," he'd said with a little choke in his voice that touched her heart.

She'd put a light hand on his shoulder. "I'm sorry, Blake. I never meant to give you pain."

He'd turned, caught the hand and brought it to his lips. "You *do* love me still, don't you? Please say you do! I don't think I could bear it if you no longer cared for me!"

His head, bent appealingly over her hand, and the hoarse tremolo of his voice had moved her to tears and caused her to make a serious mistake in both ethics and judgment: *she'd lied to him.* "Of course I still love you," she'd said, almost believing it herself.

Overjoyed at this admission, Blake had embraced her fervently. "Then don't go! I won't *let* you go!"

"But I've *told* you, Blake, that I'm promised to another. I *must* go."

He'd stared at her, his eyes desperate. "Yes, *promised* . . . to *wealth!* Bartered like a slave being sold to the highest bidder!"

"Please, my dear, don't. You know that isn't true."

"Isn't it? If it weren't low tide with me . . . if my pockets weren't all to let, your mother would be singing a different tune."

She'd let her hand brush his brow. "No good can come of this bitterness, Blake. Let's say goodbye like kind, affectionate friends."

"*Friends!*" He'd pushed her hand aside and pulled her roughly into his arms. "We will *never* be friends!" He'd looked down at her with passionate fervor for a moment, and then his eyes had lit. "Listen, my love, there is still hope. I have an uncle in Scotland who is quite ill. I haven't wanted to go to him . . . to leave you . . . until now. But if I go at once, I may be able to solve our problem. My uncle is quite fond of me, I think. If I can win him over . . . if he makes me his heir . . ."

"But, Blake, you don't understand—"

"Don't you see? His is not an enormous fortune, but it is adequate, I believe, to make your mother see that I'd no longer be behindhand in the world—"

"Blake, *listen* to me," she remonstrated. "The size of your fortune has *nothing* to do—"

"Of course it has. You're too innocent, my love. You know nothing of the way of the world. Leave it to me. You *do* love me, as you said, don't you?"

"Well, yes, but—"

"Then promise you'll wait. Wait here in London until I return."

"I'll try," she'd said weakly, wanting only to see him go. *It was Princess Priscilla, capitulating again to her tendency to avoid facing consequences by callously avoiding them.*

And thus the seeds were sown whose fruits would soon appear to cause the poor Princess years of bitter regret. But having no experience in the Thirteenth Guest's manner of delivering punishment and retribution, she watched Sir Blake take his leave without a twinge of guilt, regret or foreboding. The unpleasant scene at their parting was instantly forgotten. Sir Blake went off on his quest—to seek his fortune in Scotland

*for her sake—and she, without giving him another
thought, returned to Derbyshire with her good spirits
quite restored.*

*It was not long afterwards that the True Prince re-
turned from school and made his offer. Princess
Priscilla, who had had her fill of stylish, sophisticated
Corinthians, was rather taken with Prince Alec's awkwardness and boyish charm. His movements had a gan-
gling grace, his shoulders were broad and strong, and
his face had character. He had a way of startling a laugh
out of her with an unexpected quip or an incisive
observation. And he had a certain uprightness, an
honesty and a reliability which she admired. His mind
was so keen he would never become a bore, and his
character was too steady to weaken under pressure. He
had not yet become the Prince of her Dreams, but she
had an instinctive certainty that she would not be sorry
if she obeyed her family's wishes and married him.*

*So the Princess and the True Prince were wed. Then,
one day, the Princess chanced to fall down the Spanish
Steps in Rome, and she suddenly realized that she'd
fallen in love with him. She was not at all certain how it
had happened, or when, but as he carried her back to
the hotel that day, she found herself staring at his face
with an unexpected feeling of adoration. Her heart
seemed to swell in her chest with warmth and joy. He
was so sweet and honest and good, he made her feel un-
worthy. It was a feeling so new and powerful that the
Princess was almost frightened by it. How could this
Prince, with his keen mind, his upright character, his
youthful enthusiasms and his high standards have
chosen her to love? She was so shallow, so selfish, so
spoiled!*

*At that moment, the Princess resolved that she would
change. She would make herself over. She would read,
study, strengthen her mind and her character, and
become worthy of him. She would grow from an im-
perfect Princess to a perfect wife.*

Priss shut her eyes in pain. Those days and nights in
Italy shone like bright diamonds in her memory—

diamonds that could cut right through her. After that day of her accident, nothing—not even the weather—had interfered with her blossoming happiness. She had walked with him hand-in-hand through the streets of Rome, listening to his explanations of the ancient landmarks, filled with admiration for his knowledge. She'd lain in his arms at night quivering with pleasure at his touch. Even the prospect of the end of their wedding trip and their imminent return to London had not dampened her joy. Rather, she'd eagerly anticipated the return, for it was to be the start of her new resolve; in London she would begin to make herself into a woman he would be proud of.

But the unexpected visit from Blake Edmonds, four days after their return, had destroyed everything. *Not in her wildest dreams could poor Princess Priscilla have imagined that the small sins of her past could return to seek such retribution.* Even now, when she could review the scene with some semblance of dispassion, she couldn't quite comprehend how a foolish conversation with Blake—which had seemed to her nothing more than a minor annoyance—had grown and enlarged itself into a nightmare powerful enough to ruin her life.

Blake had heard that she had returned from abroad, and he'd come to pay a call. She had not been comfortable at the sight of him on her threshold, especially since his emotions seemed not to have changed since she'd last seen him, but she had not anticipated a *scene*. *Her* emotions had grown so far in another direction that his declarations, claims and accusations seemed unreal and silly. It was preposterous that he could still care for her—he'd had no word from her for months. It seemed to her that he'd exaggerated everything that had passed between them. Their relationship had so far receded from her consciousness that it now seemed no more significant in her memory than a dance at a ball held years before. She felt sorry for Blake, of course, but only as one might feel for an unfortunate stranger. It didn't occur to her that Alec might take the incident seriously.

She'd been *glad* when Alec had come into the room that evening. Her husband, she believed innocently, would be able to explain to Blake (much better than she'd been able to) that she was a happily married woman and could no longer have anything to do with suitors from the past. Alec would be direct and blunt, and he'd promptly show the fellow the door.

But as she'd heard Blake repeat his nonsensical allegations to her husband, she'd begun to realize how dreadful they might sound to Alec. Innocent and inexperienced in the ways of society, he might very well misinterpret what he'd heard. Then she'd taken a good look at her husband's face and realized that he'd been affected even more deeply than she'd imagined. His lips had whitened, his cheeks were like chalk, and his eyes had become almost blank with pain. And she'd been stricken with fear—chilling and ominous fear.

At that moment, Princess Priscilla became aware that her fairy-tale days were coming to an end. Somehow, her hitherto charmed life had fallen apart. She saw her husband move toward the door, and she tried desperately to hold him back . . . to explain. But he broke from her and ran from the room.

For three days she waited, silent and numb, at the window. But he didn't return. Everything seemed unreal . . . nightmarish. She didn't believe what was happening. It was impossible, she told herself, that he didn't realize how deeply she loved him. He would soon remember their happiness in Italy and, at any moment, he would return to her, ready to listen to her explanation, ready to forgive, ready to take her into his arms again.

But he didn't come. Instead, his solicitor appeared in her doorway with the news that he had gone to Spain. She listened, apparently calm, to what he had to say, told him in a steady voice that she would not agree to any decree of nullity or divorce at this time, thanked him for coming, saw him to the door . . . and fainted dead away. When she awoke, she was not a fairy-tale princess any more.

Priss brushed aside the familiar tears, wondering if the well from which they flowed would ever run dry. Fairy tales ended, but real life went on and on. Her story had been a dismal one ever since. She could not recover her health after she'd learned from Mr. Newkirk that Alec had bought a commission and gone to fight on the Peninsula. She was weak and listless and could barely drag herself from bed in the mornings. Desperately, she'd sent for her mother and, as soon as she'd arrived, heartbrokenly poured the entire story into her mother's ear. Together they'd decided that Priss had acted wisely in not agreeing to dissolve the marriage. They would wait—for whatever time was necessary— for Alec to return. Until that time, the world in general and the old Earl in particular would not be told of the marital difficulty. It was enough for them to know that Alec had gone abroad to fight Napoleon. As for the rest, it would be a secret known only to Mr. Newkirk and themselves. Priss was no longer a fairy-tale Princess, but she *was* Lady Braeburn . . . and Lady Braeburn she would remain.

But her defiant hold on her title was an empty gesture if Alec continued to stay away. She didn't care about being a Countess. She only wanted a chance to talk to him, to try to explain, to see if . . .

Her thoughts were interrupted by the sound of running footsteps in the corridor outside her door. She had barely time to turn from the window before her door flew open and her mother burst in. "Prissy, my love, you'll never *believe*—!" she cried in obvious agitation.

"Mama! What *is* it?"

"Come at once! It's *Alec*! They're *bringing him in now*!"

Chapter Four

Mr. Isaiah Hornbeck had been faced with a dilemma. He'd assisted Captain Tyrrell out of the inn and into a coach, but before he'd managed to worm a direction from the fellow's lips, the young officer, drunk as a fiddler, had fallen into a stertorous sleep from which he would not be roused. To make matters worse, the weather had completely changed since the two men had entered the inn. It was now raining with a steady, discouraging persistence. Hornbeck blinked perplexedly at the innkeeper who'd assisted him. "Which hotel did he say he wanted?"

The innkeeper shrugged in complete unconcern. "I didn't 'ear 'im say nothin'," he muttered as he turned to hurry back to more pressing duties.

Hornbeck scratched his head. "Where am I to take him, then?" he asked aloud.

"I know one or two 'otels that's proper fer a gent," the coachman offered, the rain dripping unnoticed over the edge of his hat brim.

"I'm stayin' at a decent lodgin' myself," Hornbeck said musingly, "but I don't know as I ought . . ."

Hornbeck had gotten himself into a most awkward fix. On the one hand, Tyrrell had distinctly said that he wanted to be taken to his hotel. He'd probably already deposited his baggage there. Hornbeck would willingly drop the fellow off at his hotel, since that was his wish, if only he could remember the name. On the other hand, the Captain had revealed that he had a home of his own right here in London. Why had he wanted to go to a hotel at all when he had a perfectly good place of his own? There was a wife there, too. A pretty little poppet, more than likely. Wouldn't she fall into a devil of a pucker if her husband failed to come home all night?

He peered into the coach at the sleeping soldier and shook his head at him. "Ye've pushed me right into the suds, ye have, Captain Tyrrell," he accused, "and there ye be, sleepin' as innocent and untroubled as a babe."

"Did ye say 'is name's Tyrrell?" the coachman asked.

"Aye, I did. Why?"

The coachman scratched his nose reflectively. "Seems I've 'eard the name. There's a place goes by the name Tyrrell 'Ouse. In 'Anover Square if I recollect rightly."

"*His* place, do ye think?" Hornbeck asked doubtfully.

The coachman shrugged. "Can't say. It ain't no lodgin' fer a mimper."

"Oh? Somewhat grand, is it?"

"Aye, ye can say that!" the coachman grinned.

Hornbeck hesitated. It could well be the wrong address, and all he'd have for his pains would be a contemptuous look from the butler and a door slammed in his face. At best, he'd be delivering the Captain to the very place he had no wish to go. But if the house in Hanover Square *did* turn out to be the Captain's home, he could at least tell the butler where he was staying, thus permitting the little wife to learn her husband's whereabouts. And he could then take the Captain off with him in good conscience.

"Well?" the coachman inquired impatiently. " 'Ave ye made up yer mind? I don't take no delight in standin' about in this 'ere downpour."

"Aye, let's be off." He climbed into the coach with an air of decision. "Hanover Square it is, then."

Lady Vickers, contrary to her daughter's expectation, had not been able to fall asleep that afternoon. She'd tossed about on her bed for almost an hour, but sleep eluded her. It was her daughter's emotional condition that kept the mother from her usual composure. The girl had been a bundle of nerves ever since the men had begun to return from Waterloo. Every knock at the door would make the poor creature start. The sound of a carriage passing on the street would bring her to the window. If her blasted son-in-law did not soon return, Lady Vickers very much feared that her daughter would become physically ill.

The sound of the rain drumming on the windowpanes did nothing to ease her restlessness. The past few years of living with her daughter in London had not been soothing to a woman of her years. First there had been the strain of helping her daughter adjust to her sudden aloneness. Then there had been the worry over Alec's safety during all those years of war. And now, even though peace had come and Alec was safe, there was no peace here in Hanover Square.

Perhaps, she thought, a glass of warm milk would be relaxing. She got up and called for her abigail, but there was no answer. Impatiently, she went to the door. The sound of strange voices from the entryway downstairs brought her to the top of the stairway. "What's amiss down there?" she asked querulously.

The butler appeared at the bottom of the stairs and looked up at her. "I'm sorry to have disturbed you, my lady, but there's a gentleman here saying the strangest things."

"Really? Who is he?" Lady Vickers asked, starting down.

Mr. Hornbeck hove into view. "Isaiah Hornbeck, ma'am," he said, removing a dripping beaver and bowing awkwardly. He stared up at her, his bristly eyebrows lifting in surprise. "I beg pardon. I must have made a mistake. Ye can't be . . ."

Lady Vickers descended the remaining steps. "I can't be *whom*, Mr. Hornbeck?"

"Cap'n Tyrrell's wife. I'd been told that this is the Tyrrell domicile."

"This *is* Tyrrell House," Lady Vickers assured him,

looking him over curiously. The man looked quite respectable, his rain-dampened clothing too stylish and substantial (despite the rather loud color of his coat) to belong to a tradesman. His manner of speech, too, was not easy to place. It was not that of a London gentleman, but it wasn't uneducated. The man was a puzzle.

But he was looking at *her* in even greater puzzlement. "I . . . er . . . didn't expect a lady of yer years . . . that is . . ." He reddened and fiddled with his hat brim awkwardly. "I do beg yer pardon, ma'am. It's just that I'm a bit surprised—"

"To find that Captain Tyrrell's wife is a woman of my advanced years?" Lady Vickers broke into a gurgling laugh.

"Oh, not *advanced*, ma'am. A man o' my age would be a fool to call a lady as young as yerself a woman of advanced years. To me y're a mere babe. But, ye see, compared to the Captain, ye'll have to admit—if ye don't mind a bit of blunt speakin'—"

"The *Captain*?" Lady Vickers' smile faded abruptly, and her breath seemed to catch in her throat. "It has just occurred to me . . . are you saying that you've *seen* the Captain?"

"Yes, my lady, I have."

"Are you . . . speaking of Captain *Alexander* Tyrrell?"

"Yes, ma'am. I've only come to inquire if he lives here."

"B-But . . . why?" She looked at him sharply. "Are you *acquainted* with him?"

"Yes, ma'am. I think ye could say that. *Does* he live here?"

"I will answer that question *after* you've answered mine," she said with a kind of nervous firmness as she tried to keep calm. "*Why do you ask*?"

"Because, my lady, I wish to leave a message with his wife."

"I see. Well, what is the message?"

"You *are* his wife, then?" Hornbeck asked suspiciously.

"All you need to know, my good man, is that you may feel quite comfortable about leaving the message with me."

The bristly eyebrows knit again. "I can't say, ma'am, that I'd feel comfortable about it at *all*. All this backin' and fillin' we seem to be doin' is makin' me feel uneasy. If ye'll excuse me, I'll just go out the way I came in."

"No!" Lady Vickers reached out a hand in alarm. "Mr. . . . er . . . Hornbeck, wait!" She took a few quick, nervous steps toward him, glanced about her at the servants (all of whom seemed to have gathered nearby to observe the curious goings-on) and hesitated. Then, in a quietly restrained voice, she said, "I'm sorry. I haven't been very polite. Please follow me, Mr. Hornbeck. We'll go into the sitting room, where we can be *private*." This last was accompanied by a formidable glare directed at the servants.

As the servants quickly dispersed, Mr. Hornbeck followed her into a small, rather dark room which had been considerably brightened by the cheerful flowered chintz which covered the windows and the two love seats flanking the fireplace. Lady Vickers motioned for him to take a seat on one of them, but Isaiah Hornbeck had a strong streak of stubbornness and would not budge from his stance just inside the doorway. "I don't intend to sit down, ma'am, though I thank ye kindly. It strikes me as not very likely that y're the lady I've come to see, so unless ye intend to lead me to her, I won't take up any more of yer time."

"It strikes *me*, Mr. Hornbeck," she retorted disapprovingly, seating herself on one of the love seats, "that you are a very truculent man, and a rudesby as well."

"P'rhaps I am, but at least I gave ye my handle. I didn't hear you givin' me *yours*," he replied in his blunt manner.

"Yes, I suppose you have me there." She held out her hand to him. "I'm Dorothea Vickers, Captain Tyrrell's mother-in-law."

Hornbeck's brow cleared instantly. "Ah, so *that's* it. Small wonder I didn't guess. Ye look too young to be mother of a grown woman.''

"Never mind this offer of Spanish coin, Mr. Horn-beck.'' A little twitch of laughter at the corners of her mouth softened the harsh words. "It comes too late. I already have your measure.''

"I'm not the man to offer Spanish coin, ma'am. But that's neither here nor there. Ye'll be wishin' me to come to the point.''

"Yes, please. You have a message for my daughter from Captain Tyrrell?''

"Well, not exactly. I only thought she'd like to know that he'll be stayin' with me at Graham's Hotel tonight.''

Lady Vickers gasped and started from her seat. "With *you* . . . ? At . . . *Graham's*? I don't understand. Do you mean he's *here in London*?

Mr. Hornbeck blinked at her, confused. "In *London*? He's right outside in the *hack*!''

Lady Vickers fell back against the cushions and gaped at him. "*Outside*?'' She put a hand up to her breast and seemed to struggle for breath. "*Here*? *Now*?''

Hornbeck had a sinking feeling that he'd made a huge mistake in coming here. He had evidently blundered into something he didn't at all comprehend. He took a backward step toward the door. "I . . . er . . . seem to have troubled ye. I'd best be off—''

At these words, Lady Vickers sprang up in alarm. She almost flew across the room, grasped both his arms and shook him. "No, *no*! You don't under*stand*. You must tell him to come *in*! *Please*! Tell him to come in at *once*!'' she cried eagerly.

Mr. Hornbeck was not comforted by her excitement. "But . . . ye see, ma'am, he said he didn't wish . . . er . . . I mean . . .''

"Nonsense. This is his *home*! He *must* . . .! Oh, my *God*, Prissy will be *beside* herself! I must go up and tell her at once! Please, Mr. Hornbeck, do as I ask. Tell him to come in.''

Hornbeck eyed her doubtfully. "He wouldn't thank me for it, ma'am. He expressly said—''

Lady Vickers dropped her hold on him and stared at the man's face in dismay. "Are you trying to tell me he doesn't intend even to *see* her? Is he still so foolishly adamant that . . .?" Her face suddenly paled in anger. "Do you mean to stand there and tell me that he's cruel enough to sit outside this very door at this moment while you inform us that he prefers to stay at a *hotel*?"

"No, ma'am. That's not quite the way it is. He's out there, all right, but he's a trifle . . . er . . . well-to-live. Not in a condition to say a word to anyone, if ye take my meanin'."

"What?" Lady Vickers raised her brows. "Are you saying that my son-in-law is *drunk*?"

"As a lord, as the sayin' goes. Hasn't he ever shot the cat before?"

"If by that dreadful expression you mean to ask if I've ever seen him drunk, I must certainly have *not*! Of course, since we haven't laid eyes on him in six years, I'm sure I couldn't say what he's been doing of late."

"What? *Six years*?"

"Yes." Lady Vickers sighed and cocked a suspicious eyebrow at Hornbeck. "Didn't he tell you?"

Hornbeck, dumbfounded, shook his head. "No. I thought . . . Ye said 'we.' Are ye tellin' me his *wife* hasn't seen him neither?"

"No, she hasn't."

"Do you mean . . . that spat they had . . . it took place *six years ago*?"

She gaped at him. "*Spat*? Is *that* what he called it?"

"No, now ye mention it." Mr. Hornbeck's bristly eyebrows came together worriedly. "I shouldn't have assumed . . . I'm the devil's own fool, I am. I should never have interfered in matters I know nothin' of. I think, ma'am, it would be best if I took him off now, if ye don't mind."

"Are you *mad*?" she cried. "Of course I mind! My daughter's been half out of her *head*, waiting . . .! *Bring him in at once*!"

Hornbeck scratched his head. "But . . . he's . . . overcome, ye might say. Out cold, ye see."

"All the more reason to bring him in. Tell Craymore, the butler, to see to it. The footmen can assist him, if they're needed."

"They'll be needed," Hornbeck said with a rueful, surrendering sigh. He turned to do as he was asked, while Lady Vickers ran up the stairs. The elderly fellow was smitten with remorse. Had he, in his ignorance, done the Captain a backhanded turn?

As the butler and his assistants ran out to the carriage, Hornbeck paced about the entryway agitatedly. Suddenly, the sound of running steps on the stairs caught his attention. He looked up to see a girl flying down toward him. One glance was enough to convince him that this was the lady he'd come to see. He had only a second in which to catch a glimpse of her (he had an immediate impression of a pale, oval face, fair hair piled carelessly on top of her head, a girlish figure under a rather faded rose-colored dress held up in front to permit her to run, and slim ankles flashing prettily from below the gown as she sped down the stairs) before she loomed up before him, her eyes wide with terror. "What did Mama *mean*, bring him in? Is he *wounded*?" she asked breathlessly.

"No, no, my lady," Hornbeck hastened to assure her. "Nothin' wrong with the lad that a night's sleep won't cure." He smiled at the girl, suddenly reassured and free of his feeling of guilt. Any man who'd object to coming home to *this* lovely creature would have to be touched in his upper works.

The girl shut her eyes and dropped her face in her hands. "Oh, thank God!" she murmured tremulously.

The footmen, four of them, carried the Captain in carefully, followed by the butler bearing the officer's shako as if he were carrying a ceremonial urn. Lady Vickers, who had followed her daughter down the stairs, led the procession into the drawing room and ordered the men to place the unconscious soldier on the sofa. Priss ran across the room to the sofa and knelt down on the floor in front of him.

Lady Vickers signaled the servants to withdraw,

leaving only Priss, Hornbeck and herself to watch over the heavily breathing Captain. Hornbeck couldn't help noting that the Captain looked unbecomingly dishevelled. His hair had become matted, his coat was carelessly undone at the neck, his complexion, sickly pale under the dark tan he'd acquired in his years of military service, looked almost green, and his mouth was slack and slightly open. It suddenly occurred to Hornbeck that perhaps Captain Tyrrell hadn't wanted to come home until he'd had a chance to make himself more presentable. Perhaps he *had* done the fellow a backhanded turn after all.

The girl stared at the Captain's face, unmoving, for a long while. Then, slowly, she reached out a trembling hand and brushed the hair from his forehead with an almost ethereal gentleness. The room was hushed, the very air seemed still and expectant. At last the girl turned her face up to her mother, her eyes sparkling with unshed tears. "Oh, Mama," she breathed softly, "isn't he *beautiful*?"

Chapter Five

Alec slept and slept. The afternoon and the rain passed, and tea time came, but he didn't show signs of awakening. Priss, however, didn't move from her place on the floor at his side. It wasn't until he sighed, snorted and rolled over, burying his face in the back cushions of the sofa where he lay, that her mother and Mr. Hornbeck dared to interrupt her vigilance. "He'll undoubtedly sleep for a long while," Lady Vickers whispered at last. "Come and take some tea."

Priss shook her head. "I'll stay here and watch him," she insisted.

Mr. Hornbeck added his support to her mother's plea. "He'll sleep through the night, more 'n likely. And ye can't even *see* him with his head turned away like that. Be a sensible lass and do as yer mother says."

But Priss would not be persuaded. While she remained with her husband in the drawing room, Mr. Hornbeck accompanied Lady Vickers to the morning room where tea awaited them. Over the cups, Mr. Hornbeck was subjected to a number of questions about his situation in life, and his answers gave her ladyship many opportunities to giggle. Mr. Hornbeck was spirited and unaffected, refreshingly immodest about his business success and humorously entertaining when describing his battle to avoid remarriage against the persistent efforts of two or three over-eager widows to capture him. When he finally took his leave, Lady Vickers urged him to call again, assuring him that *she* would make no effort to alter his single state.

Mr. Hornbeck guffawed loudly. "As if a lady o' quality like yerself could take a shine to a tattlin' old chubb like me! However, with yer permission, I *should* like to call again . . . just to see how the Captain does."

Lady Vickers, feeling tremendously grateful for his service in restoring Alec to their midst, assured him that he would be welcome at any time. After seeing him to the door, she returned to keep her daughter company at the side of the somnolent Alec. At midnight, unable to persuade her daughter to leave with her, she made her weary way to bed, leaving Priss alone to gaze at Alec undisturbed.

Obligingly, Alec soon turned on his back again. Priss bent over him and, in the dim light of the fire and the branch of guttering candles on a table behind the sofa, stared at his so-long-absent face. He was much changed. There were long lines creasing his weathered cheeks and a small scar just under his left eye. With a twinge of pain, she saw that he'd lost the boyish sweetness that she'd found so endearing in former days. Instead of the gentle sensitivity that had marked his looks before, there was a hardness, a sinewy impregnability in his face now. She had not been able to notice earlier, when his mouth had been open and slack, the extent of the change. But now she could see that his mouth and chin were firmer and somewhat grim, his face broader, and his brow lined and severe. The sensitive, questing student's face had become that of a man who was austere, steely and accustomed to command.

How had he changed *inside*? she wondered. Had his nature become as unyielding as his face? She was stricken with sudden fear. Was it possible that his *heart* had become hard and invulnerable? Wouldn't there be at least one small, open place . . . some soft remainder of his youth where she could gain a new hold on him?

He groaned, shuddered and threw an arm over his forehead. Silently, she rose, tiptoed to a chair across from him and sank into it. What would he say to her when he woke? She shivered in fearful anticipation. Shutting her eyes, she tried to imagine the scene. He would open his eyes, look round and spy her watching over him. He would stare for a moment in puzzled confusion. "Priss?" he'd murmur.

"Yes, love," she'd whisper. "I'm here."

He would put out a hand and clutch her arm. "You're not a dream? So many nights, I've thought—"

She would bend and kiss his lips. "See? Not a dream at all," she'd sigh, brushing his cheek with her fingers, smoothing the lines and the little scar into invisibility.

"I was a fool," he'd tell her then. "The greatest fool in the world, to have believed . . . Tell me that you forgive—"

"Hush," she'd say magnanimously. "There's nothing to forgive. We won't speak of it ever again. We'll just be happy . . . as happy as we ever were before . . ."

She smiled to herself blissfully. Why *shouldn't* the scene turn out just that way? After six years of absence, why shouldn't they be able to forget the foolish misunderstandings of the past? She had only to be patient for a few more hours.

Alec floated in comatose peacefulness all that night, but the next morning his brain shook itself and lurched reluctantly into painful consciousness. His first awareness was of a stiffness in his back, a constriction at his waist and a most unpleasant pounding inside his skull. Where was he, and what—? Oh, yes. He remembered. He'd been *drinking* . . . with a likeable old gentleman he'd come upon in the city. The city . . . near his solicitor's office . . . *Newkirk* . . . the *news* . . . he was *still married*! The pounding in his head was dreadful. *Damnation*, whatever possessed him to imbibe so deeply! He wasn't usually the sort who'd permit a bit of troublesome news to drive him to the bottle. With excessive caution, he lifted a shaking hand to his throbbing forehead.

Where was he now? he wondered. Hesitantly, he opened his eyes and found himself staring at a white ceiling from which hung a vaguely familiar chandelier. Where had he seen the thing bef—? Good *God*! He was *home*!

He sat up in hasty alarm. The abrupt movement made his head throb with even greater pain. He was about to groan aloud when his eye caught a glimpse of Priss, asleep in a chair at the window. The sound froze in his throat.

Blinking, he tried to fix his eyes on her face. The morning sun, pouring in through the partially drawn drapes, lit her face and hair with so bright a glow that he had to close his eyes against the glare. But the sharp brightness of the light could not keep him from a second attempt to stare at her. He couldn't see clearly in the glare, and his eyes burned irritatingly, but it seemed to him that she was less beautiful than he remembered. There were gaunt hollows in her cheeks and tiny lines at the corners of her mouth.

He was surprised by the strong tug of pity in his chest, and he frowned at himself in annoyance. Why should he pity *her*? It was *he* who'd been made to suffer!

He forced himself to turn away from her. He had no wish to see her waken and catch him staring like a moonling at her face. He bit his lip in self-disgust. How had he come here? Had that fellow—what was his name? Horner? Hornbeam?—brought him here? Well, it was too late now to worry about the means. What was important now was to get out before she wakened. He was certainly in no condition to face her today.

He looked down at himself to examine the state of his dress. He was in shirtsleeves. His coat and boots had been removed and his shirt unbuttoned at the neck. A quick glance around the room revealed that his missing articles of clothing had been neatly placed on a chair near the sofa. He tiptoed over to it, picked up his coat, put it on and buttoned it as quickly as his shaking fingers could manage. Then he silently picked up his boots and shako and carried them stealthily to the door.

"*Alec*?" Her voice was sharp with alarm. "What . . . ? Are you all right?"

He stopped in his tracks but didn't turn. "Yes."

She gave a nervous little laugh. "I fell asleep. I didn't mean to . . ."

He lowered his head. "I'm . . . sorry about this. I

didn't intend to . . . to disturb you."

He could hear her draw in her breath. "*Disturb* me? You weren't . . . you *couldn't* be . . . thinking of *leaving*?"

"Yes."

There was a beat of silence. "B-But . . ." The catch in her voice was quite noticeable, although it was plain she was making an effort to control it. "I haven't laid eyes on you in *s-six years*!"

He gave no answer. He merely reached out and put his hand on the doorknob.

She uttered a frightened little cry, jumped up and ran across the room to confront him. "Alec, *no*! You *can't* be so unkind as to leave before . . . before we've had a chance to . . . to talk to one another!"

He turned to face her, his eyes cold and his lips set in a harsh frown. "There isn't anything to talk about, ma'am," he said with finality.

She put her back against the door in a desperate attempt to block him. "You can't be serious! We've *everything* to talk about!"

Alec winced. What a time to be thrust into a confrontation! Little hammers were pounding behind his temples, his eyes burned, his tongue felt thick and his brain was sluggish. To make matters worse, he was standing before her in his stockinged feet, completely lacking in dignity. He simply *had* to get out of there. "I don't think," he declared as firmly as his impaired physical condition permitted, "that a conversation between us is at all obligatory."

"But it *is*," she insisted. "You've never given me the opportunity to *explain*—"

"I have no wish to hear any explanations, ma'am. Believe me, they are quite unnecessary."

"How can you say so when you don't even know what they *are*?" she demanded with some asperity. "And I wish you will stop calling me *ma'am* in that odious way, as if I were your maiden aunt!"

"I beg your pardon," he said stiffly, shifting the awkwardly held boots from his right hand to his left underarm. "I have no wish to offend. Please give me leave to withdraw."

"But . . . don't you have any interest in what I've been waiting six years to tell you?" she asked incredulously.

He raised an eyebrow and looked down at her in icy detachment. "After all this time, there doesn't seem to be much point. Your explanations can scarcely matter very much now, you know."

This bluntly cold response made her gasp. "Wh-What do you *mean*? Surely the preservation of our marriage is a matter of some importance to you!"

"Our marriage, ma'am," he said with withering scorn, "means less than nothing to me."

His words smote her like physical blows. She whitened, and her eyes, widening with a questioning horror, flew up to his. She stared at him as if he were a monstrous stranger, some sort of malevolent creature who had mysteriously inhabited her husband's body. Alec didn't know what to make of her obvious and unexpected vulnerability to his slurs. He was confused, puzzled and quite miserable, and he wanted only to tear his eyes from hers and run from the room. But he didn't permit himself to move a muscle. He would not reveal, by word or gesture, the slightest intimation of weakness. He would prove to himself and to her that he'd achieved at least *some* measure of strength and self-mastery in his years in military service.

As if she read this unyielding message in his face, her eyes wavered and fell. She pressed her trembling lips together and walked blindly away from the door. He watched her as she moved unsteadily toward the sofa. Her shoulders sagged pathetically, and her thin form seemed to shiver. Unaccountably, he was smitten with guilt. He felt an almost overpowering urge to offer her comfort and protection. But confound it, why *should* he? Let *Edmonds* comfort her! *He* was the man she loved, wasn't he?

It was all so blasted confusing! Alec couldn't understand why she hadn't permitted Newkirk to arrange to release her from the marriage; she could have wed Edmonds years ago! It was certainly a question he would have liked to have answered, but he was scarcely in a frame of mind at this moment to investigate anything, to make sense of anything, or to consider anything. What he needed was to find his way to the Fenton, to pull off his deucedly confining uniform and have Kellam, his batman, give him something for his head. "Am I now excused, ma'am?" he asked, making his voice harsh and unfeeling.

She made a small, hopeless gesture of acquiescence with her hand. He bowed briefly and turned once more to the door. But once more her voice stopped him. "I shall sign no papers, *sir*," she said with trembling anger, "until you and I have had a full discussion of everything that's happened."

He hesitated. Their brief exchange this morning had been quite painful enough; he had no desire to subject himself to an even lengthier and more emotional interview. However, if that was to be the price required to sever their legal ties, he supposed he'd have to agree. "As you wish, ma'am," he said curtly.

A little sob sounded deep in her throat. "*N-None* of this is as I w-wish," she murmured brokenly.

"Damn it, Priss," he burst out angrily, his nerves rubbed raw, "stop acting as if all this were *my* fault!"

She looked up quickly, her face suddenly eager. This was an Alec she could almost recognize—angry and boyish and calling her by name. Not the icy stranger of a moment ago. "Oh, Alec! Of *course* it wasn't your fault. I *never* said . . . It was all *mine*! If only you'd let me *tell* you—!"

She'd jumped to her feet as she spoke and was approaching him again. He took a hasty step backward, dropping his hat awkwardly, and held up a restraining hand. "No! Don't! I don't want to *hear*—"

"But . . . why not? Alec, you can't have become so entirely heartless as to—"

He put a weary hand to his forehead and shut his eyes. "Priss, please! Not now. I'm not up to this now. I've already agreed to discuss matters at . . . at some future time, haven't I? But at this moment, I'm in no condition to . . . that is, I . . . really must go."

Her eagerness faded, and she turned away again. "I

see. I'm . . . sorry,'' she said dejectedly. "Will you come
back soon?''

"Well, I—''

"Tomorrow?''

"*Tomorrow*?'' The alarm in his voice was unmistakable. "No . . . no. Not for a while . . .''

"How long? A week?''

He picked up the shako and turned to the door. "I
don't know,'' he said, not looking back at her. "I'm not
certain. A . . . month or two . . .''

She gasped. "A *month*?''

"I don't know. Perhaps sooner. I shall . . . send Mr.
Newkirk to arrange it.'' He threw her a brief glance. "I
wish you good day, ma'am,'' he said firmly and was
gone.

Priss stared blankly at the door he'd closed behind
him. For a second or two she felt almost like laughing.
This had not been a scene quite like the one she'd en-
visioned. Not quite. After six years of empty and
agonized waiting, this . . . *fizzle* had been the result.
She admitted to herself that she had not really believed
the foolish imaginings of the night before would truly
come to pass, but neither did she dream her reunion
with her husband would turn out to be such an utter,
hopeless *failure*!

But she didn't laugh. The waves of desolation that
washed over her were not conducive to laughter. She
would have liked to experience the blessed relief of a
flood of tears, but they didn't come either. She couldn't
seem to cry. The well seemed to have chosen the worst
time to go dry at last. She couldn't even bring herself to
get out of the room. She could only stand there immobile and stare at the door, empty, benumbed, and as
wretched as it was possible for anyone to be.

Chapter Six

The Fenton Hotel, while considered a stylish address for
tonnish visitors to London, was not the place for a war-
weary, emotionally fatigued soldier to find solace and
peace. It was noisy and overcrowded, full of bustling
servants jostling each other in the corridors and
arrogant guests constantly shouting for their attention.
After one night under its roof, Alec decided he'd had
quite enough of the place. The only balm which would
soothe his jangled nerves, he decided, was the smell of
country air. *Braeburn* was the place to be. Braeburn,
where he could see his grandfather again. The sight of
that beloved old face, the sound of the Earl's voice, the
down-to-earth practicality of his words—those more
than anything else would bring ease to his troubled
mind.

Harry Kellam, the quick-witted, energetic little
cockney who'd been his batman while he'd been abroad
and who'd asked to remain in his service after the war,
made a wry face when he learned of the Captain's plan.
"Queers me why ye'd want to go to the country, Cap'n.
Nothin's there but trees an' 'ills," he complained as he
moved busily about Alec's bedroom putting away his
freshly laundered linen.

"And what have you here in town that's better?"
Alec asked, knowing quite well that the answer would
be outrageous.

The batman grinned roguishly. "*You* know, guv.

Grog an' bobbery an' straw-'ats by the dozens.''

Alec raised an amused eyebrow. "Girls, eh? By the dozens? I envy you, Kellam. Perhaps I *shouldn't* drag you off. Drink and mischief you can probably find anywhere, but *dozens* of girls may not be so easy to come by in the country, even for a lover as gifted as yourself.''

"Oh, I ain't such a gifted lover 's all that," the batman demurred, patting his shaggy moustache with a modesty born of supreme self-confidence. "I on'y use a wheedle or two t' turn 'em up sweet.''

"Do you indeed?" Alec asked interestedly. "You wouldn't care to *share* the secrets of your prowess, would you?"

"Why not?" Kellam said generously. "All I do is t' be free an' easy wiv me brass and t' carry on a bit . . . er . . . impudent wiv 'em, y' might say."

Alec guffawed. "Well, when it comes to impudence, you're the best of the lot. Is that really all it takes to win the ladies—a pocketful of brass and a good supply of impudence? I must remember that."

Kellam frowned at his Captain in disapproval. " 'Oo said anythin' about *ladies*? Straw-'ats is one thing an' ladies another. Besides, y' already *'as* yer lady, if I might be so bold as t' remind ye."

Alec's grin faded and his expression grew remote. "You may *not* be so bold. May I remind *you* that my 'lady' as you call her, is not a subject for discussion? Now, if we may return to the problem at hand, I suppose I'd be showing you unwarranted cruelty to take you away from your London amusements—"

" 'Old on there, Cap'n. No need t' take on. If y've took it into yer noddle to go to Derbyshire, ye won't see me bawlin'. I'm a lad as gets on anywhere I light."

"So you do. But there's no need at all for such a sacrifice. We can't have half the straw-hats of London weeping in bereavement over your absence. It would be better if you remained behind."

Kellam drew himself up in offended dignity. "I thank ye fer yer kindness, guv, but I don't take it as such. If *ye're* goin' to the country, *I'm* goin'!''

"Come down from your high ropes, man. I'll only be gone a week. You may as well stay in town with your grog and your girls and, if you can find some spare time, you might look round for some suitable rooms for us to move into when I return."

The batman shrugged in reluctant acquiescence. Then he fixed a lugubrious eye on his employer. "Ain't ye *never* goin' back to Tyrrell 'Ouse, then?"

Alec glared at him. "I've already *told* you I'm not," he said shortly, "so you may as well cease your nagging."

"Suit yerself, guv'nor, suit yerself," Kellam muttered, moving in a casual but speedy fashion to the door as he spoke, "but a gent what dreams of a lady an' speaks 'er name out loud in 'is sleep, and then don't even go t' see 'er when 'e 'as the chance—well, I call 'im a dam—" But he swung the door quickly behind him before Alec could hear the unflattering epithet that issued from his lips and before the cushion that Alec had thrown at him could reach its target.

A short while later, Kellam stuck his head in the door again. "Gent 'ere t' see ye. Name of Isaiah Hornbeck. Are ye in?"

"Oh! That's the fellow who took care of me when I was drunk. Hornbeck! I wonder what he . . ." He rose from the armchair in which he'd been lounging with his copy of the *Times* and followed Kellam from the room. "Mr. Hornbeck," he greeted him warmly as they shook hands, "however did you find me?"

"Lady Vickers gave me yer direction," Hornbeck replied, twisting his hat in his hand uncomfortably.

"Lady Vickers? I didn't even know she was in London. How did *she* know—?"

Hornbeck shifted his weight from one foot to the other. "Oh, aye, she's here in town. Been stayin' with yer . . . er . . . her daughter . . . ever since ye went abroad."

Alec looked at his guest curiously. "You seem to

know a great deal about my family, Mr. Hornbeck. I thought you and I were only passing strangers."

Hornbeck gave him a quick and rather rueful grin. "So did I, Captain, so did I. Never dreamed fer a moment, when I asked ye to join me fer a drink, that I'd soon find myself up to the elbows in yer affairs."

"*Are* you up to the elbows in my affairs?" Alec asked, wavering between amusement and umbrage. "Sit down, please, and tell me how this came about."

As the portly old gentleman lowered himself into a chair, Alec signaled the curious Kellam to take himself off. The batman ignored the sign and tried to busy himself with some quite unnecessary dusting, but a glare from his employer sent him on his way. Alec seated himself opposite his guest and looked at him expectantly. He couldn't help noticing that Hornbeck's usual ebullience was under some restraint, and that an air of embarrassment clung to him like a cloak.

Hornbeck met his eyes manfully. "How it came about, Captain, is one of the reasons I'm here. Ye see, I'm very much afraid I did ye a disservice the day we met."

"Disservice?"

"Yes. Takin' ye home when ye told me not to . . ."

"So it *was* you, then. Well, there's no need to fall into dismals over it. No very great harm was done."

Hornbeck twisted his hat in his hands again. "Y're out there, Captain Tyrrell. I think—and I hope ye'll not take offense at my sayin' this—a great deal of harm was done. Not to you, p'rhaps, but . . ."

"I don't know what you mean. What harm?"

"To yer little bride. She's in the greatest affliction over yer . . . er . . . desertion, y' see."

"My *little bride*, Mr. Hornbeck," Alec cut in coldly, 'is a woman of twenty-five and has been *deserted* for six years."

Hornbeck lowered his eyes uncomfortably. "Yes, but she expected, after the war, that ye'd reconsider and—"

Alec got to his feet and went to the window, turning his back on his guest irritably. "Neither you nor I, sir," he said with a formal aloofness, "is responsible for my wife's mistaken expectations. I hope you will not feel any guilt for doing what you thought was a kindness. And although I'm very grateful to you for your care of me in my inebriated state, I hope you will take no offense when I suggest that there is no further need for you to concern yourself with my affairs."

Mr. Hornbeck gave no sign of discomfort at Alec's frank dismissal. "No offense taken, Captain. There ain't a word ye said I wouldn't have said myself if I stood in yer shoes. I only thought y' ought to know how yer wife is sufferin' over ye."

Alec couldn't deny that Hornbeck was a good-natured old fellow, but this invasion of his privacy was quite unacceptable. "If my *wife* has seen fit to take you into her confidence, Mr. Hornbeck, it is entirely her affair. *I*, however, am not given to discussing private matters with strangers. At least, not when I'm sober."

"Ye didn't say anything private even when ye were soused, Captain. Have no fear of that. And yer wife didn't spill her troubles into my ear either. What little I learned was from her mother . . . and even Lady Vickers didn't say much. I only know what my eyes could detect and my brain put together."

"Oh, I see. I'm . . . sorry." He looked over at his guest thoughtfully. "Was it Lady Vickers who asked you to come here to speak to me in her daughter's behalf?"

"No, it was my own idea. Not a very good one, I suppose. Her ladyship only gave me the name of yer hotel."

"But how did she know it? I didn't leave my address."

"She didn't. It was only a guess. A sharp woman, Lady Vickers. Knows which side is up."

"Yes, I suppose so," Alec said grudgingly, turning back to the window.

Mr. Hornbeck sighed and rose. "Well, the main purpose of my visit was to assure myself that ye'd recovered from the excess of brandy I permitted ye to pour down yer throat. Since y're obviously on yer feet and cold sober, I may as well take my leave. Good day to ye, Captain Tyrrell.''

Alec, somewhat ashamed of his churlishness, turned and crossed the room to him. ''Forgive me for my rudeness, Mr. Hornbeck. Six years of life in army camps make one a bit crusty. Please believe that I'm most grateful for your kindness to me the other day.''

Hornbeck gave a self-deprecating wave and went toward the door. But before he opened it, he hesitated. ''Hang it,'' he muttered to himself, ''I've gone this far . . .''

''What did you say?'' Alec asked.

Hornbeck turned back to him. ''Ye've already marked me fer an interfering old chubb, so I've naught to lose by goin' a bit further. Ye won't thank me fer sayin' this, Captain, but I'm goin' to say it any road. Ye're misjudgin' yer lass badly. And ye'll pay dearly fer it someday.''

Alec stiffened. ''No, I'll *not* thank you for it,'' he said angrily.

Hornbeck held up a restraining hand. ''Don't set up yer bristles, old chap. It won't harm ye to listen to a few words from an older head. I've known a quantity of females in my time, and yer little Prissy is the last one I'd take to be untrue.''

Alec felt a furious rush of blood to his face. ''Lady Vickers must be possessed of a busier tongue than I had thought,'' he said with icy hauteur.

''Nay, lad, not she. *You* were the one who told me. All by yerself.''

''I? You must be mad! Even in my *cups* I'd never have uttered such—''

''No, not directly. But ye *did* recite a bit of a poem, y' see . . .''

Alec was taken aback. ''A *poem*?''

''Aye. Can ye not remember? It was by a John Dorn or some such name. He said there ain't a true woman to be found anywhere in the world.''

''Oh.'' Alec lowered his head shamefacedly. ''John

Donne. 'And swear/ nowhere/ lives a woman true and fair.' ''

"Aye, that's the rhyme."

Alec lifted his head and looked at the older man sharply. "Are you suggesting that from those little lines you inferred . . . you managed to deduce my entire history?"

"Not then, of course. But later, I put two and two together."

"I see." Alec felt a grudging admiration for him. "Well, Mr. Hornbeck, it seems you are quite skilled at adding two and two. You *do* use your eyes and your brain to advantage, don't you?"

Hornbeck permitted himself a little smile. "Ye don't start out empty-fisted and end as owner of a cotton mill without a bit of *somethin'* in yer upper works. But about that poem, now. It's only boyish bitterness, ye know, that makes a man write words like that. I don't set myself up as bein' smarter than yer John Donne—he may be the world's finest versifier fer all I know—but the fact is that there's many a woman as true and fair as God made her."

"Perhaps, Mr. Hornbeck, perhaps." Alec turned and walked gloomily away. "But not my wife," he added quietly.

This was an unexpected admission from the hitherto reserved young man. Hornbeck stared at the soldier's rigid back with a profound sympathy. "Can ye not admit even the possibility," he asked after a long moment, "that ye may have made a mistake?"

"There was no mistake," Alec answered, his voice flat and emotionless. "She told me so herself."

Hornbeck was shocked into momentary silence. What was going on here? He could hardly bring himself to believe that the unhappy, pale-faced little poppet was faithless and dishonest. Yet the Captain was far from a fool. If he said his wife had admitted her indiscretion, it must be true. The situation was strange, and he realized that he'd interfered again where he had insufficient right and insufficient knowledge. If anyone had played the fool, it was he.

When at last he found his voice, he gave an apologetic cough and said unhappily, "I beg yer pardon, Captain. I'm a worse meddler than I thought. I shouldn't have . . . that is, I hope ye . . ." He looked in regretful embarrassment at the soldier who stood immobile in the window. "I suppose there's nothin' more to be said but to . . . to wish ye a very good day."

He hesitated for a moment at the door and then let himself out. Alec did not, this time, turn from the window to bid him goodbye.

Chapter Seven

The fortnight spent at Braeburn was not nearly as soothing as Alec had hoped. Instead, he found his load of troubles increased by two. The first addition to his woes was a new concern over the state of his grandfather's health. His joy at the reunion was instantly mitigated by his first sight of the old man's altered appearance. It was shocking to see the extent to which the Earl had aged in Alec's absence—the unsteadiness of his step, the heavy dependence on the cane, and the transparent, blue-lined skin of his hands and face. His grandfather, who had always been strong enough to be forbidding in an altercation, had suddenly become delicate, frail and in need of gentle handling.

Alec's awareness of the second problem came about more slowly because the old Earl's delight at seeing his grandson alive and well was so great that at first he would speak of nothing else. During the first few days of Alec's visit, his grandfather studied him fixedly. Tears would well up in the old man's eyes as he looked over Alec from head to foot. "You've become a man; I'll lay odds on that," he'd murmur over and over, his rheumy eyes not missing a detail of Alec's changed appearance. He took due note of the little scar under Alec's eye, the toughened lines of his mouth and chin, and his new and somewhat stony maturity. It was only after several days had passed, and conversation had become more normal, that Alec learned that his grandfather *knew nothing about his separation from Priss*.

To make matters worse, Alec realized that *he could not tell him*. It slowly became clear that Priss had been a frequent visitor during the war years and that his grandfather doted on the girl. The Earl's presumption that the marriage was a happy one gave the old man tremendous satisfaction. He repeatedly asked Alec why Priss had not come. Alec's reply (an evasion which made him feel cowardly and dishonest) was that he had wanted to be alone with his grandfather for a time.

Alec returned to London feeling more distressed than when he'd left. His grandfather, though the old man wouldn't admit it, was far from well. If he should learn, by some unlucky accident, that Alec's marriage was at an end, the effect of the news might well kill him. Unable to think of a way to solve the problem, Alec turned his frustration on his wife. *She* was to blame for *this*, too. If she had permitted Newkirk to annul the marriage at the outset, his grandfather would have adjusted to the news long before his health had become impaired! Damn the woman! Why hadn't she done as she was told those six years ago?

Kellam had found a most satisfactory set of rooms in a secluded little street called Pickering Place, only a step from St. James but hidden from the crowds on the busier thoroughfare by the narrowness of the access to it. It was not too narrow, however, to deter those who were determined to find the place, and, only minutes after Alec had settled in, a visitor arrived on the threshold. *"Ferdie!"* Alec shouted at the sight of him. "Ferdie, you old clod-crusher! Where did you spring from?"

Ex-Major Ferdinand Sellars leaned his large-boned frame in the doorway and grinned at Alec in satisfaction. Alec had been his closest friend through most of the worst of the war, and he'd been searching London for him for several days. "Where did *I* spring from, you disappearing make-bait? Why didn't you let me know where you were?"

After the explanations and apologies had been exchanged, Alec urged his friend into a chair. "I find you almost unrecognizable, Ferdie," he marvelled. "Look at that waistcoat! And those boots! You've become a veritable Dandy."

Ferdie stretched out his legs and looked admiringly down at his tasseled Hessians. "A Corinthian, my boy, a Corinthian. Top o' the trees, I am. Can't say the same for you, more's the pity. Why on earth are you still in uniform?"

"Haven't had time to set myself up. It's less than a month that I'm back, you know. They needed a few staff officers to remain behind for the cleaning up. I—"

"Don't need to tell me," Ferdie said disgustedly. "You volunteered."

"Yes. I wasn't in a pressing hurry to return."

Ferdie sighed. "I'd hoped you'd gotten over that feeling by this time. After all, the business ended six years ago."

"That's just it, Ferdie. I find it hasn't ended at all. It seems I'm still a married man."

Ferdie was quite surprised. "You don't mean it! No wonder you look so out of countenance."

"Do I? There's no reason for it, really. It's only a matter of time before my solicitor concludes the matter."

"Then, Alec, why the blazes *do* you look so Friday-faced?" his friend inquired bluntly.

Alec threw his friend a startled look. "Good heavens, are my moods as transparent as all that?" he asked. It was quite true that he'd been feeling inordinately blue-deviled since his return from abroad, but he'd had no idea that it showed so clearly on his face.

Ferdie shrugged. "Not to others, perhaps," he said with a wry smile. They had lived side by side on the battlefield, and each had learned intimately the moods and mind of the other. There was little either one of them could hide from the other's piercing eye. Ferdie studied his friend for a long moment and then sat erect and slapped his knee. "Damnation, Alec, don't you know the war is over? Three's a spirit of celebration and revelry all over the land. This is no time to sit in your room and brood.''

"I haven't been—''

"Don't interrupt when a senior officer is speaking!''

Alec grinned. "Sorry, Major. Lost my head. I had the impression you'd left the service.''

"A mere technicality. As I was saying, this is no time to sit and brood.''

"I take it, sir, that you are not merely generalizing. Have you a specific plan of action?''

"I have indeed. You are to pick yourself up at once and embark on a program of dissipation and debauchery.''

"Dissipation and debauchery?'' Alec's grin widened. "I hope, Major, that you are merely speaking figuratively.''

"Figuratively?'' Ferdie echoed in mock horror. *"Figuratively?''* He pulled himself up from his chair and towered over Alec threateningly. "Since when does an officer of the line speak *figuratively*? Up, man, up on your feet! We've things to do.''

"What things?'' Alec demanded, laughing. He was feeling relaxed and diverted for the first time in days.

"What things? Why, we've tactics to study, strategy to plan, logistics to arrange, complicated maneuvers to execute. Why are you sitting there gurgling like water in a blocked drain? This is no laughing matter. Up, man, I say!''

"You sound just like Colonel Osgood the night before Salamanca,'' Alec chuckled.

Ferdie permitted a self-satisfied smile to break through his severe expression. "Do I really? As witlessly wild as all that?''

"Yes, indeed. Remember how he ran about in all directions, shouting contradictory orders at the top of his lungs—?''

Ferdie burst into a hearty roar. "Yes, with his sash trailing along behind until he tangled his feet in it and fell over on his face!'' He fell into his chair, and the two friends threw their heads back, chortling heartily over the shared recollection. Ferdie, when he'd recovered himself, fixed a baleful eye on his friend. "But I wasn't joking, Alec, in the main thrust of what I said. It's time you got out and about."

"What?" Alec demanded, raising a satiric eyebrow. "Are you back to dissipation and debauchery?"

"Yes, I am. This is London, the center of the stylish world, and *we* are heroes . . . *heroes*, I tell you . . . in addition to being still young, charming and handsome. We have put our lives on the line for God, King and Country, and it is now time to reap the rewards. We shall have wine, women and song, Alec. Wine, women and song. It's all ours for the taking."

Alec cocked his head and favored his friend with a look of tolerant disparagement. "This hedonistic philosophy is a new side of your character. When did you develop it?"

"As soon as I divested myself of the uniform. I've been living a life of complete and vacuous pleasure-seeking, and I've been enjoying every moment of it. I've almost forgotten how it feels to wake to the sound of the bugle, to ride for endless hours in the broiling sun, to charge into a brutal melée and feel certain I'll not ride out alive . . ."

Alec nodded sympathetically. The Peninsular Campaign had been a long, harrowing experience which had left its mark on them all. Whatever means a man might choose to recover from it was probably justified. "I'm glad to hear that you've found a way of life to suit you. In what way, exactly, do you go about seeking this pleasure of yours?"

"Aha! So I've caught your interest, have I?" Ferdie chortled with satisfaction. "Then I'll be happy to tell you. I sleep away half the day—the mornings are good for nothing. At noon, I breakfast. In the afternoon I ride in the park and flirt with the ladies. I take tea wherever my fancy and the lure of a pair of pretty eyes lead me. I spend my evenings at the theater, the opera or, more often, the ballroom—I always have a number of invitations to parties, balls, and soirées, handsome bachelors being at a premium. Later I make an appearance at White's for cards or dice, and I end the evenings, as often as not, with an enchanting game-pullet of my acquaintance.''

Alec's eyebrows rose in genuine astonishment. "Are you quite serious? That is dissipation and debauchery indeed. Do you really intend to spend your life so wastefully?''

"Perhaps not all of it. I shall settle down, I suppose, in due course. I'll become, no doubt, a good husband, a father, a landowner, a good Englishman. But damnation, Alec, we've spent *years* in army camps and on battlefields. Aren't we *entitled* to indulge in a bit of hedonism for a while?'' He met Alec's dubious eyes with an expression of earnest defensiveness. "Hang it, man, I was on the town less than a *year* before military duty called.''

Alec dropped his eyes thoughtfully. "I've never been on the town at all,'' he admitted with a tinge of regret.

"I thought not. And what good did your rectitude ever do for you?''

"No good at all.''

"There! You see? That's exactly my point. Perhaps if you'd *had* some experience as a profligate and a rake, you'd have known better than . . .'' He stopped himself and glanced guiltily across at Alec. "I'm sorry. I shouldn't—''

"No. It's all right. I was thinking the very same thought myself.''

Ferdie's grin reappeared. "Well, then, what are we waiting for?''

Alec looked up, a dawning excitement in his eyes. "But . . . we're not boys any more, you know. Isn't it too late for this sort of nonsense?''

"Never too late!'' Ferdie exclaimed, jumping up again. "Come on, fellow, on your feet! Together we shall raise a dust the like of which London has never seen!''

Carried away by Ferdie's enthusiasm and his own

wish to change his way of living, Alec jumped up and grinned warmly at his friend. "All right," he shouted with a swing of his fist into the air, "let's *charge*!"

Under Ferdie's expert supervision, Alec ordered a complete wardrobe of civilian clothes—from stylish "shamoy" riding breeches to an evening coat of the softest superfine cut to fit like a second skin. Then, accoutred in the very height of fashion, the two set out on a round of festive doings that kept them busy most of every day and night. Alec became a member of both White's and Brook's ,as if one gambling club were not enough; he started on a round of parties and dinners, for which the number of invitations increased daily as more and more hostesses began to notice and appreciate his charm and impeccable appearance; he began to engage in sporting activities like riding, boxing and shooting, all of which he fully enjoyed; and once or twice he accompanied Ferdie to a *salon* run by members of the "muslin company," but these excursions left him feeling deucedly uncomfortable, and he wondered secretly if he were really cut out for a life of dissipation.

For some inexplicable reason, Kellam greeted his master's new, libertinish preoccupations with grunts of disapproval. "Turned in after three again, didn't ye?" he'd mutter, clucking his tongue. "I'd go bail it wuz bobbery an' ladybirds, ladybirds an' bobbery."

"Isn't that what you told me London was *for*? If maids and mischief are good enough for *you*, why not for *me*?" Alec asked reasonably.

"I don't go about callin' meself a *gentleman*," Kellam retorted cuttingly. "What I does wiv my time ain't suited fer no gent. It queers me what yer lay is, anyhow. You ain't the sort—"

"I'll thank you not to tell me what sort I am, you jackanapes. I don't see why you think I'm only suited for brooding about the house like an old dotard."

" 'Cause y'aint any 'appier now than ye wuz when ye wuz broodin', if y' asks me."

"I'm *not* asking you!"

"Y' see? Yer temper is more worser than it wuz before."

Alec grabbed his coat from his batman's hand and made for the door. "Only because my man is a 'more worser' nuisance than a vexatious mother-in-law! Goodnight, you nodcock. Don't wait up for me."

Kellam's impudent views notwithstanding, Alec was quite convinced that he was having a fine time. For the most part, Ferdie's program of dissipation suited him very well indeed. Of course there were moments when he felt bored or embarrassed or unhappy, but most of the time he enjoyed himself hugely. He was a good boxer, and his afternoons at Jackson's boxing salon were very satisfying. He liked riding in the park with Ferdie, stopping and exchanging masculine banter at every turn with the new acquaintances he'd made. He enjoyed the card games at the clubs where, for a few hours, he could actually forget to think about his troubles. He even enjoyed the evenings' social gatherings, where he noticed that several very pleasing young ladies—and several not so young—cast interested looks in his direction. Yes, he told himself, he was having a very good time.

It was not to be expected that he would enjoy every moment. He *did* have bad times once in a while. Occasionally he would be appalled at the superficiality of his pursuits. Once in a while he would be struck with an unaccountable loneliness right in the middle of a crowd. The worst moments occurred when someone would approach him and ask about his "lovely wife." Most of the *ton* had heard he was married, for Lady Braeburn was known to have been residing at Tyrrell House for years. Priss had evidently lived quietly, not going about a great deal, but she could scarcely have been expected to hide herself in the attic. She had some few acquaintances among the *ton*, and when Alec appeared in public without her, her absence was noted. He realized that several persons whispered about it behind his back. Nevertheless, it was a dashed nuisance when someone came up and asked bluntly, "Why is your lovely wife not with you? I haven't laid eyes on her these three months.'' Alec had to answer, of course. He took to murmuring something vague about her being ''otherwise engaged,'' and he became quite adept at turning the subject.

This was another instance where his life was made more difficult by his wife's stubbornness. If she'd agreed to the annulment six years ago, he would *now* be able to go about as a single man, and no one would even have known that he'd ever been married. By this time, of course, even when Mr. Newkirk managed to obtain the nullity decree, the news would be greeted with the same disapprobation, shock and gossip that a divorce would occasion. This realization exacerbated his discontent, and his irritation with his wife increased.

Another realization broke into his consciousness as his participation in the social whirl increased—*women didn't seem to permit their knowledge of his marital state to interfere with their desire to flirt with him*! He didn't admit to Ferdie that this perception shocked and repelled him. The poet John Donne had evidently been quite correct in his assessment of the female character—there wasn't a pure and faithful creature in the lot. *Unmarried* females flirted with him as readily as they did with more eligible men, and *married* women made such blatant overtures that he was often left almost speechless. At one moment a lady would whisper the most suggestive invitation into his ear, and at the next, under the eye of her husband, she would become completely innocent and demure. The game they played so well filled him with revulsion. After only a few weeks on the town, he developed a number of amusingly cutting responses to make to these invitations, he began to view the whole sex as a group of ill-disguised courtesans, and he looked upon the entire world with a new and bitter cynicism.

But, he would have insisted staunchly if anyone had asked, he was having a very good time indeed.

Chapter Eight

"I tell you, Alec, you are making a huge mistake. This one's a *diamond*!"

"Enough, Ferdie. I'm not in the least interested. I've no wish to indulge in one of those pointless little flirtations with insipid young ladies."

Ferdie shook his head and surveyed his friend with grudging admiration. Alec looked at home to a peg as he leaned against the door-jamb of the ballroom at the Chapenhams' and surveyed the dancers with an air of utter boredom. From the top of his hair (cut in a dashing "Brutus") to the tip of his shiny leather evening shoes, he was top-of-the-trees. His whole attitude suggested the jaded sophistication of the true Corinthian. He, Ferdie Sellars, had made a man-of-the-world of his once reclusive friend. The only problem was that he had not been able to convince Alec that his new-found cynicism toward women of the *ton* was becoming obsessive. His friend Alec seemed happy, indulging in all manner of sporting activities and games of chance, and he'd even found himself a *chère amie* to satisfy his need for female companionship, but he preferred to avoid all close contact with ladies of his own station. Alec had tried to convince him that it was only proper that he should do so, being still married in the strictly legal sense, but Ferdie suspected that his tendency to avoid females of the *ton* had deeper roots. The fellow seemed to hold all ladies in aversion.

Tonight was a case in point. Here was this delectable creature positively panting to meet him, and he would have none of it. "I tell you, old chap, that you're a stubborn fool. This girl is a veritable out-and-outer. Look! There she is now, on Lord Chapenham's arm. There, to your right. In the emerald-colored dress."

Alec held up his quizzing glass and scrutinized the young lady Ferdie had been trying to take him to meet. She was indeed a diamond. Her Titian hair was piled on the top of her head in a charming Grecian mode, its color startlingly attractive in contrast to the green of her gown. Her features were small and perfect, her skin fair (its light sprinkling of freckles only enhancing the perfection of her face), her form slim and graceful, and her green eyes mischievous and inviting. "Yes, I see what you mean," Alec had to admit. "You're quite right. She *is* a diamond. At least on the surface."

"And what's more," Ferdie pressed on, "she asked specifically to meet you. I don't know how you manage it, you fox. What *do* the ladies see in you?"

Alec ignored the badinage. "She asked to meet me?" he asked suspiciously. "Why?"

Ferdie shrugged. "How should I know? I *told* her I was the more interesting and agreeable fellow, but it did me little good. It's you she's after."

"What nonsense." Alec lifted his glass and studied the girl again. She was laughing flirtatiously at a remark that her elderly escort had made, and something in the way she held her head reminded him of Priss when she . . . But he didn't permit himself to finish the thought.

"Come now, Alec," Ferdie persisted. "You must have some curiosity as to why such a tasty morsel wants to meet you."

"No. None at all."

"Well, if you don't, I do. Besides, what harm can there be in it? Come along and let me introduce you."

Alec shrugged with indifferent agreement, and the two crossed the ballroom and caught up with the young lady in question just as Lord Champenham was about to hand her over to an eager young gentleman who had evidently engaged her hand for the next dance. Ferdie, however, had no intention of letting this opportunity slip through his fingers. He stepped smoothly in front of the fellow, effectively blocking his path. "Look, Clio, my dear," he said triumphantly, "I've *brought* him!"

"So you have." Clio smiled up enchantingly into Alec's eyes and held out her hand. "Well . . . Alec Tyrrell! At last!"

Before Alec could take the proffered hand, the young fellow (who had been looking forward all evening to taking his turn with this particular dancing partner) leaned around Ferdie's shoulder. "I believe this is *my* dance," he said, smiling at the girl hopefully.

Clio turned to him with a charming but obviously false expression of regret. "Oh, Mr. Beddoes, I *am* so sorry! But I really *must* sit down for a while. Will you consent to a brief postponement? You may have the . . ." She paused and studied her dance-card. "The country dance after next."

Poor Mr. Beddoes had no choice but to accept with good grace. He made a brief bow and went off. Ferdie chuckled. "That was heartlessly done."

"Was it?" The red-headed young lady turned to Alec, her eyes glinting tantalizingly. "Do you think so, too, my lord?"

Alec looked down at her with cool dispassion. "Since we haven't yet been introduced, and I don't even know your name, I think it would be decidedly improper for me to tell you *what* I think."

"I sense an air of disapproval. I suspect, Ferdie," the girl said, keeping her eyes fixed on Alec's face, "that I have been quite deliberately set down."

"Well, I warned you," Ferdie responded instantly. "I *told* you you'd be better off with me. However, you insisted that you wanted to meet this . . . this clunch, so you have only yourself to blame. I suppose you still wish me to perform my duty, don't you? Then, if I must: Miss Vickers, may I introduce—?"

Alec's eyebrows shot up. "*Vickers*?"

The girl laughed merrily. "Exactly. Clio Vickers . . .

your wife's cousin." She held out her hand for the second time.

Alec took it absently and bowed over it, his eyes never leaving her face. Priss's cousin! No wonder there were so many little ways in which she reminded him . . .

Clio Vickers was fully enjoying her effect on him. "I think I should take offense at your obvious surprise, my lord. We've met before, you know."

"Have we?" asked the bemused Alec.

"I was present at your wedding."

Alec's expression hardened. "Were you indeed? I beg your pardon, of course, but since I suspect you couldn't have been more than twelve years old at the time, I really can't be blamed for not recognizing you."

"I was past thirteen," Clio corrected, "and I was so taken with you that I followed you about all afternoon. You were forced to ask my mother to find something more suitable for me to do."

Alec had to smile. "Did you *indeed* follow after me? I cannot imagine why, for I was the dullest of dull fellows. But before we go any further, may I suggest that we find places to seat ourselves. Your Mr. Beddoes is observing us from across the floor with a most disturbed expression. You *did* tell him you wanted to sit down, you know."

Clio cast a laughing glance at Ferdie as she took them each by an arm. "Your friend is somewhat over-scrupulous, isn't he?" she remarked teasingly.

"A model of probity and rectitude. I told you you wouldn't like him," Ferdie said promptly. "He is a veritable precisionist, stiff, pedantic and methodical to a fault."

Alec laughed. "Thus speaks a man's true friend. Heaven save me from my enemies."

They found three unoccupied chairs, but Ferdie refused to join them. "I know when I'm *de trop*," he said in mock chagrin. "I can't understand why you should prefer this witling's company to my own, but since you obviously do, I shall go and drown my sorrows in champagne punch."

Alec had a momentary feeling of irritation at being left alone with this designing chit, but after a few moments of listening to her describe her early case of hero-worship of him, he found the conversation most enjoyable. In fact, when she dispatched two gentlemen (one who came to claim her for the waltz and one for a country dance) with the same heartlessness with which she'd rid herself of Mr. Beddoes, he felt not a jot of disapproval. It was only when young Beddoes reappeared, bowing stiffly and looking tense about the mouth, as if preparing for another rejection, that Alec stood up to take leave of her. He was too sensitive to pain himself to permit her to cut the vulnerable young fellow again.

Clio, as she danced off on Mr. Beddoes' arm, threw back at Alec over her escort's shoulder a look of haughty resentment. Alec, surmising that she was sufficiently irritated at his behavior to have quite finished with him, was surprised at his feeling of disappointment. But he put the entire matter out of his mind and went off to find his friend. However, just before the two of them took their leave of their hosts to head for Brook's for their usual hour or two of cards, Clio Vickers found them and brazenly elicited from Alec (although he later could not have said how she'd managed it) a promise to call and take her riding the following afternoon.

It was during that ride, while the two were engaged in a bout of truly entertaining raillery, that Alec caught sight of a familiar figure strolling across the green that the bridle path encircled. It was Sir Blake Edmonds. Alec felt himself whiten. "Good God!" he exclaimed aloud, instinctively pulling his horse to an abrupt halt.

The animal reared. "What is it?" Clio asked in surprise.

Alec tightened on the reins, regained his control of the horse and tried to restore his own equilibrium. "Nothing. Nothing at all," he muttered. "I only thought I saw . . . er . . . someone I knew."

He nudged the horse into motion again and tried to

return to the spirit of merriment that had so enlivened their earlier conversation. But he could not tear his mind away from the sight he'd just seen. Edmonds had not been alone. There had been a woman—a completely unfamiliar woman—on his arm. Who was she? Was the affair between Edmonds and his wife over? All the unanswered questions of his wife's relationship to this man flooded into his mind again. His attempts to hold a conversation with his riding companion faltered miserably. His responses to her remarks were short and brusque, and he was painfully aware that the girl was regarding him with puzzled concern.

They rounded a bend in the bridle path, and to his intense embarrassment came face to face with the strolling couple. Blake Edmonds looked up at the horseman's face and his eyes widened in recognition. "Well, well!" he exclaimed with completely unexpected conviviality. "Lord Braeburn, as I live and breathe! Back from the continent at last, are you?"

The riders pulled their horses to a stop. "How do you do, Edmonds? May I present Miss Vickers? Sir Blake Edmonds."

Clio smiled and nodded. Edmonds led his companion forth. "And this is my wife, Adela. Adela, my dear, I'm certain you've heard me speak of Lord Braeburn."

The men lifted their hats, greetings were exchanged, Clio even managed to make a quip or two, and then they parted. As he and Clio rode off, Alec's head was in a whirl. Edmonds, *married*! How could that have happened? When he'd last seen the fellow he declared with shattering vehemence that he couldn't live without *Priss*! Now here he was, strolling through the park with a wife, apparently as contented as a cat on a hearth! The entire matter was a mystery which, at this moment, he couldn't unravel.

The rest of the ride was passed in almost complete silence. It was only when he delivered Clio to her door that he realized how rude he had been. "Forgive me, Miss Vickers, for my behavior this afternoon," he apologized with a rueful smile, "but you *were* warned.

Not only did you hear Ferdie's repeated precautions, but I myself told you I was a very dull fellow."

Her green eyes, glinting enigmatically, met his. "No, my dear sir, not dull. Mysterious, perhaps. Provoking. But not dull."

"Are you provoked?" he asked with a touch of the raillery he'd employed with her earlier.

"Enough to demand that you make up for today's fizzle by taking me riding again tomorrow."

In other circumstances, he would have balked at committing himself to the increased intimacy which a third encounter in three days would signify. But his mind was on other matters, and he absently agreed. Only later would it occur to him to wonder why a young beauty would wish to waste her time with an older man she knew to be completely ineligible.

Meanwhile, he returned home, closeted himself in his bedroom with a glass of brandy and tried to unravel the mystery of Blake Edmonds' relationship with his wife. He shouldn't let it concern him, he knew. In leaving her six years ago, he'd made it plain that her romantic life was no longer any business of his. But he had been so convinced that he would return to find her married to Edmonds that this latest development threw him completely for a loss.

Alec knew quite well that he was not adept at understanding the thinking and behavior of members of the *ton*, so he suspected that the solution to the mystery was beyond him. But he attempted to think the matter through by using the same logical procedures he would have used to solve a problem in battle strategy—by listing all the possible alternatives and evaluating each of them one by one. In the matter now before him, the alternatives could be narrowed down to only two: either Edmonds had changed his mind about his feelings for Priss, or Priss had changed her mind about her feelings for Edmonds. Good logical reasoning so far, he congratulated himself sardonically. Now to the evaluation:

Presumption Number One: *that Edmonds had fallen out of love with Priss.* Circumstantial evidence seemed to support this thesis, for it was Edmonds who had married. However, this was an extremely unlikely situation, evidence notwithstanding, for two reasons—first, that Edmonds declaration of love for Priss on that fateful night had been so passionate and genuine that the probability that such feelings could fade seemed remote; and second, that Edmonds wife did not seem to be the sort who could easily steal a man's affections from a girl like Priss. Alec had to admit that his knowledge of Edmonds' wife was far from adequate—a brief glimpse in the park was certainly an unfair way of making a judgment—but the woman had appeared to be rather plain in appearance, and her personality was far from sparkling. Tentative conclusion: *Presumption Number One—unlikely.*

Presumption Number Two: *that Priss had fallen out of love with Edmonds.* The evidence to support this theory was very appealing. Blake Edmonds had never struck Alec as a man of strength or character, and perhaps Priss had discovered this for herself and had cried off. But Alec had learned in his military experiences that those theories which one most wished were true were the very ones to guard against. Wishes or desires were very powerful deterrents to objective evaluation. When wishes or desires were involved, it was more important than ever to draw conclusions from *facts alone.* And what were the facts in this case? He had only one: Priss had told him with her own lips that she loved Blake. Love, of course, was not a permanent condition. People *did* fall out of love. But he had no evidence at all to show that Priss had done so. Tentative conclusion: *Presumption Number Two—insufficiently proved.*

With both his presumptions seeming to be unlikely, a third possibility nagged at the back of his mind. But it was one that he didn't want to face. It was a theory that had been gnawing at him for many weeks, even before he'd come upon Edmonds and his wife. Even now, however, it made him sick in the stomach to contemplate it. It was this feeling in his insides that, every time the idea had popped into his head before, had always been strong enough to deter him from examining the matter more fully. He'd pushed it out of his mind with a sense of relief.

But his military training had taught him that the propositions one doesn't wish to face are precisely the ones which can wipe out an army. He had seen with his own eyes how Wellington would demand to hear the worst news first, how he would face the most alarming facts with firm-lipped dispassion and make the most unwelcome decisions because of them—decisions which later turned out to be wise judgments. Perhaps wisdom in one's private life could be achieved by demanding of oneself the same mental rigor.

Very well, then. Presumption Number Three: *that Priss and Edmonds had not fallen out of love at all . . . that instead they were or had been engaging in a clandestine affair*. The evidence to support this theory was considerable. Priss had evidently married Alec in the first place because of her (or her mother's) desire for financial advantage. (Edmonds had said something that night about having come into an inheritance, but it was unlikely that his legacy could compare to Alec's present and future worth.) Six years ago Alec had been too naive to believe that a girl of Priss's quality could be induced to marry for wealth, but his recent exposure to society had revealed that such marriages were commonplace. Perhaps (and here the feeling in his stomach became almost unbearably oppressive) Priss had decided to hold on to her financial advantage by remaining married to him while at the same time indulging in a romantic liaison with her lover. It would not be the first time such things had happened. Hadn't he himself been invited more than once to participate in just such liaisons?

Of course, Edmonds now had a wife. Would he have married while maintaining a clandestine love affair with another? The answer was obvious: *why not*? A proper wife, submissive and undemanding, would be the perfect mask for any illicit dealings. What a perfect way for

Priss and Edmonds to have their cake and eat it too! Conclusion? *It was damnably obvious*!

Alec threw his brandy glass against the wall where it splintered into fragments that flew all over the room. The sound of the crash brought Kellam pounding on the door in alarm, but Alec ignored him and paced about the room in sick despair. He'd already lived through those painful months six years ago when he'd realized that the wife he'd adored had tricked him; must he *still* feel like a cuckold even though he hadn't lived with his wife in all this time? He despised and hated her now, and it made him ill to think they were still tied in legal bonds that prevented him from being free of her. He could still feel her like a heavy lead weight round his neck pulling him down into a bottomless abyss, unless he did something . . . *anything* . . . to cut free of her at last.

"Cap'n! *Cap'n*!" Kellam was shouting. "Wot's *wrong* in there? Lemme *in*, will ye? Open th' ruddy door!"

Alec snatched up his coat and threw the door open. He strode past the open-mouthed batman without a word. Kellam cast a hasty glance into the room and gawked at the broken glass and the trail of brandy dripping down the wall. Then he turned and ran down the hall after Alec in near-distraction. "Wot 'appened? Wot's wrong? Where're ye off to?" he asked in quick succession.

"I'm going to see my damned *solicitor*!" Alec said furiously, and he slammed the door behind him.

Chapter Nine

Fortunately for Mr. Newkirk, Alec arrived at the solicitor's office so late in the day that he found the place closed. By the time he reappeared the following morning, his temper had cooled. His intention to sever his marriage, however, was as strong as it had been the day before, and he made it abundantly clear to the patient solicitor that he would brook no further delays.

"But my lord," Mr. Newkirk pointed out calmly, "it is only *you* who are delaying matters. We are waiting for those documents you promised to obtain."

"Documents?" Alec asked blankly. "What documents?"

"Can you have forgotten? They were to attest to the existence of a valid pre-contract agreement."

"I don't know what you're speaking of."

"You see, my lord, we have need of some documentation declaring that Lady Braeburn had entered into a valid pre-nuptial contract with Sir Blake Edmonds. As we told you before, those are the only grounds on which we can base a case for nullity."

"Oh, yes, I remember now. But I really don't understand just what we're talking about. Just what *is* a valid pre-nuptial contract?"

"You see, my lord, a decree of nullity is awarded only when a marriage can be shown to have been *illegal* when first entered into, as when one of the parties gives a false identity, or the parties had no knowledge that they were closely related by blood . . . that sort of thing."

"I see. But those instances certainly don't apply here."

"Yes, that's correct. But we hope to establish, by means of two clear steps, that there *was* an illegality in your marriage contract: one, that your wife and Sir Blake Edmonds had exchanged *bona fide* vows of intent to wed before your marriage, and two, that your wife was then *coerced* into the contract with you. We hope, by this reasoning, to prove illegality." The solicitor had made the reasoning seem quite simple, but in truth he was not at all sure of the outcome. Decrees of nullity were not any easier to come by than divorces, and Mr. Newkirk was not certain that the courts would be convinced that a true illegality existed in this case. But there was no need to make his lordship uneasy at this stage. It was best to put forth a confident exterior.

"But as I recall," Alec was saying, "Lady Braeburn refused to sign such documents."

"No, my lord, she did not. She merely said she would not sign them at *our* behest. She insists on seeing you first."

Alec felt trapped. There was nothing he wanted less than an interview with Priss. "Bother the documents!" he said in disgust. "Apply for a divorce decree and have done."

The solicitor glanced up at his client with a sigh of frustration. He had always been fond of the Tyrrells and had done his best for them. But this matter troubled him deeply. He'd felt tremendous sympathy for the young Tyrrell when the boy had stumbled into the office six years ago, wild-eyed with agony. He'd helped the lad buy his commission, had supervised all his preparations to leave the country and had even seen him to the ship. He'd had every intention of doing his best to sever the marriage that had caused the young man such pain. Then he'd met Lady Braeburn, and his perception of the matter had changed. Whatever the young woman may or may not have done, she was as miserable over her husband's departure as any loving wife could have been. He'd convinced himself, as Lady Braeburn had, that it would be wise to delay the annulment proceedings until young Tyrrell's return . . . that by the time the war came to an end, his bitterness would have abated and the marriage could be resumed. Evidently, however, such a resumption was not to be. Tyrrell was as adamant as ever. Mr. Newkirk, however reluctantly, was willing to proceed, but he was *not* prepared to take the route his client was now suggesting. *That* course would be a tragic one for the lady in question.

He removed his spectacles and rubbed the bridge of his nose while he tried to determine just how to proceed. Then he rose and walked round his desk. "Sit down, my lord, please," he suggested with unusual firmness. "There are certain facts I think you should know."

Alec, who had been pacing impatiently about the small room, shook his head. "No, thank you, Newkirk. Spare me the details of this matter. I want to be rid of this marriage once and for all, and I want it done quickly. I don't much care about the legal niceties."

"Please, my lord," the solicitor insisted, indicating the room's one extra chair. "I feel I must apprise you of certain important and quite relevant facts."

This time, the solicitor's use of the first-person-singular struck Alec's ear. The lawyer had actually dropped his formal "we" for the more personal "I." Did that mean he wanted to talk to Alec *informally*—man-to-man, as it were? He had never before done so! Alec took the seat and looked up at his solicitor with renewed interest.

Mr. Newkirk leaned on the edge of his desk, his eyes fixed on Alec's face. "Do you have any idea," he asked suddenly, pointing his spectacles at Alec accusingly, "of the number of couples who have been divorced in the last two hundred years?"

Alec blinked at the unexpectedness of it. "I have no idea at all. Why?"

"I'd like you to hazard a guess."

"I've never given the matter any thought. Several thousand, I would suppose."

"Not more than *three hundred*!" Mr. Newkirk said dramatically, emphasizing his point by punctuating the air with his glasses. "*Three hundred divorces in two centuries*! Does this fact suggest anything to you?''

"Well, no . . . except that it's a surprisingly small number," Alec said wonderingly.

"Yes, indeed. *Shockingly* small. And do you know *why* the number is so small?''

"No. It can't be because most marriages are so satisfying. Most of them that I've observed have precious little to recommend them."

Newkirk nodded like a schoolteacher with a bright pupil. "Just so. Then doesn't it occur to you to wonder why so *few* unhappy couples have seen fit to resort to divorce to end their misery?''

"Yes, it does *now*," Alec replied, leaning forward interestedly. "Why?''

"Because, my boy, the laws of divorcement haven't changed since the *Middle Ages*! A divorce is extremely difficult to obtain, relying on unbelievably narrow and complicated grounds, taking an inordinate amount of time, horrendous expense and resulting in complete social ostracism for the lady, a life of criticism and gossip for the man and the inability of either of the parties to remarry *ever*. The parties, more often than not, are forced to flee the country and live as outcasts if they are to have any life at all. Do you realize the import of what I'm saying?''

"I'm not sure. You're not suggesting, are you, that I *remain married*?''

"That would be the best solution, yes. But the decree of nullity is, in your case, a possible alternative."

Alec got up and resumed his pacing. "Very well, then, Newkirk. I'll stop ranting on about a divorce. Get me the nullity decree and I'll be satisfied."

Mr. Newkirk nodded, replaced his spectacles and returned to his seat behind the desk. "Then, we take it that you will visit her ladyship in due course?''

Alec grinned at the resumption of the formal "we."

"Yes, Newkirk, you may so take it. Will you inform her ladyship that I'll drop by for a *brief* interview this afternoon? Let's say about four." He turned to take his leave.

"But—" the solicitor began.

At the same moment, Alec remembered something. "Damnation," he muttered, turning back, "I've promised to take a young lady riding at four. Do you think Lady Braeburn will be content with a morning call tomorrow?"

"No, my lord, we don't. We feel that this matter should be handled with the greatest delicacy."

Alec raised an eyebrow. "Oh? A morning call is indelicate, then?"

The solicitor sighed in strained patience, took out a handkerchief and dabbed at his forehead. "Perhaps not, but it would be more . . . er . . . tactful, we believe, if you gave her ladyship a bit more notice."

Alec, too, sighed. "Very well, Newkirk, what do you suggest?"

Mr. Newkirk threw him a hesitant glance. "Next Friday? Shall we say three?"

"Next—? That's *ten days* fr—! Oh, very well, have it your way. Next Friday at three."

"Thank you, my lord. We shall see if her ladyship is agreeable. If so, we shall send the papers round to your rooms the day before. You need only ask Lady Braeburn to affix her signature to the place indicated—three copies, if you please. As soon as we have the signed documents in our possession, we will proceed."

"And when do 'we' expect that I'll finally be relieved of these matrimonial bonds?"

"That's difficult to say. Three or four months, we should think."

Alec sighed in frustration, shook his head disgustedly at poor Newkirk and, with a wave of his hand that expressed both appreciation and helplessness, took himself off without another word.

The visit to his solicitor did not lighten his black mood. His conviction that his own once-beloved wife might have been (and might still be) behaving in an immoral fashion served to deepen his already growing cynicism. The entire world seemed to him to be steeped in corruption. Truth, honor and moral rectitude were

no longer the ideals by which mankind lived, he
decided, but were merely words behind which they hid
their base behavior. The so-called "polite world" was a
place of hypocrisy and sham, and he'd been a fool to
ever have believed otherwise. How Priss must have
laughed at him when he came from school those years
ago, gullible and trusting, and fell like a green plum into
her arms.

But he was no longer a credulous, naive, green youth.
He intended to show the world—and himself—that he'd
learned to play the game. He threw himself into
dissipation with a vengeance. He tried to involve himself
in the pleasure of the moment—cards or sport or flirtations—without taking any of it seriously. He regarded
everyone with a detached suspicion, making dozens of
new acquaintances without taking one intimate. Even
with Ferdie he maintained a laughing, fun-loving exterior without revealing anything of his inner doubts
and discontents.

While he waited with growing misgivings for his appointment with his wife, Alec spent a good deal of time
with Clio Vickers. The hours with her became the most
satisfying time of his day. He knew perfectly well that
she was as superficial, as flirtatious, as potentially per-
fidious as any lady of the *ton*, but she was beautiful,
amusing and obviously quite taken with him. Years
before, with his wife, he had always felt that *he'd* been
the more vulnerable of the pair—the one who cared
more . . . the one who could be more easily hurt. This
relationship with Clio was quite different. It was a
pleasant change to be the one in control. *His* emotions
were not deeply engaged, so he could manage the affair
with an aloof dispassion, while *she*, despite the immodest self-confidence her appearance and manner had
given her, was as susceptible as a fragile bird to his least
unkindness.

Their time together became more frequent; he took
her riding almost daily, he accompanied her occasionally on shopping trips, and when they met at
evening functions (which was not infrequent, since they
had many acquaintances in common) he stood up with

her for several dances. He soon began to suspect that they were being whispered about. This gossip did not surprise him; after all, society was well aware that he had a wife. At first he had been surprised at Clio's lack of concern about her reputation, but he soon realized that her indifference to being seen so much in the company of a married man was merely another sign of the general corruption. He shrugged the entire matter off—if *Clio* didn't mind being the subject of gossip, there was no reason for *him* to trouble himself.

One evening, however, they chanced to overhear the gossip quite directly. Alec had invited Clio to accompany him, Ferdie and a few other ladies and gentlemen to the Drury Lane Theater to see Kean play Iago. The fiery young actor had been bringing to his Shakespearean roles a new and electric zest, and all of London was flocking to see him perform. The evening had begun very well. All the members of the party were congenial, the theater was crowded with famous and wealthy patrons, and the performance was quite as dynamic and thrilling as they had been led to believe. At the intermission after the second act, with Iago's *"So will I turn her virtue into pitch"* speech ringing in their ears, the group left the box to find refreshment. Alec, however, had been much affected by the play. It had touched his own life too closely. He began to wonder if he, like Othello, was too prone to believe the worst. A sense of guilt and doubt troubled him, and he didn't join in the jesting banter of the others. Clio, noting his abstraction, asked if he'd like to return to the box. Alec accepted the suggestion with alacrity, and the two returned to the empty box.

Before they could take their seats, however, they heard a voice in the next box mention Clio's name. Instinctively, without even exchanging a glance of agreement between them, they stopped—still back in the shadows—to listen. Two dowagers in the next box, neither of whom was known to Alec, had evidently recognized them earlier and felt free to discuss them as soon as their backs were turned. "And that shameless baggage, Clio Vickers, has only been out a year," one of them was saying.

"Poor Lady Braeburn!" the other said. "How disturbing it must be for a lady of her retiring nature—and I have met her, you know, and found her to be the most unassuming creature—to hear her husband's indiscretions bandied about on everyone's lips."

"Shocking!" the first agreed. "But I place all the blame on the head of the Vickers chit. What brazen effrontery to appear everywhere on the arm of a married man!"

"I don't agree," the other demurred. "They do say that Braeburn can charm the birds from the trees with that devastatingly cynical smile of his. It may well be that the fault lies right at *his* door."

Alec, who'd been frozen into immobility, had heard all he could stand. Stepping forward, he leaned over toward the next box and smiled with the most devastatingly cynical smile he could manage. "Good evening, ladies," he said with excessively formal politeness. "May I bring each of you a glass of champagne? Your throats must be quite dry after so much strain."

The ladies colored and paled in quick succession, struck quite dumb in embarrassment. Alec turned away from them and didn't even notice when, in the middle of the third act, they crept from the box. (Kean, however, *did* take notice and was said to have remarked to his dresser during the next interval that the straitlaced old biddies who'd left the theater during the third act didn't have the courage to endure the virility of his performance.)

Alec was very much aware that Clio watched the rest of the performance with her lips tightened and her expression grim. When they were alone in his carriage later, he took her hand in his. "I'm truly sorry, my dear," he said quietly. "I suspected that our companionship would set tongues wagging, but I didn't think the gossip would be as ugly as that."

"It was the most dreadful slander I've ever heard!"

Clio burst out, her voice choked with suppressed tears.

"No, my dear," Alec corrected her. "That's the worst of this situation. Most of what they said was quite true."

Her eyes flew up to his in distress. "Oh, Alec!" she cried helplessly.

He squeezed her hand. "Don't be distressed. Gossip dies down as quickly as it fires up. All we need do is stop seeing each other—"

"Alec, *no*! I *can't*—! You m-mustn't—!" The tears she'd been holding back burst forth, and she fell weeping into his arms.

He held her gently for a while, but when her sobs subsided, he lifted her face and forced her to look at him. "We must be sensible, Clio. You must have known all along that something like this would happen. Did it never occur to you that the friendship of an ineligible like me would bring a storm of criticism on your head?"

"Yes, of c-course it did. My Mama has been nagging at me for weeks! But I didn't c-care until—"

He raised an eyebrow in surprise. "Didn't *care*? Why not?"

She lowered her eyes. "Surely you know. I've been madly in love with you since . . . since I was thirteen!"

Alec's sensibilities were somewhat jarred by the unexpected unreserve of the declaration, but after a moment's thought he decided that she couldn't have meant it seriously. "Come now, my girl, let's not indulge in irrelevant nonsense. It has no—"

"*Nonsense*?" She lifted her eyes in startled denial. "I meant every word!"

He shook his head. "Don't be a wet-goose. You told me of your girlish hero-worship, but a child's infatuation can scarcely be taken seriously. Infatuations don't last, you know."

"But my dear, *dear* Alec," she said with her self-assured smile, "it *has* lasted."

He began to feel uncomfortable. "You can't mean what you're saying, Clio. It makes no sense at all."

"No? Why not?"

"Well, because, for one thing, the boy you think you

fell in love with at thirteen . . . why, he no longer even *exists*.''

Clio didn't understand what he meant, and she had no real interest in asking him to explain. She was single-mindedly seeking a response to her declaration, and she would not be dissuaded from her goal. ''*Now* who's speaking nonsense?'' she asked, dispensing with his objection. ''I see that boy in you even now.'' She studied his face with a sudden worried little frown. ''Is this your way of telling me, Alec, that . . . that you d-don't love *me*?''

Alec was taken aback. He'd never considered the matter before. ''Well, *no*, not exactly. I—''

But his denial was all she wanted to hear. Her eyes brightened in glowing relief. She slid her arms around his waist. ''Then you *do* love me!'' she sighed, nestling her head on his shoulder.

''I didn't say that, either,'' he said quickly, trying to extricate himself. ''See here, Clio, we can't discuss love between us. I have no right—''

''Really, Alec,'' the girl said in a tone that combined amusement, affection and rebuke, ''sometimes I think you're as straitlaced as my mother! Are you going to harp on that marriage of yours again? Everyone knows it's a marriage in name only.''

''Nevertheless, it *is* a marriage. And my wife is your *cousin*. Have you no shame, girl?''

Clio giggled. ''None at all. I always knew that cousin Priscilla was not quite up to the mark. Not for a man like you. You need someone with more charm, more sparkle, more beauty . . .''

Alec frowned at her in disapproval. ''Besides having no shame, Miss Vanity, you seem to have no modesty. If you want the truth of it, your cousin had more charm, more sparkle and more beauty than any man could wish.''

Clio, snuggling confidently in his arms, would not be deflated. ''Did she?'' she asked complacently. ''More than *I*?''

Alec's eyes took on a faraway glaze. ''More than any woman I've ever known,'' he said softly.

"Alec!" Clio sat bolt upright in immediate affront.

He brought himself back to the present by sheer force of will. "I hope, Miss," he said to her with an avuncular smile, "that I've given you a sufficient douse of cold water to dampen your excessive self-esteem."

She flounced to the far corner of the seat. "You *don't* love me, then," she pouted. "Is that what you're trying to tell me?"

"I don't know. I haven't given the matter any thought."

"Wh-What? Never?"

"Never."

"Oh."

Her voice was low, and the pathetic little monosyllable was delivered with the merest quaver. This little indication of weakness and bravery touched him more than anything else that had passed between them that evening. Perhaps she *was* brazen and forward on the outside, as the world of the *ton* had required her to be, but inside, he thought, she was as insecure and needful of protection as a kitten. "Come here, you little ninny," he said fondly, and he pulled her back into his arms. "If it will lift your spirits, I shall reveal a secret to you, and then we must have done with talk of love and marriage."

"A s-secret?" she asked, looking up into his face hopefully.

"Yes. So you must not speak of it until I give you leave. My solicitor tells me that in a few months he will make me a free man—as free as I was before the marriage occurred. At that time, if you still wish it, I shall think about whether or not I love you."

"Oh, *Alec!*" she breathed, completely restored to happiness. "Do you truly *mean* it? We can be *married*?"

He fixed a mock-disapproving eye on her again. "Now, that is quite enough of that sort of thing. I said we must end the discussion on this subject. Really, I don't know what you were thinking of to bring the matter up at all. What could you have expected of me when you knew I was not free? You didn't want me to offer you a *carte blanche*, did you?"

She giggled. "No, of course not. But I did think . . ." She hesitated and looked up at him askance.

"Well, what disreputable suggestion were you about to make? Out with it, or you'll have me thinking the worst."

"I thought we might . . . run off . . ." she said with a pretty blush.

"*Run off*?" He stared at her, appalled.

"Yes. Well, you needn't look as if I'd suggested we carry off the crown jewels. It's not unheard of, you know. I thought we might run away to Paris or Vienna . . . like Lady Waterton and her French lover. It would be quite exciting to live like romantic outcasts, wouldn't it? Couldn't we, Alec?"

"I should say not! Romantic outcasts, indeed. I've never heard such drivel. What sort of nonsensical drivel does your mother permit your to read?"

"It is not nonsensical drivel. It was a very good suggestion, especially if you were not going to be a free man. However, under the circumstances, I suppose it would be more sensible to wait."

"Under the circumstances, my girl, I suggest we drop the entire subject until the proper time. And until then, I had best keep a discreet distance from you so that tongues will not be wagging. Therefore, if you please, you may remove these very pretty arms from about my neck and sit over there."

Clio, her confidence completely restored and her hopes for the future high, did as she was bid. "But really, Alec," she laughed as she adjusted her cloak to lie primly about her, "I never noticed before, but underneath your dashing exterior, I think you're a positive *Puritan*!"

Chapter Ten

In the house in Hanover Square, Priss, making herself ready for her long-awaited visit from Alec, sat at her dressing table brushing her hair, but her eyes were on the note from Mr. Newkirk which lay open before her. She read over the words for the hundredth time: *Dear Lady Braeburn, We have been requested by his lordship, Alexander Tyrrell, to arrange for the honor of an interview with you in the near future. If Friday, the 16th of October, at three P.M. should chance to be a convenient hour, we shall be happy to have him wait upon you at that time. With the very best wishes for your continued good health, we remain your most sincere and humble servant, etc. F. L. Newkirk.*

The forbidding formality of the note, and the fact that Alec hadn't written himself, had filled her with foreboding. Her mother, too, had found the letter upsetting. "It certainly is a most unencouraging document," Lady Vickers had said as they'd sat over their morning coffees discussing it. "I truly dislike to douse your hopes after you've waited so eagerly to hear from him, but I find nothing in this missive to cause you to rejoice."

Priss did not rejoice over the letter, but she did permit herself to hope just a little. At least she would *see* him, and that was the most hopeful news she'd had in weeks.

The days between the receipt of the letter and today, when she would actually be seeing him, had been spent on a see-saw of emotions. Sometimes she would convince herself that he truly loved her—that the man who had carried her so adoringly through the streets of Rome had surely shown a passion beyond the ordinary —and would be readily coaxed back into her arms. At other times she felt equally positive that he had forgotten his feeling for her entirely and that her attempts to convince him that the entire business with Blake was insignificant would come too late to interest him at all.

She had heard from more than one of her callers that her husband had been much in evidence in the season's social activities. They usually spoke of him with great admiration—his caustic wit, his lean and weathered good looks and his cool unattainability all made him a favorite of the ladies. But one or two of the more vicious gossips dropped all too obvious hints that he had been seen in the company of one particular lady more often than was seemly. Her one intimate friend, a modest, unmarried girl named Ariadne Courdepass, tried to convince her not to let the gossip disturb her. Ariadne had remarked with practical good sense that a gentleman on the town, especially one who had been away from home fighting a war for so many years, could hardly be expected to eschew all female companionship. But when one of the gossips dropped—oh, so casually—the name of Clio Vickers, Priss felt quite sick with jealousy.

She had not told her mother what she'd learned, but Lady Vickers had her own sources of information. "I shouldn't take the gossip at all to heart, my love," her mother advised her. "A man always needs to sow *some* wild oats during a lifetime." And she went on to caution her daughter against mentioning a word to Alec on the subject during the forthcoming interview. "It will not do, at such a time," she said wisely, "to throw *his* indiscretions in his teeth, especially when you are apologizing for your own."

Her mother was right, of course. It was not a topic she would care to discuss in this, the first real conversation she would have with Alec in six years. The problem was, however, that she wasn't sure just what topic she *should* discuss. Her weakness in dealing with the importunities of Blake Edmonds so long ago hardly seemed, after all these years, sufficiently sinful to have caused such a rift between Alec and herself. What *really* was troubling her husband? She had no clue to the true state of his mind and his feelings. The bitterness he'd exhibited that morning when he'd awakened in the drawing room those weeks ago had been quite baffling to her.

Of course he'd been suffering the aftereffects of excessive indulgence in drink, and he was obviously not himself. But even after he'd recovered, he had not seen fit to come to her. He seemed to have convinced himself that she'd betrayed him in some way, but the substance of that betrayal was not at all clear. Over and over she rehearsed what she would say to him, but since his motivation was a blur, she had no assurance that her words would be an adequate bridge over the gulf between them.

On this fateful Friday morning, she had permitted her mother's dresser to arrange her hair. She wanted to look as lovely as possible, for she needed all the self-confidence she could command. The dresser had devised a very complicated and modish arrangement, with small ringlets lining the forehead and a number of bouncy curls gathered tightly at the temples and permitted to fall over the ears in a bushy mass. Priss thanked the abigail and dismissed her, but as soon as the dresser had left, Priss had picked up her hairbrush and brushed out the entire coiffure. She had enough to strain her nerves without giving herself the added distraction of worrying about the effect of an over-elaborate hairstyle on a husband who no longer was familiar with his wife's appearance.

She brushed for half an hour before the crimping which the dresser's hot iron had impressed into each strand had been smoothed out. Then she tied the entire mane into a single knot at the nape of her neck—as she had done every day for years—and went over to her bed

to select one of the four gowns she had laid out on it.
The first one she put on was a mauve jaconet with a
ruffle of soft lace at the neck and a row of acorns
embroidered in purple along the hem. But after a glance
in her mirror, she decided it was insipid, and she took it
off. Next she tried the sapphire-blue lustring, which
some gentleman whose identity she no longer remembered had told her brought out the blue of her eyes,
but she discarded *that* because it was too daring for
afternoon wear. A pink round-gown of Persian silk was
next discarded because of its tendency to cling too
suggestively to her thighs, and the gray crape with its
row of silver buttons down the front was rejected for
making her look like an evangelical. She had gone back
to the mauve and was buttoning the back when her
mother tapped on the door and came in.

"Don't tell me you haven't finished dressing! It's after *two*! And what have you done to your *hair*?" Lady
Vickers exclaimed nervously.

Priss turned to her with an expression of dismay. "I
look a veritable dowd, don't I? Oh, Mama, I don't
know if I can go through with this!"

Lady Vickers was immediately conscience-stricken
for adding to her daughter's nervousness. "Nonsense,
my love, of course you'll go through with it. Everything
will be fine, I know it! I shall find you both in each
other's arms before an hour goes by. You look
positively lovely. You always do, even *without* a proper
coiffure."

Lady Vickers believed every word she'd said. In her
eyes, her daughter's beauty was so marked, it would
shine through any disguise, resist any embellishment,
overcome any unflattering costume. Of course, the way
the girl had pulled back her hair *was* rather severe, and
the dress she'd chosen was perhaps somewhat un-
pretentious, but since it was far too late to do anything
about it, it was best to put a good face on it.

And as far as the interview with Alec was concerned,
Lady Vickers didn't see why it should not go well. Mr.
Hornbeck, who had paid a call just yesterday—the dear

man had taken to paying a call each fortnight, when he came to London on business with his bank—had agreed that there was every reason to hope. Priss had not done anything so very terrible to Alec that she should be past forgiveness. She had, admittedly, been a silly chit in her handling of that *cloying* Edmonds fellow, but she'd been a mere child. Certainly a man of Alec's character could see by this time that the entire matter had no relationship to their marriage.

With murmurings of optimistic encouragement, she urged her daughter out of the room. It was time to go downstairs, to make sure that everything in the drawing room had been polished and dusted to perfection, that fresh flowers had been arranged in all the vases, that the tea things in the sitting room had been set out properly and that all the servants had been warned against any intrusion. Nothing—not the slightest little detail—must go wrong today.

Priss twisted her fingers together nervously as they descended the stairs. At the bottom, she turned to her mother with a troubled hesitancy. "Mama . . . promise you won't take offense if . . ."

"What is it, dearest? Don't tell me you think *my* hair is overdone!"

"Oh, Mama, *no!*" the girl exclaimed with a quick laugh. "Your hair is exactly as it ought to be. I only . . . wish to ask if you would mind *terribly* if I greeted Alec alone."

"Mind? No, of course I don't. You are quite right to wish to do so, and I should have thought of it myself. If I were present, there would be a great deal of time wasted in polite interrogations and empty responses, and then I should have to make a patently obvious excuse for leaving the room—"

"Exactly. And, if all goes well, you shall see him later at the tea table—"

"When conversation shall be much more delightful and relaxed!" Lady Vickers concluded happily. "Go on, then. Into the drawing room with you. I shall be waiting in the sitting room until you're through. And

Prissy, my love, do not hurry the interview on my account. I shall be quite content with my embroidery, I assure you.''

Priss watched as her mother disappeared into the sitting room where the tea table had been set with the finest china and plate in the house and decorated with a huge centerpiece of yellow mums and pink-edged snapdragons in the hope that, a short while later, it would be the scene of a festive celebration. As the door closed behind Lady Vickers, Priss felt a tremor in her stomach. It was almost time. By the time she'd instructed Craymore on his part in the affair and waited for him to bring a decanter of the best Madeira to the drawing room, Alec would be knocking at the door.

She was not at all sure she could endure the suspense. She took a deep breath, grimaced and clenched her fists. She *had* to endure it. Her entire future depended on the way she would handle herself this afternoon. All her hopes and desires had somehow centered themselves on the little drama to be played out in her drawing room today, and she had to rise to the occasion. She had, if necessary, to be calm, wise, loving, forgiving, understanding, brave, serene and true. She had to play Jeanne d'Arc, Elizabeth, Beatrice or Portia—whatever the occasion should demand. The only trouble was that she almost didn't know how to play *herself* any more!

Well, there was no more time for reflection, except perhaps for one more quick look at her own reflection in the mirror. The face that stared back at her was a stranger's—a pale woman whose frightened eyes seemed much too large for the pallid little face. She shut the eyes, sent a silent little prayer to the heavens for pity and aid, and then went off to find the butler.

From the time *he* awoke on the Friday of his appointment with his wife, Alec, too, found himself unreasonably tense. A morning ride in the park with Ferdie failed to ease the churning in his stomach. A quiet luncheon in his own dining room, with only the *Times* for companionship, gave him a brief breathing spell, but when he went into his dressing room to change into appropriate clothing for the call to Hanover Square, the flutterings and mutterings of the usually indifferent Kellam threatened almost to undo his nerves entirely.

Kellam made such a complete and unwarranted furor over the trappings of his costume that Alec could only stare at the fellow in baffled fascination. Kellam wavered in unaccustomed agony over the choice between the oriental or the *trone d'amour* as the proper fold for the neckcloth; he lingered pensively over the waistcoats, swinging between the apricot cassimere and the striped linen in a torment of indecision; and finally, he was completely unable to make up his mind between the Lincoln green superfine and the *cachou de Laval* in the matter of the coat. At last, Alec's patience snapped, and he pulled the brown coat from the fellow's grasp and shrugged into it. "What on earth has gotten into you today, Kellam?" he asked irritably.

"Nothin', Cap'n. On'y tryin' t' be a bit 'elpful-like. Thought t' meself that ye'd wish t' look yer best today."

Alec glared at him depressingly. "There's nothing so very special about today, I tell you."

"So ye say. But ye needn't think t' tip me a rise. Y're as jittery as a frog on a washin' block, an' that's the truth."

"Perhaps so," Alec acknowledged, turning to the mirror for a last look, "but I don't see why *you* should be so greatly affected."

"Why not, I asks ye? '*Oo*, I'd like t' know, wuz the tom-doodle 'oo sat up nights listenin' to ye cryin' out 'er name?"

"What has that to say to anything? First of all, I've long since gotten over that. And second, I'm going to see her to obtain her agreement for an annulment, *not*, as I've told you a dozen times, for a *reconciliation*!"

Kellam's mobile face indicated his profound disappointment. "But ye could *try*, couldn't ye? Wiv 'ow y're lookin' like a reg'lar dash an' all, I'd go bail she'll like ye again."

"Will you never cease your blasted nagging? I don't *want* her to like me again! I don't like *her* any more!"

"Oh, very likely!" the batman said with heavy irony. "I ain't no fool, ye know. I ain't blind, neither. I see wot I see."

"Then buy yourself a pair of spectacles!" Alec said sourly, picking up the envelope that Newkirk had sent round and striding to the door. "When I return, I'll be well-nigh a single man again. And as merry as a mouse in the malt over it!"

"Ye don't say. Then the more fool *you*!" Kellam shouted after him as Alec slammed the door.

The altercation with Kellam had so churned his stomach that Alec decided not to take his carriage for the ride to Tyrrell House. A brisk walk, he hoped, would settle his agitation. He set off with energetic strides toward his destination, but he couldn't seem to shake Kellam's words from his mind. Why on earth was the fellow so eager for him to be reunited with Priss? The unpredictable batman had never even *met* the lady! Alec knew that Kellam had his best interests at heart—during the dark nights of the campaign they had each confided to the other the details of their lives and had come, each of them, to care deeply for the welfare of the other—but what made Kellam believe that a reconciliation would be the answer to Alec's prayers? Alec couldn't remember painting a picture of Priss for the fellow that would put her in so favorable a light, yet Kellam persisted in believing the best of her. The way the fellow spoke of her, one would almost believe he'd been intimately acquainted with her for years! He seemed even to know what she *looked* like! It was very strange indeed.

So deep was he in his ruminations that he failed to hear his name being called from a passing hack. It was not until the occupant of the carriage jumped out and ran toward him that he awoke from his reverie. "I say, Alec! *Alec Tyrrell*! *Ho*, there!" the fellow was shouting as he ran toward him.

Alec gaped. "Good lord, it's *Gar*!"

Garvin Danforth thrust out a hand in enthusiastic greeting. "I can't believe my good luck! I was just on my way to Tyrrell House to see you!"

Alec flushed. He had not seen his school friend since Gar had stood up with him at the wedding. They had exchanged a few letters during the war, but Alec hadn't written a word about his separation from his wife. "I'm no longer . . . er . . . staying at Tyrrell House," he said awkwardly.

"No? Then where have you and Prissy moved? It *was* a stroke of luck, then, that I spotted you. And look at you! I hardly *knew* you when I first saw you. You've turned into a . . . well, I may as well say it . . . a veritable *Corinthian*! I don't think I've ever laid eyes on such a marvelous coat. And that beaver at an angle . . . and the silver-headed cane! You've come a long way from our Oxford days, old man. But let's not stand here. Come up in the hack and I'll take you home. You're a sight for sore eyes, I can tell you. And I'm impatient to see your beautiful wife as well."

Alec hesitated. He had neither the time nor the inclination to explain matters to Gar here on the street. "I can't now, old fellow," he said embarrassedly. "I'm on my way to a long-standing and important . . . er . . . meeting. I'll explain later. Where are you staying?"

Gar's face fell. "I'm putting up at Long's, in Clifford Street. I'm only in town for a fortnight. I've been so deucedly immersed in my bibliographical work—but you don't know about that, do you? Well, in any case, Lord Hawthorne—it's his library I'm reorganizing—practically ordered me to take a holiday, and I immediately thought of you. I was certain you'd have sold out of the army by this time, so I thought we could spend some time together . . ."

"And so we shall," Alec assured him. "In fact, you can put up at my place. Plenty of room there, and you'll like it better than a hotel."

Gar brightened at the invitation. "That *would* be grand! But perhaps you'd better ask Prissy first. Females have an aversion to unexpected guests and surprise visits and that sort of thing."

"Good lord, Gar, you sound like a married man! Don't tell me you've taken yourself a wife!"

Gar laughed. "Me? Not likely. Too wrapped up in my work to be in the petticoat line. But Lady Hawthorne—my employer's wife, you know—never likes unexpected guests, so I thought—"

"Don't worry about it. I'll come by your hotel later and explain everything. But now I must rush off. See you later, Gar."

He hurried down the street, uncomfortably aware that Gar was watching him. The encounter had not done a bit of good for his spirits. It had merely reminded him of the awkwardness of his situation. Even after the decree of nullity would have been acquired, he realized, he would be beset with difficulties. Everyone he'd ever known as a married man would have to be informed. Old friends, like Gar, would be shocked and disapproving. And . . . good God! . . . what would his *grandfather* feel when he learned the truth?

With his mind in a troubled whirl, he tapped his cane irritably on the door of Tyrrell House. Above and beyond all his worries, the necessity of facing Priss now was the worst prospect. His bitterness toward her was so strong he wondered if he could manage to behave in a civilized fashion. Perhaps it would be the better part of valor to retreat and face her another day, when he might feel less hostile.

But Craymore, the butler, opened the door at that moment, and it was too late to escape. The aging butler had known Alec since childhood (when both his parents were alive and occupied this very house), and the warmth of his greeting shone through his butlerish impassivity. In fact, Craymore permitted himself the liberty of pumping his lordship's hand enthusiastically and remarking how very glad he was to see him back. "Her ladyship's expecting you, my lord," he said as soon as the greetings were exchanged. "If you'll just step this way to the drawing room . . ."

Chapter Eleven

Alec could see, in the butler's prompt closing of the drawing room doors behind him and the absence of anyone else in the room but Priss, who was standing in the window embrasure, that his wife had taken pains to ensure their privacy. She had evidently been watching for him, for she turned from the window with a smile of relief. "I was beginning to fear you wouldn't come," she said, crossing to him and holding out her hand.

He bowed over it with formal remoteness. "I *am* late. I'm sorry."

She withdrew her hand with nervous haste. "I did not m-mean to reproach you," she offered timidly. "You are not so *very* late, after all."

Her painful shyness was not the sort of response he'd expected. She had always been such a spirited, self-assured creature that this unwonted meekness startled him. He peered at her intently.

He had not really seen her closely in six years (having been too unsteady in body and mind and too bemused by the circumstances of their last meeting to have taken a proper look), and the change in her struck him profoundly. It was not that she'd lost her looks—if anything, she was more beautiful than he remembered. But she'd changed in a way he had not expected: the years seemed to have somehow . . . his mind struggled for a word . . . *refined* her. Her face had a chiseled

look—the hollows and planes more pronounced, the
lines on the forehead and round the mouth a little
darker. Her hair, bound in the back in a simple knot,
had lost some of its vibrancy and seemed paler than
before. Her skin, too, had lost the golden quality he
remembered and was now almost as white as an
alabaster sculpture. But what he found most surprising
in her appearance was not that she'd lost her bloom but
that she'd gained (in appearance at least) what so few of
the women he'd met in society seemed to possess—
character.

Balderdash, he thought, steeling himself against the
penetration of any vestige of tenderness or admiration
for her, *appearances are always said to be deceiving*.
She was probably still too young for her corruption to
have left its marks upon her face. And how many stories
had been told about women who *appeared* to be as pure
as saints and yet were as faithless as Satan?

Priss blushed under his intense scrutiny. "I think you
find me much changed," she murmured, her hand flying
to her hair as if she feared a strand had become loose.

"Time has not been unkind to you, ma'am, if that is
what you're asking."

At the sound of the repulsive "ma'am" her back
became rigid, and she frowned. "I was not asking for
flattery, sir," she said with a touch of her old spirit,
"and if you think time has been *kind* to me, you much
mistake the matter."

She turned and walked away from him, her hands
tightly clenched at her sides. When she reached the table
that stood between the tall windows at the far side of the
room, she stopped, leaned her hands upon it and
lowered her head. "I promised myself that I would
n-not behave missishly today. Forgive me." She tried,
by means of a couple of deep breaths to gather herself
together, and she turned round to face him with a small,
strained smile. "Please, Alec, do sit down. Would you
care for a glass of Madeira?"

"No, thank you. I hope this business will not be long.

I know you have something to say to me, and I'm here to listen, but we neither of us need to waste our time with these social niceties.''

"Very well, we'll dispense with the Madeira," she said dispiritedly and took a seat on the sofa. Indicating the wing chair facing her, she asked with the slightest touch of asperity, "Is taking a seat too much of a social nicety as well?"

Without responding, he placed his hat and cane on a small table near the sofa and sat down.

She raised her eyes to his face. Studying him with a brave directness, her mouth curved up again in an unwitting smile. "*You* certainly have changed, Alec. I never dreamed you'd turn yourself into a Corinthian. I don't think I've ever laid eyes on such a dashing coat."

He had a sudden, vivid recollection of the coat he'd worn the night he'd offered for her, from which his wrists had hung down so awkwardly from the too-short sleeves, and he couldn't help smiling himself. "Not much like the coats I wore in my younger days, is it?" he admitted.

"I would never have surmised that you'd turn into a Dandy. Do you have a valet who polishes your Hessians with champagne and spends hours tying your neckcloths?" she asked, letting her eyes roam over his finery with amused appreciation.

"I have my former batman who fusses over me like a mother hen, but he'd be more likely to *drink* the champagne than to use it on my boots."

Her smile broadened. "Remember that evening in Paris when you remarked to the Compte d'Estegrize that you saw no need for valets when almost any fool could manage to dress himself after the age of five—?"

Alec, who had for so many years strictly prevented himself from indulging in reminiscences of his honeymoon tour, was drawn into the memory before he had time to set up his defenses. He burst into an unwitting guffaw and nodded in quick recollection. "And the Compte stiffened up, looked at me through his quizzing glass and said, 'Zat, milor' Braeburn, is because you Eengleesh, you dress for ze warmth, but we French, we dress for *le style*!' ''

For the first time that day, Priss laughed out loud. It was not the humor of the story but the release from the tension of the day that brought it out. She was so delighted that she'd managed to shake Alec from the sullen stiffness of his earlier manner that her reaction was a bit extravagant.

He, of course, noticed and immediately froze. What had gotten into him to so forget himself? he wondered. "Yes . . ." he said quickly, "but perhaps we should get down to business, ma'am. What is it you wish to say to me?"

Her face clouded over. "I've gone over in my mind a thousand times . . . just how I should explain . . ." She looked at his face, as if searching for a sign of interest or warmth, but there was only an impenetrable impassivity. Her eyes flickered down uncertainly to the hands folded in her lap, and she went bravely on. "But I'm no longer clear about what it is that troubles you. Surely you must have realized by this time that the cause for which you left this house six years ago was something more imaginary than real."

His right eyebrow shot up, and he gave her a disdainful smile. "I don't know anything of the sort, ma'am."

"What do you *mean*?" she asked incredulously. "You don't *still* believe I was in love with Blake?"

"Why not? You told me so yourself."

She leaned forward and looked at him with earnest intensity. "I told you I *had* loved him. I never said I loved him when we married. You surely can *not* believe I cared for him after we'd been wed!"

Alec jumped up from his seat in acute discomfort. "I find speaking of these matters deucedly awkward, ma'am. What good does it do to rake up all this again?"

"We *must* talk about it, Alec! I want you back again. I want to be your *wife*!"

He wheeled on her. "Your *wants* no longer concern me, don't you understand? You've had what you want for too long."

The vehemence of his tone startled her. "How can you *say* that? I've waited six interminable *years* for what I want . . ."

"Spare me, please, from any more lies. I'm no longer the green boy I was when you wheedled me into marriage."

"*Wheedled* you!" She stared at him, aghast. "What sort of . . . of *coxcomb* have you become?"

"If I *am* a coxcomb, I don't see why you wish to have me as a husband," he retorted coldly.

She started to utter a rejoinder but found herself speechless. Putting her hands to her mouth, she shut her eyes, drew in her breath and endeavored to gain control of herself again. After a moment, she straightened up, lifted her head, folded her hands in her lap again and looked up at him. "We mustn't let this meeting degenerate into a silly quarrel, my dear. Please sit down again. Let me try to understand you. Will you answer a few questions for me?"

"Yes, I suppose so," he said reluctantly and took his seat again.

"Are you telling me, by these terribly . . . *unexpected* responses you've been making, that you believe I really *was* in love with Blake when you married me?"

His jaw tensed. "Yes. Why else would I have left?"

"And you still believe it?"

"Yes. I see no reason why I should change my mind."

"And you will not take my word that you are mistaken?"

"Why should I take your word?" he asked icily. "You were not, as I remember, a model of truthfulness, were you?"

She winced in real pain. "I might have indulged in some girlish deceits, yes, but I would never lie about something as important as *that*!"

"Wouldn't you?" He stood up and looked down at her in scorn, his mouth twisted, his jaw set, his eyes hard. "I think you are quite like most ladies in society. You say whatever will bring you what you want, whether it's the truth or not. Perhaps you don't consider it lying. Perhaps you and your kind don't understand what truth is at all.''

Her face, turned up to him, expressed sheer astonishment. Alec had never, as long as she'd known him, spoken with such unfeeling cynicism. She could barely believe this was the man she had been waiting for. Slowly, without her being aware of it, the corners of her eyes filled, and two tears spilled over and ran unheeded down her cheeks. ''Oh, my dear Alec,'' she murmured, ''what has *happened* to you?''

''Whatever it is, ma'am,'' he answered, completely unmoved, ''it keeps me from succumbing to tears and deceits as easily as I did before.''

For a long moment, she couldn't move. This icy stranger that Alec had become had numbed her to the core. She didn't know what to do, or what to say to him. ''Do you honestly mean,'' she asked helplessly, ''that nothing I can say would move you to reconsider—?''

''Nothing. You needn't look at me with that horrified stare. I *did* warn you . . .''

She lowered her eyes, but the horror remained inside her. She felt empty and too frozen to know quite what was happening. Later, she supposed, she would be able to understand, to sort it all out, to cry. Now she only knew that everything was over . . . all hope for her marriage, her happiness, her future. The love she'd carried in her breast unnourished for so long . . . even *that* was at an end. She felt nothing. ''What is it Mr. Newkirk wants me to sign?'' she asked at last, her voice flat and emotionless.

He hesitated for a moment, struck by the unfathomable look in her eyes. Then he pulled the envelope from his inner coat pocket and unfolded the contents. ''As I understand it, the document merely vouches for the fact that you and Edmonds had agreed to wed each other before you married me,'' he explained briefly.

''But . . .'' She blinked as if awakening from a stupor. ''But that's not *true*!''

He stiffened up again. "Now, see *here*! I thought we'd finished with this lying game of yours."

She put her chin up in angry defiance. "I *never* agreed to marry Blake. It's *you*, with your documents, who are engaged in playing lying games!"

"But Edmonds stood right here in this room and *told* me—!"

"I don't care *what* he told you! I never agreed to marry him, and I will not sign anything that says I did!"

Alec felt a tidal wave of rage start from his knotted stomach, swell up into his chest and flood into his head. He grasped Priss by the shoulders in a grip so painful she cried out. "Damn it, woman, haven't you put me through *enough*? I'm no longer such a fool that I don't know why you are continuing to perpetrate this pretense of a marriage. If my blasted fortune means so much to you, tell me your price for your signature. Well, don't gape at me! What is the price you'll take for my freedom?"

"*Price*?" With a sudden wrench of her body, she broke free of his hold, and without quite realizing what she was doing, she swung her arm with all the force at her command and slapped his face.

Alec reeled back a couple of steps, put out a hand to steady himself against a chair and stared at her. He could feel his cheek burning, but, strangely, his fiery anger seemed to have died down. He had to admit to a grudging admiration for her. When pressed, she was still a woman of considerable spirit.

Priss, seeing the growing red mark on his cheek, recoiled in horror. "I'm . . . *sorry*!" she whispered, holding out a trembling hand. "I didn't mean . . ." Then, bursting into tears, she put her face in her hands and dropped down on the sofa. Her shoulders shook as she gave way to the flood of sobs that had been threatening all through the interview to overwhelm her.

Alec stood watching her, his insides torn with conflicting desires. Something in him seemed to be almost physically compelling him to move to the sofa and take the weeping girl in his arms. But the rules he'd established in six years of rigid control over the sentimental yearnings of his nature pulled him to remain aloof. Twice he found himself taking a step toward her and twice he stopped himself. Finally, he forced himself to go to the window where he stood staring out into the street until her wracking sobs had abated. When at last he could hear the deep gasps subsiding to weak sniffles muffled by her handkerchief, he forced himself to speak. "I was *afraid* that a discussion of this sort would come to this—meaningless at best and ugly and bitter at worst," he said quietly.

"It's *you* who's m-made it ugly and b-bitter," she accused, dashing the last of her tears from her reddened eyes. "And I kn-know *why* you've done it, too."

He turned from the window, arrested. "What do you mean?"

She bit her lip and twisted the soggy handkerchief in her fingers. She hadn't intended to bring the matter up. She'd thought about it deeply and decided against it. She knew instinctively that she was making a mistake, but this entire conversation had gotten beyond her control, and she couldn't seem to help herself. "I'm n-not such a ninnyhammer as you evidently think me! Accusing *me* of lying and h-having b-base motives . . . when all the while, it's *you* who are lying and base! Do you think I've heard nothing of your doings with my c-calculating little cousin Clio?"

"So . . . you've heard that, have you?" He strode across the room and placed himself squarely before her. "Whatever you may choose to think, ma'am, Clio Vickers has nothing whatever to do with this. I learned a thing or two while I was abroad, you know, and one of the things I learned was that one can often salvage what seems to be a losing campaign by creating a diversion. You women are *born*, I think, with instincts for battle strategy. But don't think you can use Miss Vickers as a diversionary strategy *here*. It won't wash. Your admitted infidelity with Edmonds is the issue, not some unsubstantiated and malicious gossip concerning your cousin and myself."

"Dash it, Alec, there *was no infidelity* between Blake and me!" she cried.

He waved away her words with an impatient gesture. "Please! Not another denial. Repetition does not make it convincing."

"Only because you don't wish to be convinced. If you did, I shouldn't need to say anything. The obvious fact that I didn't marry him would have been convincing enough."

"Well, I do not find it so."

"So I see. Nor the fact—or haven't you yet heard it?—that Blake has been married these three years or more?" It was a last hope, and she suggested it with a faint elevation of her spirits, but Alec had been so distant, so strange, so unwontedly cruel throughout this meeting that any means of touching him seemed remote indeed.

"No. That fact, ma'am, merely substantiates my conclusions."

This response quite confounded her. "What conclusions?" she asked.

"Yours is not the only case, you know," he said distantly, "in which a lady has found it more convenient to be married to *one* man while she bestowed her favors on another."

Priss's eyes flew to his face in shock. "What is it you're *saying*?" she queried, her mind refusing to take in his hideous suggestion.

He fixed a steely eye on her. "If you insist on the whole truth, my dear, you may have it. You married me at the insistence of your mother, who convinced you that your possession of my considerable fortune had decided advantages over a life of impecunious romance with Edmonds. As all ladies of society with an ounce of sophistication soon discover, a married woman, especially one with a pitifully naive husband such as I was, has considerable freedom to do as she likes. What better way to have a life of luxury and a lover as well? And if that lover is *also* married, the cloak of respectability is double-thick, isn't it?"

Like someone in a hypnotic trance, she rose from her seat. Her lips were ashen and her eyes wide. "*You think . . . that Blake and I . . .?*" Her voice was a mere whisper, so great was her effort to speak.

"That is *exactly* what I think."

"And that we *still*—?"

"I have no interest in the present state of your affair, ma'am."

The floor seemed to lurch beneath her feet. Her hand reached out until it found support on the arm of the sofa, but her eyes never left his face. She could feel her limbs trembling and the blood pounding in her ears. She did not know what had happened to cause the change, but this man was not the Alec she'd married. She was filled with such revulsion that she felt physically ill. If she were a man, she would have set at him at once with sword or pistol and not ceased until he lay bleeding at her feet. If she were a simple country girl, she would have scratched his eyes out. But she was neither of these. She was merely a discarded wife . . . a foolish, romantic dreamer . . . with a ruined past she could no longer bear to remember, and an empty future she did not dare to contemplate.

But for the present, she knew only one thing. This creature standing before her filled her with loathing. "Give me the papers!" she said with venom. "I'll sign them! I'll sign *anything* that will allow me never to set eyes on you again!"

Chapter Twelve

It had been a shattering scene. If it had occurred on a stage, a curtain would have fallen on her ringing declaration of disdain. But this was not a play. No curtains fall on the dramas of real life; the scenes just continue, on and on. In this case, the continuation turned the drama into a farce—for there was neither pen nor inkstand to be found in the drawing room!

It was an embarrassing and futile anti-climax, during which Priss stormed helplessly around the room to find an inkstand that wasn't there (for all the writing tables were located either in the library or the upstairs or downstairs sitting rooms), acutely aware that Alec was observing her movements with an expression of distaste—much as one might watch a child having a temper tantrum. This only served to increase her fury, and she snatched the papers from his hand, ran out of the room and across the hall to the sitting room, Alec forced to follow behind.

She flung open the sitting room door, surprising her mother into a glad outcry. "Prissy, my love, is it over? Have you kissed and made—? Good heavens, what's the matter?"

Her daughter had brushed past her, her face stiff and unreadable, and made straight for the writing table in the corner. And Alec, equally stiff, had not crossed the threshold of the room but stood waiting in the doorway. "Alec! What's happening? Aren't you and Priss—?"

"No, Mama, we're *not*!" Priss muttered between clenched teeth as she hurriedly scratched her name on the three sheets. "You're not to say a *word* to him! Not a *word*!"

Lady Vickers, paling in alarm, looked helplessly from one to the other. "But . . . isn't he even to stay . . . to take tea? Everything's all laid out . . . the silver . . . the flowers . . .!"

Priss threw down the pen, scattering droplets of ink heedlessly across the desk top. "Bother the tea and the silver!" she muttered, wheeling about and crossing back to the doorway again. As she passed the table, she flung out her arm. "And bother the *flowers*, too!" With a violent swing she sent the vase toppling over and rolling across the table, scattering blooms and foliage all over the floor and sending the water in the vase spilling on the white linen to run unchecked over the table's edge. "*Here*!" She thrust the papers at him roughly. "You have what you came for! Now, please, leave this house! If you should ever have need to communicate with me again, you can do it through Mr. Newkirk." She pushed him aside and ran past him to the stairs.

Lady Vickers clasped a trembling hand to her bosom. Alec stared after Priss, thunderstruck. In spite of all his supposed sophistication, he had never before seen a woman in a genuine frenzy. He knew he should leave—he *wanted* to leave. But it seemed quite heartless, somehow, to go without a word. "Priss? . . . er . . . *ma'am* . . .?" he called after her awkwardly.

She had already run up the first few steps, but at his voice she stopped, her hand on the bannister. But she did not turn or acknowledge in any other way that she'd heard him.

He took a faltering step toward the staircase. "I . . . I just wanted to say that . . . if you have need of . . . of . . . er . . . of anything . . . you have only to ask Mr. Newkirk, and—"

She whirled around in a fury, her eyes blazing. "Do you m-mean *money*? You . . . you *dastard*! If you think I would take a *penny* of your blasted fortune, you're a greater fool than even *I* think you! I wouldn't *touch* your money . . . not even if I had to go b-begging for *b-bread* . . . *b-barefoot* . . . in the *snow*!'' And she turned and ran up the stairs and out of sight.

He looked after her in stupefaction until he heard her door slam shut. Then he turned to Lady Vickers, who had remained frozen to the spot during the entire altercation. ''I hope you'll tell your daughter, Lady Vickers,'' he said, his lips curling sardonically, ''that it will not be necessary for her to 'go b-begging b-barefoot in the snow.' I fully intend to make a substantial settlement—''

''I shall tell her nothing of the sort,'' Lady Vickers declared, drawing herself up to her full height and fixing him with a glare of withering scorn. She crossed to the door and, stalking past Alec with a forbidding frown, she added, ''She will want nothing of your settlements. If you ask *me*, Alec Tyrrell, you are the *world's prize idiot*, and Priss is well rid of you!'' Without another glance, she followed her daughter up the stairs.

For a moment Alec stood rooted to the floor, torn between two conflicting impulses—one to shout up the stairway some very choice epithets of his own, and the other to kick the furniture. But he realized that, although both these activities would afford him a pleasurable sense of release, neither would elevate him in the ladies' esteem—or his own. A discreet cough from the shadows made any other sequel impractical: Craymore was observing him from behind the stairs.

The butler emerged from hiding. ''You'll be wanting your hat and stick, my lord,'' he said, proffering the items with an air of unmistakable disapproval.

''I can tell from your expression, Craymore, that you want to say something,'' Alec said with a sigh. ''Go ahead and speak your mind . . . if you must.''

The butler shook his head, all his earlier warmth gone. ''It's not my place to say what I think, my lord. But if I were your father (and since I'm acquainted with your lordship since you were a babe in arms and your sainted mother permitted me to dandle you on my knees, I have sometimes felt like a substitute parent, you might say), I would say that you've acted mighty like a . . . a . . ."

Alec held up a restraining hand. "I know. A fool."

"Yes, my lord."

"Thank you, Craymore. Good day."

He stepped out into the fading sunlight and sighed in considerable relief as the door closed behind him. But his ordeal was not yet over. No sooner had he reached the street than he came face to face with Isaiah Hornbeck, obviously bound for the place he had just left. The older man grinned and grasped his hand. "Afternoon, Lord Braeburn. Y're lookin' at home to a peg. But are ye leavin' already? Don't tell me I've missed tea—her ladyship distinctly said to present myself at four—" He stopped himself abruptly, and his expression changed with the suddenness of the daylight when a small cloud obscures the sun. "Oh, no!" he exclaimed with alarm. "Ye haven't gone and cut yer wife *again*!"

"If by that expression you mean to suggest that Lady Braeburn and I have not reconciled," Alec answered stiffly, "you are quite right." He met Mr. Hornbeck's glower of disapproval with one of his own. "And if you're about to tell me that I'm a fool, you needn't bother. I've already heard it from four different quarters this very afternoon!" He lifted his hat, nodded brusquely and strode off down the street.

Alec found his spirits not a little depressed by the encounters, and his return home did not bring him the relief he'd hoped to find, for Kellam's attitude was so marked in its disapproval that Alec was not permitted to forget what caused it. The batman went about his household duties with his nose decidedly out of joint. The fellow did not deign to speak to his employer with anything but the rudest of monosyllables, and in all ways was so impossible that Alec almost considered terminating his employment. When he mentioned the possibility aloud, however, Kellam merely snorted, for

both of them knew that they were too tightly bound for
Alec ever to take such a drastic step.

Even his evening's festivities at White's, in the company of Ferdie, failed to cheer him, and when he suddenly realized, with an exclamation of self-condem-
nation, that he'd forgotten all about his promise to Gar,
he knew that his evening was quite ruined. He took
himself round to Gar's hotel as soon as he could make
good his escape from the club, but his friend, whom he
awakened from a deep sleep, was groggy, sullen and
piqued over Alec's neglect. It took all of Alec's talent
for persuasion to bring himself back into Gar's good
graces.

Gar moved in with him the next day, but even that
turned out to be less agreeable than he'd anticipated.
Garvin Danforth had changed, of course, yet in many
ways he'd remained disturbingly the same. His mind
was still in the ivory tower world of scholarship. He was
completely absorbed by the work he was doing for his
uncle, Lord Hawthorne, whose collection of many
thousands of volumes of scholarly tomes had been sadly
in need of organization before Gar had come on the
scene. The fellow could speak of nothing else but his
bibliographical discoveries. Alec could easily sym-
pathize with Gar's excitement over having discovered an
unknown translation of Tacitus or an unfamiliar edition
of Erasmus' *The Praise of Folly*, but the fellow did tend
to prose on at inordinate length over these triumphs. To
make matters worse, Gar tended to disapprove of
everything Alec did, and he did not hesitate to voice his
disapproval very frankly and at great length. "I had no
idea you were a *gambler*, Alec," he'd say. "Lord
Hawthorne says that gambling is the scourge of the upper classes, and I am inclined to agree—"

Alec would try to put in a few words in self-defense.
"A few games of cards can hardly be considered—"
he'd begin.

But Gar would not be stopped. "A game of cards
leads so easily to a game of Faro, and before one knows
it, one is *gaming*, you know. I've heard that twenty

thousand pounds can be lost in one evening at your club! Twenty thousand! Isn't that monstrous? Why, entire estates can be lost in such profligacy! And it is such an addiction that the gamester soon begins betting on anything—a race between two flies on the wall, or whether or not a certain lady will succumb to a certain gentleman's wiles! Can you not see the way in which the corruption deepens?''

Gar's disapproval over Alec's pursuits and interests did not stop with gambling. He was appalled at the size of Alec's wardrobe, remarking that the excessive number of his coats indicated "a shocking extravagance and a tendency toward vanity." According to Gar, Alec's entire life was reprehensible: he rose too late in the morning, went to bed too late at night and was completely decadent in between. Alec's friends, Gar said, were too frivolous, his pursuits too mindless and his habits too self-indulgent.

This stream of criticism became so irritating to Alec that he was often tempted to suggest to Gar that he was wasting his time as a bibliographer—that his talent for *preaching* indicated a decided bent for holy orders. But he held his tongue, for in moments of detachment he recognized with amusement that he, Alec, could have been quite the same sort of pedantic nuisance if his life after Oxford had continued as predicted.

But there was a good reason why Gar hammered away at Alec with such irritating persistence. Alec had been the friend he'd most admired, the fellow he'd always tried to emulate. Alec, in their school days, could do no wrong. Gar admired his thinking, his appearance, his character and even the woman Alec had chosen to wed. His devotion to his old friend had been so deeply ingrained that, even now, it would not waver.

Garvin Danforth considered himself an idealist, and it had troubled him deeply when he first began to see the extent to which his friend Alec had changed. Alec seemed to have lost *his* ideals. But he suspected that his separation from his wife had caused Alec great pain, and he soon began to realize that Alec's descent into dissipation was an escape from the unpleasant reality of his life. Gar understood, and in his mind, he forgave Alec completely.

But understanding and forgiving did not necessarily mean, in Gar's view, approving. He *could not* and *would not* approve of Alec's behavior. While he had a breath in his body, he would fight to save Alec from a descent into a life of waste and corruption.

For Alec, however, Gar's endless sermons were more irritating than uplifting. Although his affection for his old friend remained, his desire to be in the fellow's company decreased markedly. Ferdie, on the other hand, became more welcome than ever. Ferdie, with his easy disregard for rules and conventions and his outspoken lust for pure, mindless pleasure, seemed to be a companion more suited to a grown man who had faced the realities of life. Gar seemed still a boy, full of romantic illusions. Despite Gar's patent disapproval, Alec continued to accompany Ferdie on any dissipated course the ex-Major suggested. Alec invited Gar to join them, but more often than not, Gar chose to remain behind. Alec did not often reject Ferdie's invitations in order to stay at home with Gar, even though he felt guilty for leaving his old friend behind. Now more than ever, he needed the escape from his thoughts which his adventures with Ferdie provided.

Gar, of course, felt rejected during these times when Alec and Ferdie went off without him. He wavered between an urge to cut his holiday short and return to work and a contradictory inclination to remain here with Alec and fight Ferdie for Alec's character. Musing over this decision one evening, sitting in Alec's drawing room and brooding in a chair by the fire, he was interrupted by a cough from Kellam, who stood nervously in the doorway. "Yes, what is it, Kellam?"

"Pardon, Mr. Danforth, but there's a lady 'ere . . ."

"A *lady*? To see me?"

"To see the Cap'n. But she says she wants t' wait fer 'im. Where 'm I t' put 'er, eh?"

"Put her? I don't know what you mean."

"I mean where's she t' wait? We ain't got no sittin' rooms fer ladies in this 'ere place. This 'ere drawin' room's the on'y place what's right to put a lady . . ."

"Oh, I see." Gar pulled himself to his feet in haste, putting up one hand to smooth his hair and the other to straighten his neckcloth. "I suppose you'd better bring her in here, then."

Kellam shrugged and disappeared. In a moment he was back, leading in the most spectacular young lady Gar had ever seen. "In 'ere, Miss Vickers. The Cap'n's chum Mr. Danforth'll keep ye company."

"Thank you, Kellam," the lady said with a gracious smile and crossed over the threshold. She held out her hand to Gar. "Mr. Danforth, how do you do? I had *heard* that Lord Braeburn had an old school friend staying with him."

Gar bowed over her hand and then stood fidgeting in awkward discomfort. He didn't know what to say or do—the situation was not one which he felt competent to handle. In the first place, the lady had brought no companion with her. He had never before heard of a lady of breeding who would pay a call on a gentleman at night without chaperonage of any kind. In the second place, Kellam had taken himself off without properly introducing them. Gar hadn't even caught her name! And in the third place, the lady herself was so gaudily attired, and her gown was cut so low over her bosom, that Gar didn't know where to look.

The lady, sensing his discomfiture, laughed coquettishly. "Well, Mr. Danforth, are you going to stand there eyeing me like a fish, or will you ask me to sit down?"

"Oh! Ah . . . yes. Please. Do sit down, Miss . . . er . . . Miss . . ."

"Vickers. Clio Vickers." She pulled off the shawl that had been hanging from her arms, placed it on the back of the chair facing the one he'd been occupying and settled herself into it comfortably.

"Vickers?" he asked, his brow clearing in some relief. "Oh, I *see*! You're *family*, then."

"I would hardly say that, Mr. Danforth. I *am* his wife's cousin, but I barely know the woman. Won't *you* sit down, please? I shall get a stiff neck if I have to look up at you all evening."

Gar obediently sat down opposite her and colored to the ears as she looked him over in cool appraisal. From the corner of his eye, he appraised her too. He found little to approve of. Her hair, he had to admit, was marvelous, its gleaming redness brushed into a modish Greek style that permitted dozens of little ringlets to frame her face, but she was otherwise shockingly indecorous. The gown she wore was of bright pink which clashed horridly with her hair—he wondered how she managed to look so attractive in spite of it. It was the low *décolletage*, he supposed, that made her look so lovely. It was indecently revealing, but he couldn't deny that it was effective. In addition, she had seated herself in a most unladylike way—one leg outstretched so that the ankle showed below the hem of her dress and one arm raised and bent enticingly behind her to support her head. She certainly showed no embarrassment or shyness about being in a gentleman's flat in the company of a strange man.

"I've seen you before, I think," she remarked. "Weren't you the fellow who stood up for Alec at his wedding?"

"Yes, I was. Were *you* there?" He looked at her in surprise, but, meeting her eye, he uncomfortably looked away again. "I'm sorry. That was rude, I suppose. It's only that I can't imagine why I don't remember you."

"I was a mere child in those days and quite beneath your notice," she said, her green eyes glinting at him distractingly. "But you weren't at all rude, you know. You paid me a compliment."

"I? A compliment?"

"Yes, didn't you realize it? You implied that, if I'd looked in those days as I do now, you couldn't have forgotten me, isn't that right?"

"Well, yes . . . I suppose I—"

"That was very nice, Mr. Danforth," she said, a little gurgle in her voice.

She was obviously quizzing him. He must appear like a bumbling gawk to such a worldly, self-assured creature. "You are teasing me, I think," he said, stung. "I'm afraid I'm not . . . er . . . accustomed to . . . er . . . paying compliments to ladies."

"Or entertaining them in privacy, like this?" she suggested with a grin.

He nodded, threw her a quick glance and quickly looked away again. There was something about her that made it almost impossible for him to speak comfortably. When speaking, one was supposed to look directly into the eyes of the person one addressed, yet with this girl he didn't know where his eyes would land. He felt himself staring at her *décolletage*, or at her ankle, or at the line of her thighs which showed clearly through the thin, clinging fabric of her gown. (He'd heard that some ladies—very dashing ones—were wont to damp their petticoats to make their dresses cling. He had little doubt that Miss Vickers had employed that technique this evening.) He was very much afraid that Miss Vickers was *fast*! But he couldn't continue to sit here staring at his boots. "Was Alec . . . er . . . Lord Braeburn . . . expecting you?" he asked, meeting her mocking eyes bravely.

"No, he wasn't."

"Oh, I see."

"And you may call him Alec to me, you know. We are *very* well acquainted."

"Oh, I see."

She laughed again and shook her head at him. "Do you know, Mr. Danforth, that you have a habit of saying 'Oh, I see,' when you disapprove of something?"

He blushed. "Do I? Oh . . . I . . . I beg your pardon. I wouldn't presume to disapprove . . . I mean . . . I have no right to . . . that is . . ."

"No, you haven't any right. But you *do* disapprove of me, don't you?"

He felt himself redden even more. "I don't see how you . . . that is, I didn't want to . . . to . . ." he stammered. "I hope I haven't said anything to . . . to offend . . ."

"No, you haven't," she said, propping her chin in her hand, her elbow resting on the arm of the chair, and looking at him frankly, "but I wish you would. It would be more interesting than to make fruitless conversation about nothing at all."

He would have enjoyed making interesting remarks to her, shocking her in some way and shaking the supercilious gleam from her eyes when she looked at him. But what could he say? He certainly couldn't tell the lady that he thought she was fast! "But you can't expect . . . I mean, I don't know you long enough to . . ." His voice petered out. He had sounded like a tongue-tied schoolboy. How had a mere slip of a girl—she couldn't be much older than nineteen—have put him at such a disadvantage?

She looked at him for a moment with her disdainful smile and then rose from her chair. "Well, I see I am making you uncomfortable, Mr. Danforth," she said, picking up her shawl.

He stumbled to his feet. "No, no. Not at all," he said hurriedly.

"Yes, I am. You think this visit is improper, don't you?"

"Well, I—"

"There, you *see*? You *do* think so. And you are quite right. If Mama knew I had come here, she would have an attack of the vapors. Will you give Alec a message for me?"

"Yes, of course, Miss Vickers," he said, feeling a flood of relief that this painful interlude was coming to an end.

"Tell him that I've had quite enough of this severence he's imposed upon us. I care not a whit about the gossip. Tell him I shall expect him to wait upon me tomorrow, to take me riding. Tomorrow, I say. And if he fails, tell him I shall run off with the coachman. Or

Ferdie. Or . . ." She looked at him with her teasing smile, tossed her shawl over her shoulders and sauntered to the door. "Or *you*!" She gave her gurgling laugh just before she disappeared from sight.

Gar stared after her, completely appalled. Was Alec *involved* with Miss Vickers? From the sound of the message, it certainly seemed so. Had Alec sunk so low that he could entangle himself with so brazen a female as *that*? Why, the girl was worse than fast! She was . . . *shameless*!

But her visit had done him *some* good. It had made up his mind for him. He would not return to the Hawthornes just yet. Alec, even if he didn't realize it, required his help and guidance . . . and he, Garvin Danforth, was going to supply it. He would be the anchor in the stormy sea of Alec's life. He would stand by Alec's side to caution him against corrupt indulgences . . . and to save him from whatever tragic results would come if Alec didn't heed his advice.

He went to the writing table and dashed off a note to Lord Hawthorne saying that he might not find it possible to return to work as soon as he'd expected. His friend needed him!

Chapter Thirteen

Lady Vickers never learned what Alec had said to her daughter during that fateful interview, but she knew it must have been dreadful—dreadful enough to have shaken the girl out of a six-year lethargy. She felt, of course, a profound sympathy for her daughter's suffering (for although Priss had not been seen to shed a single tear since Friday, there was something one could see in the back of her eyes and the set of her mouth that told of her deep inner pain) and she couldn't help but be glad that the waiting was over. Priss had for much too long been playing the part of Patient Griselda, and Lady Vickers had seen quite enough of it. It was a relief to learn that her daughter's spirit had been awakened at last from its six-year nap.

Lady Vickers' new friend, Isaiah Hornbeck, had been furious with Alec when he'd heard her account of the interview. "I'd like to give the boy the thrashin' he deserves," he'd said to Lady Vickers.

"Well, we really don't *know* what transpired, Mr. Hornbeck. A man must be presumed innocent, after all—"

"*Innocent*! When I see the look in the little lass's eyes, I could wring the fellow's neck!"

Lady Vickers sighed. "I know. It quite breaks my heart to see her. I'd give my ruby brooch (and just between us, my friend, it's the only decent piece of jewelry I own) to find out what that beast said to her. But I can't bring myself to ask. I think it would hurt Priss too much to talk about it.''

Hornbeck nodded. ''Y're right, ma'am. Least said, soonest mended, as they say. Best that ye all forget him and go about yer lives.''

That was just what Priss intended to do. The very same Friday evening after the fateful altercation, Priss announced that they were moving back to Three Oaks in Derbyshire.

''Oh, Priss, do you mean it? How I've been *yearning* to go home again!'' her mother sighed. ''But why now?''

''This house is Alec's,'' Priss said flatly. ''I won't live in it a day longer than I have to.''

The two ladies set about the enormous task of packing. Priss was determined that nothing belonging to Alec Tyrrell should find its way into their boxes; on the other hand, there were paintings and other household items which she'd brought with her to the house which she was equally determined he should not have. With her mother, she went through every room in the house, carefully sorting through all the furnishings and housewares to determine their ownership.

Mr. Hornbeck, with his talent for organization, his skill in management and his knowledge of the business of shipping goods, was an invaluable aid to them. He provided them with sturdy boxes, sound advice and the name of an honest drayman to transport their possessions to Derbyshire. And, in great embarrassment, he took Lady Vickers aside one evening and made a sincere, if awkward, offer of financial assistance ''if yer ladyship should find yerself a wee bit scorched.'' He assured her it would ''pleasure me mightily'' to aid her in this regard, since he was ''nicely beforehand in the world and very well to pass.''

She laughingly turned the offer aside, assuring him that she was quite plump in the pocket, having been provided with an adequate, if not luxurious, jointure by her late husband. In secret, she *was* somewhat worried about financial matters, for prices had risen alarmingly since the war's end, and she was not at all sure that her meager inheritance would be sufficient for the needs of both herself and her daughter since her daughter had completely stopped drawing on the account that Alec had always left at her disposal. However, it was a problem that they didn't need to face at once. There was enough on their minds at the moment to worry over. The rest could wait.

Priss was busier and more active than she'd been in years. She moved through the days with a dogged energy, supervising the packing, helping to clean the rooms and cover the furniture with the Holland covers, writing to the housekeeper at Three Oaks to make certain all would be in readiness for their arrival, and paying calls on a few select friends to say her goodbyes. Lady Vickers was surprised and somewhat pleased to note that Priss began—as in the days of her come-out—to wear more daring gowns when she went out. She chose brighter colors, too, and put a dashing ostrich plume on her favorite bonnet. It was only when the girl emerged one evening from her dressing room (after being closeted with Lady Vickers' hairdresser for two hours) with her hair cut short that Lady Vickers voiced an objection. Priss had done her hair in a style like the notorious Lady Caro Lamb. Her head was covered with soft, bouncy curls, none of them more than three inches long. "Aren't you going a bit far, my dear?" she asked mildly.

"Perhaps. But I'm tired of looking like a dowd. Ariadne thinks I will look all the crack. Besides, if Rosalind Wilkes can walk about town with a muff as huge as a bear, and your niece Clio can appear in public in a garish, pink gown cut down to *here*, I can certainly be permitted to wear my hair like Caro Lamb."

Lady Vickers withdrew her objections. Her daughter's hairstyle was charming and made her look years younger. And if the gossips wanted to whisper about it, let them. In less than a week, they would be returning to Derbyshire. London gossip would make very little difference to them there.

With Priss driving everyone in the household to work at peak energy, the task of packing and closing the house was soon completed. But just when the last of the boxes was about to be tied, the last of the rooms to be swaddled with Holland covers and the last of the good-byes to be said, a letter was delivered which threw the ladies into complete turmoil and threatened to undo all their plans.

It was addressed to Priss, and it was brought to the dining room—the last of the rooms to be closed—where Priss and Lady Vickers were packing the china. They had rolled up their sleeves and, enveloped in huge aprons, they had carefully wrapped and crated each piece of a one hundred and forty piece set of Worcester Royal Porcelain with the famous "willow" pattern which Lady Vickers had given to her daughter as a wedding gift. The task had just been completed when the footman came in with the letter. Lady Vickers instructed the footman to nail the lid on the fully packed crate, while Priss went to the window to read the missive. It was from the Earl. *My dearest granddaughter,* he'd written, *it has been so many weeks since I heard from you and Alec that I've begun to wonder what's become of you. Of course, I'd lay odds that, after a separation of six years, a loving couple has a need to spend some time in seclusion. However, I will admit to a feeling of loneliness since Alec's last visit, autumn being a season when one grows increasingly aware of the swift passage of time and the fragility of life. It makes one wish to have one's family close by. Is it selfish of an old man to say these things?*

But I don't mean to sound melancholy. In truth, I am very cheerful at the moment, having just had a visit from my doctor who tells me that I am much improved. This being the case, I would like to make a suggestion. Why don't we open up Braeburn for a splendid house party, as we used to do before the wars? We have not properly celebrated Alec's return, and since I am feeling relatively hale, this might be the most favorable time. We can invite some of your London friends—as many

*or as few as you like—and anyone else you may think
of. I'd lay odds that we could have a rousing good time.
It would certainly be a blessing for an old man to hear
the sounds of merriment again in this quiet old house.*

*If you and Alec favor the idea, write and let me know
when you would find it convenient to make the trip, so
that I can begin the preparations.*

*Hoping this finds you both—and Lady Vickers, too,
of course—in the very best of health, I remain your
loving grandfather, Braeburn.*

Lady Vickers was so intent on preserving the china
from destruction that she didn't take her eyes off the
footman until the fellow had put in the last nail. When
she finally looked up, she was appalled to see her
daughter staring out absently at nothing at all, her face
a picture of intense distress. "My *dear*! What is it
now?" she cried, waving the footman from the room.

"The Earl! How could I have forgotten—?" With a
trembling hand she held the letter out to her mother.
"The poor darling. How are we to *face* him now?"

Lady Vickers scanned the note quickly. "I didn't
know he'd been ill. He says he's *improved*. Does that
mean he's on his way to a cure or that he's contracted
some lingering affliction?"

Priss shook her head as she sank upon the wooden
packing case. "I don't know. His heart has not been
strong these last years. Perhaps he's been stricken with
an attack . . ."

"Good heavens, do you think so?" Lady Vickers
began to pace about the room. "If his heart is weak,
how will he stand the news that . . . that . . .?"

"Exactly! How can we *tell* him?"

Lady Vickers threw her daughter a look of dawning
horror. "But how can we *not* tell him? If we are to live
at Three Oaks—practically on his doorstep—he's bound
to find out!"

"Mama! The news might . . . *kill* him!"

Lady Vickers sank down beside her daughter. "He
and your father wanted that accursed marriage for so

long . . . and the Earl was so overjoyed that you and Alec were happy. It was the dream of a lifetime come true for him."

Priss looked at her mother aghast. "What are we to *do*? We can't possibly return to Three Oaks now!"

Later that afternoon, Kellam popped his head in the door of the drawing room but found only Garvin Danforth, in his shirtsleeves, seated in his favorite armchair reading a frayed copy of Virgil's *Eclogues* in the original Latin. "Oh," Kellam muttered, "ain't the Cap'n 'ere?"

"He's changing into his riding togs, as any good manservant ought to know for himself," Gar responded, not looking up from the page.

"Well, I'm too busy bein' butler an' kitchen maid to be doin' valet service too, y'know. Lady Vickers is 'ere t' see 'im."

"What, *again*?" Having been too deeply immersed in his reading, he was aware only of the "Vickers" in Kellam's announcement, and thought Clio had returned. He dropped the book and leaped to his feet. "Are you letting her *in*? I *don't* . . ." He paused, fingered his neckcloth nervously and said reluctantly, "Oh, very well. Tell her to come in here until Alec is ready."

Kellam, who had been watching him with an expression that was obviously and offensively scornful, merely nodded and disappeared. By the time Lady Vickers was heard in the corridor, Gar had thrown on his coat, taken a quick look into the mirror over the mantelpiece and posed himself in a stance of casual welcome a few feet from the doorway. As soon as he heard a footstep and the rustle of a gown, he smiled, put out his hand and began the speech he'd hastily prepared: "Well, ma'am, didn't you trust me to deliver your mes—? *Oh!*"

Lady Vickers' surprise was as great as his. She blinked at him in complete puzzlement, but after a moment her brow cleared. "Mr. *Danforth*, of course!

How very nice to see you after all these years. Were you saying something about delivering a *message* for me?''

Gar blushed, bowed awkwardly over her hand and stammered an incoherent apology. ''*Lady* Vickers . . . delighted to see you . . . No, no message at all . . . just a bit of a misunderstanding. Won't you sit down?''

Gar spent the next few minutes trying to make polite conversation, but he had been so disconcerted by his mistake that he continued to stumble and stammer. Fortunately, Alec appeared on the threshold almost immediately, buttoning his riding coat hastily, his brow wrinkled in puzzled concern. Gar quickly excused himself and left the room.

Alec didn't waste a moment on amenities. ''Is something wrong with Priss?'' he asked tensely.

Lady Vickers, whose polite smile had faded the moment her estranged son-in-law had made his appearance, raised her eyebrows haughtily. ''If there were, my lord,'' she said coldly, ''you would be the *last* person to whom I would turn. I believe you made it clear that you were no longer interested in matters relating to my daughter.''

''I shall always have such an interest, ma'am. I am not made of stone, you know. However, since it is not Priss's health which brings you, may I ask to what I owe the honor of this visit?''

''Yes, you may. It is this.'' She handed over to him the letter Priss had received earlier. ''I believe that this is a matter which concerns you even more than it does us; therefore I decided to bring it to your attention.''

Something in her ladyship's use of pronouns struck his ear. Before he opened the letter, he couldn't resist asking, ''Doesn't your daughter know you've come?''

Lady Vickers' eyes flickered and fell. ''My daughter does not see fit to mention your name. I took it upon myself to come to you without mentioning it to her.''

''I see.'' He opened the letter and read it through, shut his eyes in pain and read it again. Then he sat down on a chair opposite hers. ''I've been shamefully neglectful,'' he muttered, half to himself. ''Do you have any idea what might be the nature of the illness he mentions?"

"No, I'm afraid not. Priss believes it is his heart."

"His *heart*?" Alec ran a worried hand through his hair. "I had no idea—!"

Lady Vickers felt a small softening toward him. She leaned forward and patted his arm. "You needn't blame yourself. The Earl *did* develop a weakness in his heart while you were abroad, but it was not thought to be incapacitating, and he made us promise not to tell you. *Now*, however, if it has become more serious, I thought you should be aware . . ."

"Yes. I thank you, Lady Vickers. It was thoughtful of you to come."

"I didn't come merely to inform you of the condition of the Earl's health. There's more to it."

"You mean the party he suggests? We can make some excuse. I'll go up and stay with him for a while. I can invent some reason why Priss isn't with me."

"You don't understand. Priss and I had intended to return to Derbyshire ourselves. Permanently."

Alec looked at her in considerable surprise. "Do you mean Three Oaks? But, I thought . . . that is, I was given to understand that Priss . . . and you, of course . . . were fixed in *London* permanently."

"I don't know why you should have been told such a thing. I, for one, never intended to remain in London after you had returned."

"But Priss . . . surely she's been . . . er . . . happy here, hasn't she?"

"*Happy*? You must be mad! What had she here in London to make her happy?" Lady Vickers asked scornfully.

"But she has friends and . . . er . . . friends . . ." he said lamely. He couldn't very well, he realized belated, suggest to her *mother* that Priss had a lover in the vicinity.

"Her London friends are quite beside the point, my lord. Now that matters between you have been—how shall I put it?—severed, she no longer *has* a London home. Naturally, she plans to return to Derbyshire with me.''

"No longer has a *home*? What on earth are you talking about?" Alec demanded, rising from his seat.

"Tyrrell House is *yours*, my lord, as well you know. Priss has no intention of—''

"Did she think I was going to *put her out*? Has she lost her *wits*? Of all the *muttonheaded*—!''

"Will you please stop shouting at me, Alec? None of this is *my* doing, you know. Besides, we are straying from the point.''

Alec sat down again and rubbed his eyes. "What point?''

Lady Vickers viewed him in considerable annoyance. "Haven't you yet grasped it? You've placed my daughter and me in a very awkward situation. We are reluctant to return to Three Oaks if our appearance there will reveal to your grandfather the truth about your marriage. Yet we have no other choice—''

"You *have* another choice," Alec said impatiently. "You can remain in London. At Tyrrell House.''

"But Priss does not *wish* to remain in your house.''

He met her eye angrily, but the weakness of his position gave him pause. He had no right to tell Priss where to live. She couldn't be expected to remain in London to please *him*. "If you are determined to go back to Derbyshire . . . well, then I'll . . . have to tell him," he said worriedly.

"But that's just the point. If you tell the Earl about you and Priss . . . well, Priss thinks it may . . .''

"Kill him?" Alec looked at her helplessly. "Then what am I to *do*?''

"I don't know. If I had a solution to this impasse you've gotten us into, I wouldn't have demeaned myself by coming here.''

"Your daughter had a hand in creating this 'impasse,' ma'am, even if you're unwilling to admit it," he muttered resentfully.

"If you are going to try to tell me that my daughter's innocuous little peccadillo caused this monstrous predicament, I shall stand up and scream!" Lady Vickers snapped.

His eyebrows went up in sardonic scorn. "I wasn't referring to your daughter's 'innocuous little peccadillo.' I meant that if she'd let my solicitor proceed with the annulment six years ago, my grandfather would have learned the truth at a time when he could have managed to survive it!"

"If there is anything in this world I most dislike, Alec Tyrrell, it is the phrase 'if you had only.' Hindsight comes cheap, young man. What I'd like to know is what you intend to do *now*?"

"I have no idea, ma'am," he said coldly, rising from his chair. "But as a first step, I'd like to ask if you came in your carriage and if you intend to return to Hanover Square at once."

"The answer is yes to both questions," she replied in some surprise. "Why?"

"Because I'd be obliged if you'd take me up."

"If you like. Do you wish me to drop you somewhere?"

"Yes. At Tyrrell House. I have a couple of matters that I think I had better discuss with *my wife*."

Chapter Fourteen

When the carriage arrived at Hanover Square, Alec jumped out and strode angrily up the steps of the house without waiting for Lady Vickers. It was undoubtedly an act of extreme rudeness, but since they'd spent the time during the ride engaged in a vehement quarrel, he'd already passed beyond the bounds of polite behavior anyway. The argument had centered around the wisdom of his paying a call on Priss at this time. Lady Vickers, anticipating with considerable trepidation an explosion of wrath from her daughter merely because she'd taken the liberty of visiting Alec without permission, did not want to accept the additional responsibility of bringing him back with her to make this unannounced visit.

"But it is not your responsibility, ma'am," Alec said reasonably. "It is all mine, I assure you."

But her ladyship was not reassured. She tried every argument she could think of to dissuade him. Alec, after several fruitless attempts to reason with her, quite lost his temper. "Your daughter and I are both of us old enough," he told his mother-in-law coldly, "to make our own decisions about our lives without requiring parental permission at every turn." And to forestall any further argument, he leaped out of the carriage as soon as it rolled to a stop.

He brushed by Craymore and strode into the hallway, but there he stopped abruptly. The appearance of the house was a shock to him. Every bit of furniture had been covered, and the windows of the rooms into which he could see were shuttered and draped. The house looked dark and lifeless. The last time he'd seen it this way was after his mother's death. "What on *earth*—?" he asked angrily, turning on the butler. "Have they closed the house already?"

The elderly servant shrugged. "All but the bedrooms and the morning room. May I take your hat, my lord?"

"No, don't bother. I don't intend to make a long stay." He placed his hat on what he knew, under its sheet, was the hall table and looked at Craymore with a troubled frown. "I say, Craymore, her ladyship hasn't given *you* notice, has she?"

The butler gave a slight smile. "Oh, no, my lord, don't worry about that. I'm to stay on as caretaker. I'll be right as rain."

Alec nodded. "Will you ask Lady Braeburn to come down? I'd like to see her on some rather urgent business."

Lady Vickers loomed up in the outer doorway. "Never mind, Craymore. I'll tell her myself." And she marched to the stairs, passing her son-in-law without so much as a nod in his direction, her nose very decidedly out of joint.

But before she'd climbed three steps, her daughter appeared at the top. She was backing down the stairway carrying, with the help of a housemaid, a tall, elaborately framed looking glass. She was holding up one end and the maid the other.

Lady Vickers was horror-struck. Not only was her daughter doing a heavy, menial task, but her costume was even less dignified than that of the housemaid who accompanied her. The housemaid was wearing a neat apron and a frilled mobcap, but Priss had covered *her* hair with a shabby scarf and pinned up her skirts so that her legs, in their thin white stockings, were exposed to the knees! "Priss!" she cried. "What in heaven's name are you *doing*?"

"Hush, Mama. Don't distract me." Carefully looking over her shoulder at the step below, she cautiously began to back down. "It's Grandmother Vickers' Venetian looking . . . glass . . ." she explained, her breath a bit short from her exertions. "Becky and I . . . decided it would be safer to pack it . . . downstairs in the hallway . . . than upstairs in all that . . . confusion."

"But why couldn't you ask Craymore, or one of the footmen—?"

"I didn't want . . . to take any chances with it." Her pace was now more certain, and the mirror was carried down several steps during this exchange.

The maid, who was facing front, could see a gentleman gaping at them from below. "Pssst, my lady," she whispered to Priss, "ye've got a gent—"

"Hush, Becky. Save your . . . breath. Wait 'til we . . . get down," Priss ordered, taking another gingerly step backward.

Lady Vickers threw Alec an agonized, I-told-you-so glance. Clearly this was not the time for him to be paying unexpected calls on his wife. Lady Vickers would at least have liked to have had an opportunity to warn her daughter that he was here, but she very much feared that, if she told Priss now, a broken mirror might be the result. "Priss, my love, you *will* hang on to that glass carefully, won't you? But I think you ought to know . . ." she began dubiously.

"What, Mama? Goodness, this is . . . heavier than I thought. But . . . we're almost down. There! The last step, Becky. Let's set it down right here 'til I catch my breath."

They set the mirror down carefully, leaning one end against the wall. "Well, Mama, that's—" At that moment, she caught a glimpse in the glass of a man standing behind her and whirled around. "Oh, my *God*! *Alec*!"

"I *told* him not to—" Lady Vickers said in a hasty attempt to exonerate herself from blame.

But Alec cut in. "Excuse me for intruding," he said, his emotions swinging wildly between his residual anger at her and amusement at her obvious embarrassment, "but I have some urgent matters which I must discuss with you."

"I *told* him," Lady Vickers began again firmly, "that he should wait for a more propitious moment."

Priss, her heart beating much too rapidly to bear, clenched her fists to keep herself in control. "As far as I'm concerned," she said with icy breathlessness, "he needn't have bothered at all. I have not the slightest intention in the world of speaking to him. If he will take the trouble to think back to our last conversation, he might recollect that we had agreed that all communication between us would be handled by Mr. Newkirk." She turned her back on him, but the sight of herself in the mirror made her gasp. Humiliated, she snatched off the scarf from her head and hastily unpinned her skirts.

"This is not a matter in Mr. Newkirk's province—" Alec was saying, but suddenly his eye was caught by a shocking change in her appearance. "Good *lord*, Priss! What have you done to your *hair*?"

"What?" Her hand flew uncertainly to her head. "Oh. I've cut it, as you can see. Although I'd like to remind you it's not the slightest business of yours."

He frowned and turned away, disturbed by a feeling of completely unwarranted annoyance. "No, you're quite right. It is *not* my business. If you want to surrender to every foolish impulse and every turn of fashion, it means less than nothing to me." He made an angry turn about the hallway and circled back. "But I would just like to mention," he said venomously, "that the looking glass, if it is the one from the large bedroom, is *not* Venetian glass and was *not* your grandmother's. It is Stourbridge and was rolled—at very great expense, I understand—especially to my mother's specifications a decade before I was born."

"That's not *so*!" Priss cried, outraged. "I remember *distinctly* that my mother gave me the Venetian glass for our . . . for the bedroom! Didn't you, Mama?"

"Well, I *think* so," Lady Vickers said, thrown suddenly in doubt, "although it is *possible*, I suppose, that the Venetian piece is still at home in Derbyshire."

"It is *not*! I recall distinctly receiving it and ordering it to be placed upstairs," Priss insisted.

"I know my mother's looking glass when I see it," Alec said, brushing a fleck of dust from his sleeve with casual indifference, "although I would be delighted to let you have it. Especially if it will encourage you to step into the drawing room so that we may have our talk." He glanced depressingly at Lady Vickers, Craymore and the maid Becky, all of whom were following the scene with rapt attention. "In private," he added pointedly.

Craymore and the housemaid scurried off, but Lady Vickers held her ground. "You needn't agree to see him, my love," she advised her daughter. "If I were you, I should send him packing. He can return at *your* convenience, instead of demanding *your* time at *his*."

"It's important, ma'am. There are a number of matters which should be cleared up between us," Alec pressed.

Priss met his eye, her chin up proudly. "Very well, since you've come. But I have only a few minutes to spare. We are very busy here, as you can see." She marched into the drawing room without a backward glance. Alec, after nodding to his mother-in-law in some satisfaction, followed after her and closed the door behind him.

"Now, then, my lord," Priss said with brisk formality, "what do you want of me?"

"I want to wring your neck!" he responded promptly, striding to the sofa and pulling off its sheet-like cover. "How *dared* you say to the world that this is not your home?" He crossed to the wing chair and whipped the dustcover from that, too.

"I did *not* say it to the world! Only to Mama. Why on earth are you pulling off the covers?" she asked in annoyance.

"I *hate* covered rooms," he said, pulling off the rest of them in a showy display of temper. "They are ugly, dreary and oppressive."

"Then you needn't stay. Oh, *look* at what you're *doing*! You're crushing those Hollands dreadfully . . . and dragging them on the *floor*. At least give them to me and let me fold them."

"I shall do no such thing," he said, dropping them in a pile behind a chair. "I am waiting for a proper answer, ma'am. Why do you say this is not your house?"

"Because it isn't."

He came across the room and confronted her. "What sort of ogre do you think me, ma'am? Do I pull wings from flies for sport, or beat little children? Do you seriously believe that I would permit you to, as you so charmingly put it, 'go b-begging for b-bread in the snow'? Did you really think I would leave you without a roof over your head or a sufficient competence to permit you to live in comfort?"

"I don't know if you're an ogre or not," she answered slowly, searching his face. "I don't know *anything* about you any more." She stared up at him for a moment with an expression he found completely unreadable. Then she turned her back on him. "I only know that I was quite sincere when I told you I would take nothing from you. Understand me, Alec. I shall take *nothing.*"

He wanted to shake her. "I don't require your permission, you know. This house is yours, whether you like it or no, as well as anything else I choose to bestow upon you."

"Then you will, of course, do as you like. I can't stop you. But I can't be coerced into *using* what you choose to bestow, can I?" She turned back to face him. "Is that all you wish to say? If so, I must ask you to excuse me. I have a great deal of work to do."

"Hang it all, Priss," he said, grasping her shoulders angrily. "Why must you behave in this childishly pig-headed fashion? There is no *need* for this sort of upheaval! I never meant to uproot you like this."

"I have no stomach for charity, especially yours," she said proudly.

"But it is *not* charity!"

"A decree of nullity, as I understand it, means that the marriage never truly existed, isn't that right? Then I have never been your wife, and this house has never been, nor can ever be, mine. Therefore, if you give it to me, what else can it be but charity? And your bruising my arms will not alter the facts."

He let her go, shamed and speechless. She went to the door. "Good day, my lord," she said quietly.

"You are adamant, then?" he asked in a choked voice. "About returning to Three Oaks?"

"Yes, I am."

"No matter what it means . . . to your life . . . and to Grandfather's?"

With her hand on the knob, she hesitated. *"Grandfather?"* She turned around, her eyes wide. "The letter! You *saw* it, didn't you? Did *Mama* . . .?"

"Yes, she did."

Priss frowned in chagrin. "She needn't have done so. I fully intended to send it round to you myself."

"Thank you. That would have been most kind."

She came a few steps toward him. "You know I wouldn't go back home," she said, her brow furrowed with worry, "if I had anywhere else . . ."

Alec turned to the window and stared out with unseeing eyes. "I suppose that it isn't possible for you to return to Three Oaks without revealing to Grandfather the truth of our situation."

"How can I fail to do so? Mama and I can't stay hidden in the house . . . and since you will not be with me, how else can I explain to him . . .?"

"Yes. Yes, of course you're right."

"Besides, this sort of thing is bound to leak out sooner or later. Any chance encounter . . . a visitor from London . . . a servant . . ."

"Yes," Alec said sadly. "I must tell him, then."

"I . . . I'm sorry, Alec. I don't know what else to do. I've been racking my brain all day . . ."

"Thank you." He sighed hopelessly. "Can't be helped, I suppose."

"Do you think . . . would it be easier for him if we . . . told him together?"

He turned round and studied her wonderingly. "Would you be *willing* to do that?"

She sank down on the sofa, her head lowered. "I'd find it painful in the extreme. But if you think it would help . . ."

He came a few steps toward her. "It would help even more, you know," he suggested hopefully, "if you remained *here* and let him continue to believe . . ."

She turned her face away. "I c-can't, Alec. You shouldn't ask it of me."

"But why not? It would be doing me the most enormous favor . . . and thus it couldn't be considered charity."

She looked up at him, her face tortured. "This house is . . . a prison to me now."

He stared at her. "A *prison*? But . . . why?"

She lowered her head and made a little gesture with her hand, as if to say the matter was too difficult to speak of. "Don't ask me! You wouldn't understand."

He knelt before her and tried to see her face. "Try me. Please."

"I . . . it's . . . too full of . . . painful memories, don't you see? I *can't* . . ."

He looked at her wonderingly, the thought occurring for the first time that perhaps he had made a mistake about her life during these past six years. "I had no *idea*—" he murmured.

Her head came up, her eyes blazing. "Of *course* you had no idea! You told me quite clearly what you think of m-me! But I have *not* . . . m-made merry . . . behind your back and under your roof, whatever you may choose to think! To me there is nothing in this house now but gloom and horrid m-memories, and I won't stay here a day longer than I must!" And she turned away from him again and hid her face in her hands.

He stood up, feeling completely bemused and ashamed. Had he been wrong about her liaison with Edmonds during his absence? Had she truly spent the last six years alone in this house waiting for him and trying to make amends? His throat burned, and his heart ached in sudden sympathy for her. No wonder she wanted to leave this house!

It would make a difference in his feeling for her, of course, if she were truly repentent over what she'd done to him earlier. If it was indeed true that she had lived the life of a woman of character since he'd left her, he couldn't *hate* her. It could *not*, however, make up for her original deception. Whatever had or had not occurred since, it was still true that she'd married him while loving another and had made a mockery of what he had believed was the most joyful time of his life. For *that* he could never forgive her. Nevertheless, he didn't wish her to spend a lifetime suffering for it.

He took a seat on the sofa beside her, pulled her hands from her face and held them. "Forgive me," he said quietly. "I should not have asked you to remain here. I have no right to ask you to make such a sacrifice."

"B-But . . . if the Earl should . . . die . . . because of m-me . . ."

"Perhaps we are taking too dim a view of that. He is a man of deep inner resources. If we tell him together, after you've taken up residence in your mother's house, it is quite possible that the news won't strike him with so great a blow as we fear."

"I hope you're right," she said, withdrawing her hands from his grasp and moving a small distance away from him.

The movement was not lost on him. He got to his feet. "Well, I needn't keep you any longer. Thank you for your concern for my grandfather. Under the . . . er . . . circumstances, it is more than kind."

She swallowed and dashed the tears from her eyes with the back of her hands. "You needn't thank me," she said unsteadily. "I l-love him too, you know."

"Yes, I know. He spoke to me of your frequent visits and kind attentions to him while I was abroad." He tried to go on, to express his gratitude, but he felt uncomfortable, guilty and uncertain. It had been easier to despise her as a completely artful deceiver than to feel this ambivalent, divided emotion. Meanwhile, she was giving him no sign of dismissal. Did she want him to go or stay? He hesitated, not knowing what to do next.

"It's heartbreaking that the Earl can't have his party," Priss said, half to herself.

"Yes. It would seem to be such a small thing to do for him. And yet there is no possible way . . ."

Priss's eyes filled with tears again, and one trickled down her cheek. "It would have given him such pleasure . . ."

He sighed. "There's little point in crying over it, my dear. If there's no possibility . . ." His brow knit as a preposterous thought struck him. "Or *is* there?"

She lifted her head. "What? Have you thought of something?"

"Yes. Something quite maggoty. It doesn't bear scrutiny. Never mind. We shall have to manage with the plan we have."

"But what *is* it? Surely we can examine it a bit."

He looked at her speculatively. "I'm embarrassed even to *suggest* it. Believe me, my dear, it's a very foolish idea indeed."

"Really Alec," she said with a touch of asperity, "you are making me itch with curiosity. What *is* it?"

"I'm certain you'd never *consider* such a scheme. I was going to suggest that we simply *pretend* to be happily married and *have* the blasted party."

She gaped at him. "*Pretend*? How?"

He flushed. "It was only a passing conceit, a product of a desperate and fevered imagination. Forget that I ever—"

"Oh, for goodness sake, Alec, stop behaving like a bobbing-block! Sit down and explain yourself."

"Well, you see," he said sheepishly, seating himself beside her again, "it would only be for a fortnight, after all—or even less, if matters became unmanageable. All we need do, really, is invite a small, select group of people whom we can trust, warn them not to breathe a word about our separation, and make our appearance at Braeburn hand-in-hand, as if nothing had ever happened between us. The only requirement for us would be to behave with civilized politeness toward each other—that's all the affection other married couples of my acquaintance seem to show, at least in public—and let Grandfather enjoy the sight of us. He could have his merriment and his festivities, just as he wishes."

"But . . . that would solve nothing! After the party ended, we would be right where we are now!"

He shrugged. "I didn't promise you a miracle, my dear. Only a party. After it ended, we would tell him the truth, just as we've decided to do in any case. Only . . .

he would have had his party first, that's all.''

She stared at him as if he were a loony. "No, no! It's an impossible scheme. I couldn't possibly go through with it.''

"I can readily understand that.'' Alec patted her hand comfortingly and got to his feet. "I knew it was a preposterous suggestion.''

"Yes, it was. There would be a *thousand* difficulties. Why, I could never even look you in the eye. I could never convince *anyone*, much less a man as shrewd as the Earl, that everything was loving and good between us. Neither could you, for that matter—you never had the slightest skill in dissembling. One or the other of us would be bound to give the show away. Or even if *we* managed it, one of the guests would say something wrong and spoil everything. And if Grandfather learned the truth *that* way, it might be the worst possible thing for him. Besides, I'd counted on my time at Three Oaks to start a *new* life for myself, not prolong the old. I need to wash away all these memories. I've wasted so much time already. I want to start living a life of some meaning and purpose. And furthermore, there's the matter of wardrobe. It's been so long since I attended any parties, I no longer have the sort of clothing one needs for an entire fortnight of festivities. I'd need at least three new dinner gowns and a pair of dancing slippers and all *sorts* of trumperies, because there would *have* to be one or two evenings of music and dancing, you know, and truly, I haven't the stomach for that sort of thing now. I sincerely doubt that my face could stand so long a period of false smiles and artificial merrymaking. And—''

"All right, Priss! Enough!'' Smiling wryly, he held up his hand to stop her. "I *do* understand. Truly. And I completely agree with everything you've said. It's an impossible scheme.''

"Yes. Yes, it is. I'll do it.''

He couldn't have understood her. "What?''

"I'll *do* it. I'll write to him tonight and tell him we accept his invitation. Shall we say the beginning of next month?''

"Priss! Do you *mean* it?"

"I shall probably detest the entire affair," she said bravely, "but he deserves to have a small bit of celebrating before he . . . at this time of his life. So let's go ahead and do it for him."

He studied her for a moment, torn again between gratitude and suspicion. Reluctantly, he uttered a reminder. "You *do* realize, don't you, that nothing fundamental will be changed by all of this? And that, at the end of the fortnight, we must face him and tell him the truth?"

Her face tightened immediately, and she gave him a glance of withering scorn. "You didn't need to remind me. It will be a fact constantly at the forefront of my mind. If you wish to have the truth, I can hardly wait for all this to be over . . . so that I may see the last of you."

She swept to the door and held it open for him. As he passed into the hallway, now deserted, he turned back to her. "Thank you for your generosity in this, my dear. Whatever else is wrong between us, this will be something that will ever deserve my gratitude."

"There is not the least need for pretty speeches, my lord," she said, starting for the stairs. "I'm not doing this for *you*." As she put her foot on the first step, her eye fell on the looking glass. Looking over her shoulder, she asked curiously, "Is that mirror really your mother's?"

He tossed her a sidelong glance as he picked up his hat. "Well, you see . . . I was quite furious with you—"

She could not follow the non sequitur. "What?" she asked.

"For cutting off all your lovely hair, you know."

"Alec! . . . Do you mean to say that you . . . you . . .?" she sputtered.

He set his hat on his head jauntily and opened the front door. "Yes, I'm afraid I lied. My mother never had a Stourbridge looking glass at all, as far as I know," he said, grinning broadly.

"Well, of all the *toplofty*—!" she began furiously.

But he'd whisked himself out of the house and shut the door.

Chapter Fifteen

It became evident almost at once that the deceptive little plot would not be as easy to execute as Alec had expected. The first stumbling block occurred when Alec sent his list of suggested guests to Priss for her approval. Telling her that she was free to add whomever she wished, he had listed only three names: Garvin Danforth (who had insisted on being invited, claiming that he'd already written to his employer that he would not return to his post for another month and that he had no wish to spend the time in London without Alec), Clio Vickers (who had informed Alec flatly, when he'd confided his plans to her, that she had no intention of permitting him to go gallivanting off on an intimate fortnight with her cousin Priscilla unless she was present to protect her interests), and Ferdinand Sellars (who'd told him frankly that he hated the country, but who'd agreed to go along when Alec pleaded that he needed Ferdie close by to protect his sanity.)

He received an icy response from Priss, telling him that if *that* was the sort of female companionship he liked, he could jolly well make up the rest of the guest list himself, so long as he included one of *her* friends, a Miss Ariadne Courdepass of Upper Brook Street, who was demure and modest and would in no way interfere with Miss Clio Vickers' desire to make a conquest of every man in sight.

Alec, in considerable irritation, showed the letter to

Ferdie, but the ex-Major, an unflappable campaigner in both the romantic and the military wars, only laughed. "Your wife has a waspish temper, hasn't she? I think I'm going to like her. But I don't know why I'm laughing. The news in this letter bodes ill for me."

"Why is that?" Alec asked curiously.

"Well, with Clio having eyes only for you, and your wife under the necessity of showing devotion to you as well, the only available female for *me* will be this Miss Courtplaster—"

"Courdepass, you make-bait. Courdepass."

"She sounds like a courtplaster to me. A sticky little thing, no doubt, being so 'modest and demure,' who hangs on to a fellow's arm for dear life, saying 'Oh, do you really think so?' to everything he says. You know, Alec, I think I shall match her up with your friend Danforth the moment we arrive."

Alec guffawed. "A perfect idea. Go to it. Do you see why I need you there, old man? You're practically indispensible."

The second stumbling block was Priss's determination to settle into her mother's house as soon as possible. But what would his grandfather think, Alec asked her worriedly, when he heard that she'd arrived at Three Oaks several days before the party and without her husband? After a long and somewhat heated discussion, Lady Vickers conceived an idea which overcame the hurdle. She composed a cheerful letter to the Earl, telling him that she'd grown quite tired of London and had decided, at long last, to come home and open up her Derbyshire house. *After all*, she wrote, *Priss doesn't need me now that Alec has returned. It's about time that I took up residence at Three Oaks, the place where I feel most at home. Believe me, my dear friend, there is nothing in the whole of London so pleasing as the Derbyshire air.*

By the way, Priss insists on coming along to help me settle in—these young upstarts, once they come of age, do enjoy treating their parents like doddering old fools, don't they?—so she asks me to tell you that she will be near you for a full week before your house party. In that way, she says, she'll be available to give you all sorts of assistance (when she's not assisting her doddering old mother, of course) in your preparations before the others arrive for the festivities. Alec, of course, pretends to have fallen into the sullens over the fact that he and Priss will be parted for a few days, but in truth he'll be busily occupied in entertaining his friend Garvin Danforth (who has extended his holiday so that he can attend your party) and, as I told my son-in-law, any couple, no matter how loving, can certainly endure a minor separation such as this.

Alec and Priss agreed that the letter was a masterpiece of cunning subterfuge and congratulated the author on her talent for deception. But Alec, as he sent the letter on its way, made a fervent wish that this was the last stumbling block he'd have to overcome.

Priss and her mother (with the help of a houseful of servants, the drayman and his three assistants, Alec, Gar and an officious and managing Mr. Hornbeck) succeeded in dispatching their possessions and themselves to Derbyshire only eleven hours behind schedule. And a week later, an entourage of four carriages of assorted styles set out for Braeburn and a fortnight of country pleasure. The sun shone, the early November wind was brisk, and the spirits of the three gentlemen who climbed aboard the first carriage (a dignified and somewhat antiquated phaeton handed down to Ferdie from a wealthy uncle) were high despite the fact that each of them had reason to anticipate the coming festivities with mixed emotions.

The second carriage began the journey vacant, for it was intended for the use of the ladies of the party who were waiting at their respective residences to be taken up. The third vehicle carried the baggage and was already burdened with fifteen bulging boxes and bags. Bringing up the rear was Alec's barouche-landau, in which sat two antagonistic passengers: Harry Kellam, ex-batman, and George Archibald Smoot, *Valet Extraordinaire* to Mr. Ferdinand Sellars. The valet, having taken one look at Kellam's casual dress and shaggy moustache, had decided the fellow was beneath his touch; and Kellam, taking immediate note of Smoot's mincing walk and the ruby ring which he wore on his index finger (which anyone with half an eye could see was paste), decided the fellow was a hypocritical fop (or, as he would have put it, a 'bubblin' sprag'). As a result, neither exchanged a word with the other but kept looking at each other with either surreptitious or blatant disgust.

When the procession stopped at Upper Brook Street to take up Miss Courdepass and her abigail, both Alec and Ferdie hopped out of their carriage to assist, for they had not yet met the lady and their curiosity had been piqued by Priss's terse description of her. Ariadne Courdepass turned out to be a young lady of about twenty-five, with a not-unpleasing figure, a somewhat flat face, a retroussé nose, a remarkably pretty mouth and long, silky hair which she wore twisted into a long coil and wound around her head like a coronet. She carried on her arm a huge, wooden-handled workbag, and after she and her abigail had been helped aboard the second carriage, she extracted from the bag a piece of knitting at which she worked steadily almost without ceasing during the entire two-day journey.

Her portmanteau, trunk and three bandboxes having been stowed aboard the third carriage, the entourage set out for Clio Vicker's residence. There they were kept waiting for more than half-an-hour, but when the lady at last emerged, her enchanting appearance won their immediate forgiveness. She was absolutely captivating in a blue velvet pelisse trimmed with matching satin welting, an enormous fur muff, and a remarkable bonnet with soft blue feathers which waved gracefully over the poke like little fingers trying to grasp at her red curls. All three gentlemen eagerly rushed to her assistance, handed her into the carriage and lingered, with many hearty quips and asides, over the introductions. A reproving cough from the street made them aware that Miss Vickers' companion, a middle-aged and dour-faced lady who was much too dignified to be called an abigail, was waiting to be assisted aboard. This was promptly attended to, the great number of boxes and trunks which Miss Vickers had assembled for the trip were loaded into and on top of the baggage coach, and the procession lumbered off toward its destination to the north.

The journey was a merry one, with much exchanging of passengers between the first two carriages, much laughter, a headlong and dangerous race between them down a long hill, and other pastimes that inventive minds can devise to pass away the hours. When they stopped for the night at an inn a mile north of Market Harborough, Alec took the opportunity (while they were all together at dinner) to remind them not to reveal by word or expression while they were at Braeburn that there was anything at all amiss between his wife and himself. They all hastened to assure him of their support, Miss Courdepass remarking bluntly, her eyes all the while on her knitting, that as far as *she* was concerned, Alec and Priss *were* man and wife and that was all that she—or anyone else, for that matter—need know about it.

They arrived at Braeburn the following afternoon, to find the Earl, his face beaming, standing before the high oak doors of the house to welcome them. Just behind him, a strained, shy smile on her face, was Priss. Alec was the first to disembark, and he ran up the stone steps two at a time. After embracing the Earl warmly, he leaned down and kissed Priss's cheek. "Hello, my dear," he said heartily. "I've missed you."

Clio Vickers, a blue-clad vision, ran up to her great-uncle the Earl and enveloped him in an enthusiastic embrace. Priss looked from Alec to her cousin and back again. "I'm *certain* you missed me, my dear," she said with an almost imperceptible touch of venom and went off to greet the guests.

After the details of the arrival—the greetings, the

unloading of the carriages and the dispersal of the baggage to the various bedrooms—had been attended to, the Earl herded them all into the library, where a lavish tea had been laid. It was then that Priss took the opportunity to whisper to Alec that she had to speak to him urgently. Alec promptly announced to the assemblage that, not having laid eyes on his lovely wife for a week, he trusted they would all excuse them if they took a few moments in private. With the Earl's glowing approval, he put an arm about her waist and walked her from the room.

As soon as the library doors had closed behind them, he let her go. "What's gone wrong?" he asked her at once. "Dash it, Priss, the old man looks so well, I can't believe it's the same fellow I saw here a month ago. If anything or anyone has put a spoke into the wheel, I'll—"

"Hush, Alec. The problem may not be crucial. Come away from those doors. Let's go into the morning room where we won't be overheard."

They crossed the hall and closed the door of the morning room quietly. But even in the safety and seclusion of their surroundings, Priss found it difficult to explain. "The Earl has made the most awkward arrangements, Alec. And I don't know how to tell him they won't do."

"Arrangements? What arrangements?"

"For our . . . er . . . sleeping accommodations. He's given us the large corner bedroom, you see."

"Us? *Both* of us?"

She felt herself blushing. "Yes. You see, he remembered that, when we came home from our . . . honeymoon . . . that I'd said . . . I'd said . . ."

He grimaced. "You'd said that you didn't like separate bedrooms! He *remembered* that?"

"Worse, he positively *dotes* on it. I wouldn't be at all surprised if—" She put her hands up to her burning cheeks. "—if he *bragged* about it to his *cronies*! Alec, it's a . . . a . . . gold and white *love nest*!"

Alec fought back a laugh. "You don't mean it!

Romantic old dog, isn't he? Well, I don't think we need concern ourselves too much. If you don't mind sleeping in a gold and white love nest, I can always bed down with Ferdie.''

"But, Alec, Grandfather's room is just down the hall! If you bedded down with Ferdie, he'd be *bound* to discover it!''

"Yes, confound it, I suppose that's true.'' He took a few turns around the room. "Hang it all, Priss, you've been here a week! Why couldn't you have told him we're . . . we're not so . . . so full of youthful ardor any more?''

She drew herself up angrily. "I might have known you would throw this all back at me! It's truly wonderful how you manage to make everything *my* fault!''

"I'm sorry. You're quite right—it isn't your fault. I'm beginning to think I should never have suggested this ridiculous plot.''

She sighed. "No, it's not ridiculous. You've *seen* how happy he is.''

"Yes, but I fail to see what we're to do about this latest coil.''

"Neither do I. I did *try*, you know. A dozen times I started to say to him that we've grown accustomed to separate bedrooms in our . . . mature years—''

Alec broke into a laugh. "Did you truly try to say that?''

"Indeed I did. But I just couldn't bring it to my tongue, for I was certain he'd see it as a rift between us. You do realize what your grandfather has in the back of his mind, don't you?''

"No. What do you mean?''

"A great-grandchild, of course. I'm convinced that he believes that since the London environs did not yet produce one, the country air will. Hence all the sheer drapery and the gold cupids and the paintings of cherubs on the walls—''

His eyebrows rose in amused repugnance. "Good heavens, is it as bad as that?''

"Wait until you see for yourself.''

Alec saw it for himself when the company dispersed later that afternoon to dress for dinner. The bedroom was large and pleasant, with panelled walls and large casements, but the old Earl had had it decorated with too lavish a hand. An enormous bed dominated the room, its voluminous hangings (now pulled back and tied against each post) seeming to be wide enough to surround the bed several times over. The cornices which bridged the bedposts were arched, and at the high point of each arch, a gilded Cupid reclined, its bow and arrow at the ready. The gilt-edged headboard was painted to represent a blue sky on which floated a number of puffy little clouds bearing dimpled, pink cherubs on their backs. All the other furniture in the room, from the triangular basin-stand in the corner to the high, double chest of drawers at the right of the door was gilded, fretted, inlaid, festooned, splayed, stenciled, molded, rosetted, frogged and filigreed to such an extent that the entire effect was overpowering. For a long moment, Alec stared at the display with open-mouthed stupefaction. Then he sat down on the bed and gave way to such whoops of laughter that his wife, eyeing him askance from the doorway, feared he'd be heard all over the house. "Alec, hush!" she warned, checking to ascertain that the door had been properly closed. "You don't want the world to hear you! And I don't see anything to laugh about, in spite of this room's being so ludicrously overdone. What are we to do?"

Alec wiped his streaming eyes, rose and looked about. "Where do those doors lead?" he asked. "I don't remember much about this part of the house."

"That one is my dressing room. It was once a guest bedroom—the little blue bedroom, remember?—but Grandfather converted it into a dressing room especially for me. Don't go looking into it, for you'll only go into whoops again. And *this* door leads to *your* dressing room. I suppose you may look there, for the furnishings are relatively unremarkable."

He opened the door and peered inside. "I say, Priss, this may be the solution to our problem. It's adequately large and has a door to the corridor. If you wouldn't mind it, I could have Kellam set up a camp-cot in here.''

She came up behind him. "A camp-cot? But . . . shall you be able to sleep in such cramped quarters for an entire fortnight?''

"My dear girl, I've slept in much worse." He looked down at her with a grin. "The question is, will *you* be able to sleep surrounded by all those Cupids?''

She gave him a small smile and walked away, but he could see she was still troubled. He followed after her, his forehead furrowed in concern. "This is asking a great deal of you, I know. The proximity of these living quarters . . . they'll make for more intimacy than you had anticipated, is that what's troubling you?''

"Well, you couldn't *always* use that other door without being detected, any more than you could successfully have bunked with Ferdie. You'd have to come in here, and . . . it would be extremely awkward . . .''

"Yes, I suppose it would. Shall we call it off? Grandfather looks surprisingly hale—I can go to him now, if you like, and tell him the whole.''

She shook her head. "No. I suppose we can contrive somehow.''

"Good girl!" he said, relieved. "I shall not be a bother at all, I promise you. I shall go straight to my little *chambre* the moment we come in, and I shall not emerge until you knock and tell me it is permissable for me to do so.''

She shrugged in reluctant acquiescence. "Very well. Then you'd best go into your *chambre* right now, for if we don't hurry and dress for dinner, we shall be scandalously late.''

Priss dressed in hurried distraction, for Alec's presence so close by made her strangely uncomfortable. Then she dismissed the abigail the Earl had thoughtfully provided for her and examined herself critically in the tall mirror set into her dressing room door. She was not pleased with what she saw. Her gown, a rose-colored Tiffany silk which she'd chosen in the hope that the color would relieve her pallor, was pretty enough, she supposed, with its high, shirred waist which permitted the skirt to fall in soft folds and to swing gracefully when she moved. But it lacked dash, and she was certain that whatever Clio would have chosen to wear would by far outshine *her* choice.

Then there was her hair. Why, oh why, had she ever permitted herself to cut her hair? Alec was quite right to dislike those short curls. Only a dashing beauty like Caro Lamb could carry off such a gamin-like hairstyle. Once she had felt herself the equal of any of the reigning beauties—she would not have been daunted by the likes of Caro Lamb, Clio Vickers or any of them—but now . . .

She tried, in last-minute desperation, to improve the effect of her coiffure with a ribbon wound through the curls. But the result was too simperingly girlish, and she pulled the ribbon out and tossed it away. Then she hastily draped a long, diaphanously thin silk scarf over her shoulders and crossed the bedroom to Alec's door. She lifted her hand to knock, hesitated and ran back to the mirror. In a panic of indecision, she snatched off the scarf, threw it on the bed, squared her shoulders and marched back to his door. She knocked at it firmly. "I'm ready to go down," she said.

He came out promptly, tucking his watch into his waistcoat pocket. She couldn't help but admire his appearance. His high, starched shirtpoints, the fold of his snow-white neckcloth, the black gleam of his coat and the skin-tight fit of his breeches would have won the approval of Brummell.

"Well, my dear," he asked, "are you ready for your entrance for our first real performance in this little charade?"

"I'm as full of butterflies as any fledgling actress about to perform her first major role," she said with a sigh, "but I suppose we may as well begin."

"Just a moment, please." He'd noticed the scarf lying across the bed. He reached for it and carefully draped it over her shoulders. "There! No one in the 'audience' will be able to take their eyes from you, you know.''

"What a whisker!" she said disparagingly, uncomfortably aware that her pulse had begun to race. "I know what you think of this shorn head of mine."

"Do you indeed? Well, if you want the truth of it," he said, offering her his arm, "it makes me wish that I were *truly* your husband again, just so that I might run my fingers through it. And now that you've won *that* trick from me, my dear, I think we'd better go before I lose the game."

She would have loved to ask what game he meant, but his words had stirred her blood with such a tingly glow that she did not dare say anything that might spoil it. Instead, she merely colored, took his arm in meek obedience and went with him down to dinner.

Chapter Sixteen

Undressing for bed that night, Clio Vickers was far from pleased. As far as she was concerned, the first day at Braeburn had been as boring an occasion as she'd ever endured. Never before in her life—at least not since she'd come out—had she been so greatly ignored by the gentlemen in an assemblage. Not one of them had remarked on her appearance, even though she'd taken particular pains to look her best. She'd chosen to wear her saffron-colored crepe, a spicy confection on which her *modiste* had outdone herself in the cleverness of the design of the sleeves (which were cut open down the center and then lashed together with black lacings) and the elegance of the black silk embroidery around the rather rakishly revealing neckline. But no one had seen fit to mention it. She had thought that Gar, at the very least, would utter one of his *gauche* and backhanded compliments, but although she'd caught his eye on her several times in a sort of gaping fascination, she could not be sure what he'd been thinking.

And what Ferdie had been about in his obvious and embarrassing attempts to push Gar upon the Friday-faced Miss Courdepass she didn't know. It should have been clear to any greenhead that neither one of them had any interest in the other. And then, once they had sat down to dinner, none of the men seemed to have eyes for any but her unpredictable cousin Priss. Priss's rose-colored dress had struck Clio as being completely commonplace, but she'd had to admit to herself that, at the table in the glow of the candlelight, the color had seemed to light up the irritating creature's face. Priss had seemed to have a particular sparkle this evening, and, seated at the foot of the table as she had been, with the Earl at the head and Alec at her right, Priss had been the cynosure of all eyes. Her demeanor had been gracious, she'd given her attention equally to all the diners, she'd laughed pleasantly at the quips and even had got off one or two of her own. In short, Priss had been a perfect hostess, blast her.

Lady Vickers had come over from Three Oaks for the evening, and she, too, had been outstandingly charming. Bright-eyed and obviously in the best of humor, she had received a great deal of notice. She'd told a very amusing story about, of all things, a dog that had gotten himself trapped inside a cotton mill, a tale that captivated all the listeners but Clio, who felt it went on far too long.

And even the platter-faced Miss Courdepass had had her moment, and *that* had occurred at Clio's expense. It humiliated Clio just to *remember* the exchange. She'd been trying to win some attention to *herself*, but none of her remarks had been particularly noted. Then, during a lull in the conversation, she'd said rather loudly to Miss Courdepass, who'd been seated opposite her, that *she* hadn't yet been heard from. "Don't you think, Miss Courdepass, that this conversation would be made more brilliant with a flash of *your* wit?" she'd asked.

Even to her own ears, the tone of her question had been surprisingly old-cattish, and she immediately felt the others at the table stiffen and eye her in disapproval. All but Miss Courdepass, who'd merely looked at her with a glance of imperturbable placidity and responded, "It often seems to me, Miss Vickers, that there are many conversations which would be made a great deal more brilliant by occasional flashes of *silence*."

Everyone had laughed heartily, Ferdie raised his glass to Miss Courdepass and crowed, "A hit, Miss Courdepass, a positive hit!" and the Earl had cackled,

"Hear, hear!" And Clio had wanted nothing more than to crawl away and hide in a dark corner.

Worst of all, when she'd tried to make excuses for her behavior to Alec later, he hadn't known what she was talking about. He seemed to have been engrossed in other thoughts. And it occurred to Clio that Alec might be in love with his wife after all.

But tomorrow would be another day, she consoled herself as she climbed into bed. She would play the game better tomorrow, and then she would see what she would see.

For Priss, also reviewing the events of the evening in her mind as she readied herself for bed, the results of the evening seemed quite different. She'd enjoyed herself hugely. It was wonderful to be Alec's wife again, seeing him smile at her in unspoken approval, feeling him at her side to support and sustain her, even if it was only a pretense. Her heart had jumped up and down alarmingly every time she became aware that his eyes were on her, and her skin had positively prickled with excitement whenever he'd taken her arm. But the very best moment of all, she thought with a happy sigh as she sank into the pillows, was that moment in this very room when he'd said he wished he could touch her hair.

She pulled the covers up to her neck and snuggled into the softness of the bed like a contented kitten. But suddenly she sat bolt upright. What was she *thinking* of? How could she have forgotten her situation? It had all been a performance! He'd only been *playacting*. It would all come to an end in less than a fortnight's time.

Whatever happened in the next two weeks, she must remember to keep a closer guard on her emotions. She mustn't let herself slip into this easy fog of happiness, for it was not based on anything real. At the end of the allotted time, he would be gone forever from her life. *That* was the reality that had to be faced. It would not do to let herself forget it for a moment, or the fortnight's end would bring her greater pain than before.

She lay back against the pillows and pulled the covers

up again. Her eyes, growing accustomed to the dark, could make out the door behind which he was sleeping. Or was he, too, lying awake and looking at the door? Would he ever, in the strange, unreal days ahead, feel tempted to *open* that door? The thought sent a shudder of excitement right through her. But, she warned herself severely, that was another direction along which her mind had better not travel. The best thing to do was to shut her eyes tight and will herself to sleep.

In truth, Alec was *not* looking at the door, nor was he entertaining any such romantic thoughts as his wife imagined. He was shifting himself about on the narrow little cot, trying to find a position comfortable enough to permit him to sleep. In this he was not successful. At last, he gave up the struggle, settled himself on his back, his hands folded under his head, and stared up at the ceiling. He was feeling disturbingly irritated at his grandfather, at Ferdie and at everyone who'd spoken to him about Priss this evening. It had started, after a perfectly pleasant dinner, with a comment made by Lady Vickers when he'd seen her out to her carriage. "You make a charming couple, you know," she'd said as he handed her up. "It's too bad you are too stupid to see it."

A short while later, Gar had taken him aside and delivered a long and uninvited lecture in which he'd indicated, in his usual pompous and verbose manner, that Alec didn't really know what he was doing in regard to his marital situation. "I don't pretend to know the details of your problem," he'd admitted, "and I don't wish to appear to pry into anyone's private affairs, even those of my very best friend, but I can't believe, seeing your very lovely wife presiding over tonight's festivities, that there could be anything reprehensible in her character. If ever you should decide to review the situation . . . to talk to a friend, if you know what I mean . . . I wish you to know that you are free to call on me for advice at any time. At any time at all."

Alec had held back a sharp answer with what he

thought was admirable restraint, but that was not the last time that evening he'd had to restrain himself. Shortly afterwards, he'd accompanied his grandfather upstairs to his bedroom. The old man looked tired, but his eyes sparkled brightly. "A delightful evening, wasn't it?" he chuckled before he said his goodnights. "Everything was just as it ought to be, I thought. I'd lay odds everyone enjoyed it." He nudged his grandson and gave him a conspiratorial wink. "We were a couple of sharp old birds, Vickers and I, when we paired you and Priss in your cradles." And off he went to bed, crowing with self-satisfaction, leaving Alec standing in the corridor looking after him in frustration and wondering how on earth he would manage to break the news to him—as he would have to do before too long—that his long-laid plans were nothing but dream castles built on air.

Then Ferdie had accosted him briefly with the remark that he was an idiot. "If I had a wife like that, I would not be such a dunderhead as to give her up, no matter *what* tricks she'd played on me in her youth," Ferdie had whispered.

Alec hadn't deigned to reply but merely tossed his friend a look of contemptuous disdain and turned on his heel.

But the last straw had occurred here in this stuffy dressing room in which he was to be confined for the duration of the house party. Kellam, while he made up the camp-cot which he'd managed with his usual ingenuity to procure, had prosed on at great length about Priss's virtues. "She's just the very sort o' lady I wuz expectin'," he grinned as he plumped the pillows, "an' too good fer yer likes, if ye was t' ask me."

"I suggest, you chaffer-mouth," Alec had muttered angrily as he pushed him out the door, "that you keep your comments to yourself until I *do* ask you. And I'm as likely to ask you for your comments as you are to talk sense."

He threw himself onto the cot fuming. What was the matter with everyone? He had graduated with honors from Oxford and had led a company of soldiers with distinction, hadn't he? Then how was it that half the world had made it plain that they thought him no better than a fool? But the ceiling at which he'd been frowning in such intensity, brought no answers, and after a while he turned on his side and fell asleep.

The weather, during the next few days, was extremely kind. The days were sunny and brisk and the evenings not quite as chilly and damp as one would expect in November. The gentlemen spent their days in hunting and riding (the Earl having given them the freedom of his admirable stables), leaving the ladies to lounge about, read, or stroll in the sunshine. In the late afternoon, the entire party gathered for tea and then went their own way until it was time to assemble for dinner. That meal was usually long and leisurely, for both the food and the conversation were meant to be savored. The evenings were spent by indulging in all manner of country pleasures: there was usually some time spent in the music room listening to Priss play a selection on the pianoforte and Clio sing an air or two in a very pleasing and confident soprano; then tables of cards were set up, Lady Vickers and the Earl usually snaring Miss Courdepass and one of the others for their favorite whist while the others played copper-loo; a play reading was organized by Gar when he discovered in the Earl's fine library an unfamiliar translation of *The Phormio*, a romantic comedy by Terence (for which everyone was given a role to read and which occasioned so much laughter and good spirits that the reading required several evenings to complete, with such good results that Gar, to his delight, was requested to find another play for them to do); and, interspersed in all the other activity, a great amount of flirting and teasing was indulged in, instigated by Ferdie and leading to no particular matching of pairs—at least none that anyone could notice.

By the time five days had passed, life had taken on a familiar and pleasant routine for everyone but Clio. She was finding the evenings passable enough (for by this time both Ferdie and Gar had indicated sufficient admiration for her charms, and she had even managed to see Alec alone once or twice), but she found the days impossible. She was forced to stroll about the grounds or to take brief excursions into nearby Wirksworth with only her cousin and the imperturbable Miss Courdepass for company, or, when driven to the extreme limits of boredom, to pick up a book. As soon as she found the opportunity, she made her complaints to Alec. He felt exceedingly guilt-ridden, for he had been enjoying himself a great deal and not giving her much thought. As a result, he prevailed upon the gentlemen to cut short their day of shooting and return home to spend an afternoon with the ladies. They returned from the stables a little after two, to find Miss Courdepass knitting contentedly in the drawing room, Clio gazing disconsolately out of the window, and Priss nowhere in evidence. "Where's my wife?" Alec asked.

"I've no idea," Clio answered, delighted to see that the gentlemen had returned and no longer the least bit interested in the whereabouts of her hostess. "She often disappears at this time of the afternoon."

"That's strange," Gar remarked. "Not like her at all. She's always such a perfect hostess."

"It *is* a bit strange," Alec agreed. "Is she napping, do you think?"

"No," Clio shrugged, "for I've seen her leave the house."

The Earl headed for the table where decanters of wine and glasses had been set. "Probably gone to Three Oaks to see her mother. Who's for a glass of port?" The matter so logically explained, the assemblage dropped the subject for the more interesting one of the advantages of a good port over the claims made by Ferdie for the rich-bodied Amontillado.

Priss returned shortly thereafter and was quite surprised to find the entire company assembled in the drawing room. In response to their questions she affirmed that she'd indeed been visiting her mother, and she entered into the good spirits of the group by accepting a glass of wine and fending off Ferdie's effusive compliments on her appearance with a blush and an accusation that he must have had a glass or two too many of his favorite vintage.

The rest of the day was very gay, the early return of the gentlemen from their sport having made it seem somehow special. Everyone instinctively dressed with particular elegance for dinner that night, the meal turned out to be especially lavish, and everyone at the table seemed to exude merriment and warmth. The warmth was noticeable even in the weather, which was unseasonably balmy.

When the party entered the drawing room and sat down to cards, they noticed that the air was positively stuffy. Priss excused herself from the card game and opened the windows. The windows, reaching from the floor almost to the ceiling, led to a wide, balustraded terrace which overlooked the undulating lawns, serpentine walks and clusters of shrubs and trees which had been laid out some thirty years before by the famous landscape architect, Capability Brown. All these were almost invisible now in the deepening darkness of the November night, but Priss remained staring out into the dimness. Alec, glancing up from his place at the whist table, saw her standing there, and something in her stance made him wonder if there was something disturbing her.

When he next raised his eyes she was gone. As soon as he could lay down his cards without disturbing the game, he too excused himself and went out on the terrace to find her. She had walked down to the southern end of the terrace (which extended for the entire width of the building) where the light from the drawing room windows could not reach her. It was only because of the light color of her gown that he was able to determine where she was. She was turned away from him and apparently had not heard his approaching footsteps, for when he came up to her she jumped in surprise and uttered a little cry. As she turned her face to him, he noted with astonishment that her cheeks were streaked with tears. "Good God, Priss, what's amiss here?"

She smiled in tremulous embarrassment, shook her head and wiped her cheeks hastily with the back of her hand. Lowering her head, she said in a small voice, "It's nothing at all. T-Truly. I'm only indulging in a bit of sentimentality."

He lifted her chin with one hand while he withdrew his handkerchief with the other. "Sentimentality over what?" he asked with gentle concern as he dabbed at her cheeks.

"It's too silly to speak of," she murmured. "I'm ashamed to have been caught out."

"I wish you'd tell me," he persisted, keeping her face tilted up to him.

Her eyes wavered under his insistent gaze. "It was only the l-leaves, you see . . ."

"The *leaves*?"

"Yes. I told you it was silly. They're turning brown and dying off so quickly, in spite of the lovely weather we've been having . . . and I couldn't help thinking that soon they'll be gone . . . and everything around us will be bare and cold . . . and I suddenly felt unaccountably depressed . . ."

"Poor Priss," he whispered with a rush of tenderness for her.

She made a little grimace of self-deprecation. "It's a very foolish wallow in melodrama. You needn't look so stricken."

Her words set off an echoing sound somewhere deep in his memory. When had she said them to him before? The scene popped into his consciousness with a crystal clarity. In Italy, of course! He'd carried her in from the Spanish Steps and laid her on the bed. He'd bent over her, torn by an agonizing fear that she'd been seriously hurt. Her face had been tilted up to his, just as it was at this moment, and she'd tried to reassure him with those very words . . . *no need to look so stricken*. And the next thing he'd known she was trembling in his arms, locked in an embrace that all the intervening years had not erased from his memory.

Suspended somewhere between the past and the present, he was not aware that he'd lowered his head and put his lips on hers. He shut his eyes and tightened his hold on her until he could feel the blood pounding in his temples. And it was Italy, and the world was whirling around in a dizzying imbalance, and he could almost believe that he was about to take his first step into manhood all over again. But in a very few moments the earth righted, the present became real, and he could feel her struggling against him, her hands pressing against his chest with urgent strength. He opened his eyes and, appalled at himself, let her go.

She stepped back, breathless and aghast. "Alec! How *dare* you—?"

He colored to the ears. How could he so have forgotten himself? Once again he'd behaved in her presence like a green youth . . . just as if all the experiences of the intervening years had never happened. How could he have permitted himself to tumble into a situation in which she could laugh at him again? "I . . . I'm very sorry. I . . . er . . . thought I heard Grandfather approaching," he mumbled, trying to cover his embarrassment with this lame excuse. "I thought it would please him to . . . er . . . catch us embracing."

"*Did* you indeed?" she responded with cool skepticism, putting her chin up in dignified disdain and marching past him toward the drawing room. "Well, in future, I hope you'll remember that I have *no intention* of pleasing him quite as much as all *that!*"

Alec was unable to fall asleep that night. The turmoil inside him failed to subside, and the fact that Priss lay sleeping on the other side of his dressing room door was in no way soothing. He had to admit that no other woman he'd encountered in six adventurous years had ever had so intense an effect on him. Perhaps Ferdie and the others were right. Perhaps he *was* being a fool to remain so unforgiving about the past. It certainly seemed as if she had been quite sincere when she said that she had not seen Edmonds after he'd left for Spain. If that were true, perhaps he *could* bring himself to forgive and forget the rest . . . to start life anew, with her as his wife again!

It was an intoxicating thought. He was almost afraid to let himself dwell on it. Besides, she would not consider it any more—not after all the cruel suspicions he'd thrown at her. Of course, she *had*, at first, expressed a willingness to take him back. If his unkindness to her in their recent talks in London had not completely killed that willingness, perhaps she might be persuaded to try again.

Suddenly it seemed a very inviting idea. There was much to recommend it. Besides winning the approbation of everyone he knew, from Ferdie to Kellam, he wouldn't have to give his grandfather the devastating news that the marriage was to be annulled, he wouldn't have to deal with the problem of Clio, and he wouldn't have to sleep in this blasted dressing room in this agonizing loneliness.

But he would not be hasty. He was not going to make a fool of himself twice. He would think about it.

But, in the morning, the idea was still amazingly appealing. As soon as the morning light filtered in through the curtains, he jumped out of bed, so filled with hopeful anticipation that even the suddenly cloudy sky and the cold wind (which seemed to be ushering in the winter with a determination to make up for the previous days' pleasantness) failed to dampen his excitement. He would ride out on his horse this morning while he mulled over the situation once more . . . and then he would present the entire plan to Priss!

The Earl and Gar both declined to ride in such ominous weather, so Ferdie and Alec set out on their own. After a while, even Ferdie decided that the wind was too biting and turned back. Alec, however, was buffered against the blow by his inward optimism, and he rode on.

His high spirits lasted only another half hour. While galloping across the roadway that marked the western boundary of his grandfather's estate, his horse almost collided with a curricle which came suddenly, and at much too high a speed, around a bend. With great presence of mind and speed of reaction, Alec managed to turn his roan aside in the nick of time. As soon as he'd brought his rearing animal under control, he leaped out of the saddle to confront the driver of the curricle in order to deliver a furious and pithy castigation on his method of taking a turn. But the sight of the driver caused not only the words to die on his lips but his entire optimistic plan for the future to explode into desolate fragments and disintegrate completely in a sea of dismay and chagrin. The driver of the curricle was Sir Blake Edmonds.

Chapter Seventeen

The threatening clouds burst open just as Priss turned into the wide avenue leading to the front portico of Braeburn, and although she ran very quickly up the drive, took a short cut across the lawn, sped along the terrace and dashed in through the drawing room windows, she was nevertheless quite thoroughly drenched. She shivered as she closed the windows and pulled off the thin Norwich shawl with which she'd attempted to protect herself from the elements. As she was about to shake it out, she found that she was being smilingly observed by her friend Ariadne Courdepass. "So there you are at last," Ariadne said pleasantly. "I was *afraid* the rain would catch you out, so I've built up the fire."

Priss smiled gratefully and went to warm herself before it. "Have you ever known the weather to make such an abrupt change? I had so hoped it would remain fine for a few more days." She heard no response, so she turned to face her friend. Ariadne was seated in a high-backed wing chair, her feet up on an ottoman, placidly and steadfastly knitting. "Where is everyone, Ariadne? Have you been sitting here alone for long?"

"Only since luncheon. You needn't look so concerned, you know. I'm quite enjoying myself."

"Are you really? You are the most amazing girl! Whatever are you knitting with such dogged patience?"

Ariadne's pretty mouth turned up in a mischievous smile. "This will be, when I've stitched all the sections together, a warm and rather colorful counterpane for my marriage bed.''

"Oh?" Priss responded with a chuckle, thinking her friend was joking. "Aren't you putting cart before horse? One would think you'd need a husband to put *in* your marriage bed before you'd need a counterpane to put *on* it."

"And what would you say, my dear, if I told you I'd found the man to put in it."

Priss gasped. "Ariadne! Are you wheedling me? Who *is* he?"

Ariadne's smile broadened. "I'm not yet at liberty to say."

Priss ran across the room and dropped down on the ottoman at her feet. "You odious wretch! You *must* tell me! You know all *my* secrets!"

"I can't just yet, Prissy," Ariadne said, permitting her needlework to fall into her lap as she leaned forward to pat Priss's shoulder affectionately. "You'll be the first to know, I promise you, as soon as I have confidence that the revelation is not premature."

"Oh, I see. You're not yet sure of him, is that it?"

"I've not yet planted the idea in his mind."

Priss giggled. "Must you do so? One would hope the fellow had enough sense to see for himself—"

Ariadne laughed, a rare, full-throated laugh. "I'm not at all sure he *has* any sense. But then, I have enough sense for both of us."

"So you do, my sensible friend, so you do. I hope he's worthy of you. Oh, dear, I'm so curious . . . can you at least tell me if I'm acquainted with the gentleman?"

"My lips are sealed. I don't wish to say anything at this time which will make me seem foolish later on."

"Yes, of course. Very sensible of you," Priss responded with a teasing smile. "I wish you good luck, dearest," she added with sincerity as her smile faded. "Better luck than I've had . . ."

"As to that," Ariadne remarked, picking up her knitting again, "I would not look so glum if I were you."

"Why? What do you mean?"

"I've been observing quite closely, you know. Alec is as much in love with you as it's possible to be."

Priss drew in her breath. "Oh! Do you *truly* believe that? I haven't wanted to . . . I try not to permit myself to . . . but it *has* seemed to me, too, that he . . ." She jumped to her feet, leaned down and enveloped her friend in a warm but rather damp hug. "Oh, Ariadne, perhaps before long we may *both* be happy!"

"We shall not be very happy if you develop an inflammation of the lungs. Go upstairs and take off that wet dress!"

Priss nodded and ran out to take the advice of her sensible friend. She had not been gone above five minutes when the drawing room door opened again to admit Ferdie who was firmly propelling a reluctant Gar into the room ahead of him. "Now, go ahead, Garvin, old fellow. *Ask* her," he said as he pushed the blushing Gar before Ariadne's chair.

"Damn you, Ferdie," Gar muttered under his breath, "if only I—"

Ariadne looked up at Gar sympathetically. "You really must not let Mr. Sellars bully you this way, Garvin. But if there's something you'd like to ask of me, you needn't hesitate. I shan't mind, whatever it is."

Gar reddened even further. "Well, Ferdie says I . . . that is, I . . ."

"What this silver-tongued *rake* is trying to ask," Ferdie put in derisively, "is to permit him to stand up with you for the first dance at Saturday's ball."

"Ball?" Ariadne gave a small shake of her head. "It is certainly not to be a *ball*. Just because the Earl is arranging for a few musicians to be present—"

"Don't quibble," Ferdie interrupted. "Even if it is not quite a ball, it is to be a fine party. I understand some of the local gentry will be invited, too. Therefore, young Sir Longshanks here wants to insure that your hand will not be snapped up by some unknown Lothario—"

"Mr. Sellars," Ariadne said in her matter-of-fact

manner, her knitting needles clicking steadily, "please be good enough to release your hold on Mr. Danforth's collar. There, that's better. Now, Garvin, I'm sure you know perfectly well that there's no need for a formal application for my hand for a dance. It is to be a quite informal party, and none of the ladies will have cards. I shall be quite delighted to stand up with you whenever you wish to ask me. And now that *that's* said, I'm certain you'd prefer browsing about in the library to standing about here making nonsensical conversation. Mr. Sellars and I are quite willing to excuse you."

"Th-Thank you, ma'am," the red-faced Gar said gratefully. "I do find dancing, especially as it's done nowadays, rather . . . er . . . too uninhibited to be quite proper. Not . . . er . . . in my style, you know. But one of the country dances . . ." He backed to the door. "I'm certain we'd enjoy . . ." And he went awkwardly from the room.

Ferdie looked after him, shaking his head hopelessly. Then he turned to frown down at the placid girl in considerable annoyance. He placed his hands on his hips, his elbows akimbo, and studied her for a few silent moments. "What on earth is the *matter* with you, Miss Courdepass?" he asked at last.

"I've told you, Mr. Sellars, to call me Ariadne."

"Ariadne then. Though it's a deucedly ridiculous name. Wherever did your mother get it?"

"From the Greeks. Ariadne was King Minos's daughter who led Theseus out of the Labyrinth by marking the way with a ball of yarn."

He looked down at her fingers, with the yarn wound between them, and grinned. "Very appropriate, I see. Wise of your mother, after all. But I was inquiring, ma'am, what is *wrong* with you?"

"Not a thing, Mr. Sellars, as far as I can tell."

"Do you care nothing for your *future*? Can it be that a lady of your obvious attributes for marriage and motherhood has no interest in fixing on a potential suitor?"

"Are you speaking of Garvin Danforth? I should

have thought, sir, that a man of your intelligence would have realized by this time that he was barking up the wrong tree.''

''Wrong tree? *Danforth* is the wrong *tree*? Why?''

Ariadne shrugged. ''The answer should be obvious.''

''Not to me. Perhaps you've not paid sufficient attention to his many fine qualities. He is tall, handsome and in good health. He has, I understand, a more than adequate competence from his father's estate, in addition to great expectations from his uncle and employer, Lord Hawthorne, who is childless and loves Gar like a son. And, most important of all, he is well-educated, scholarly, and as serious and high-minded as yourself.''

''Perhaps, Mr. Sellars, I am not as serious and high-minded as you suppose.''

He blinked. ''Aren't you? I would have said those were your most noticeable attributes.''

''If the character of a person were so easily read in his outward demeanor, matchmaking would be a much simpler art than it is.''

He cocked an offended eyebrow at her. ''Are you saying, with your usual unaffected directness, that I have no talents as a matchmaker?''

Her mouth curved up in a tiny, almost unnoticeable smile. ''You might interpret it that way, if you choose.''

''Very well then, ma'am—''

''Ariadne, please.''

''Very well then, *Ariadne*, I retire from the matchmaking business as of this moment. I give you up. I withdraw from the fray. I hope you will not have cause to regret, later, that you chose to dispense with my services. Good afternoon, ma'am.''

''Before you march off in your high dudgeon, Mr. Sellars, I wonder if you might be willing to give me a moment or two of assistance.''

''What?'' he asked turning back with a triumphant smile. ''Have you reconsidered? You've changed your mind, and you wish me to try my matchmaking skills once more?''

"No, thank you. I only want you to hold this skein of wool for me while I wind it. If you sit down there on the ottoman and hold the skein between your two hands, thus, I think we shall contrive . . ."

Trapped, Ferdie sank onto the ottoman holding the skein stretched between his two hands. For a few moments he watched silently while she rapidly wound the wool into a growing ball of yarn. After a while, he cocked his head on one side and eyed her speculatively. "If Gar is too serious for you, Ariadne, what sort of fellow *would* you find suitable?"

"Why do you ask? I don't believe there are any *other* candidates on the premises that you can dredge up for me, are there?"

He laughed. "No, I'm afraid there aren't. Just for my own edification, however, I'd like to know what sort would suit you."

"*Your* sort, I think," she said placidly, her hands steadily and rapidly winding the yarn.

Ferdie choked. "*My* sort! Are you mad?"

"You must keep your hands steady, Mr. Sellars, or you'll tangle the yarn," she cautioned mildly.

"Have you never heard what a wastrel and rake I am? Has no one ever told you that I'm thoroughly reprehensible? I've a well-earned reputation for indulging in all sorts of dissipation and profligacy, besides being past thirty and not at all plump in the pocket."

"Yes. I've heard all that."

He shook his head in bafflement. "And to *think* I had taken you for a woman of remarkable sense."

"And so I am. I'm really the only sort who could *manage* a profligate rake like yourself."

A snorting laugh was surprised out of him. "I almost believe that you could!" he declared admiringly.

"Please, Mr. Sellars, you *must* keep your hands up," she cautioned again.

"I think, Miss Ariadne Courdepass," he said, fixing her with a look of sudden and interested speculation, "that if we're to continue this very interesting conversation, you'd better begin to call me Ferdie."

At that moment, the door to the drawing room opened again. "There you are, Ferdie," Clio said, ignoring Miss Courdepass with her usual thoughtlessness. "I've been looking for you. Priss has asked me to help her decide which of the rooms would be most suitable for the dancing on Saturday, and I need your advice. The ballroom in the east wing is much too large, but there's a room on the second floor, just beyond the gallery, that I'd like you to come and look at. I can't make up my mind if—"

"Clio, I wish you'd go away," he said, not taking his eyes from Ariadne's face. "You are interrupting a very interesting conversation."

Clio gaped. "Well! I'm very *sorry*, I assure you! If a conversation with Miss Courdepass is more important than the choice of rooms for the dancing, I'm sure I can manage without your advice!" And she turned on her heel in offended dignity.

Ariadne's needles continued to click steadily away. "Why don't you ask Gar to help you, Clio, my dear? You'll find him in the library."

"What," Clio demanded, slamming the library door behind her in fury, "is the matter with Ferdie?"

Gar, perched on top of the library stepladder, a copy of Aristotle's *Metaphysics* open on his lap, started at the sound of the door slam, causing the stepladder to wobble dangerously. "Can't you come into a room with less noise?" he demanded querulously as soon as the ladder had reestablished its equilibrium.

Clio flounced across the room and dropped into an easy chair. "Don't *you* shout at me, Garvin Danforth! I've had enough high-handedness for one day. Did you know your so-called friend Ferdie is sitting in the drawing room making sheep's eyes at your *innamorata*?"

"I have no *innamorata*. If you are referring to Miss Courdepass, Ferdie is probably only trying to persuade her to save the first dance for me on Saturday night,'' Gar explained uninterestedly, returning his attention to the book on his lap.

"Hmmmph! If that's what he's doing, he's certainly going about it strangely. If you're not careful, you'll find that he's snatched her right from under your nose.''

"He's welcome to her. If you don't mind, Miss Vickers, I'm more interested in Aristotle than in Ferdie's flirts.''

"Oh, don't be such a grind, Gar. Come down from there! Are you going to sit up there and *read*, while Ferdie takes the exciting Miss Courdepass for himself?''

"What a lot of balderdash! You know perfectly well that Ferdie is not going to turn sheep's eyes at Miss Courdepass while you . . . that is, while there are other ladies about who are so much more . . . more . . .''

Her petulant expression cleared. "More *what*, Garvin, my dear?'' she asked with a sudden twinkle.

"Nothing.''

She got up from the chair and went to the foot of the ladder. "*What* have I more of than Miss Courdepass?''

Gar turned a page ostentatiously. "You know perfectly well what your charms are,'' he said, his eyes fixed on the book.

"No, I don't. Please come down. If you don't, I'll shake this ladder until you topple off.''

He didn't look up or bother to answer.

She shook the ladder, but not enough to trouble him. "*You* don't think I have any charms at all. I've had the decided impression that you disapprove of me.''

"Your impression is correct,'' Gar said, turning another page with excessive deliberation.

"Then what did you mean by saying that Ferdie would not look at Miss Courdepass while I'm present?''

"I did *not* say that, although it's probably true. Ferdie is not a man of particular discrimination.''

This time she really did shake the ladder. "I hope you fall and break your neck!'' she said with venom.

"Stop that! This is not at all amusing, Miss Vickers!

A fall from this height could lead to serious injury!"

She turned away and walked thoughtfully to the fireplace. Staring at the flames, she asked in sudden seriousness, "Why don't you approve of me?"

He shut the book and turned himself around to look at her. "It is not my place to say, ma'am."

"But I give you my permission. I truly want to know."

"If I say anything, you'll only lose your temper and—"

"I shall be as meek as a lamb, I promise."

"Well, then, for one thing, your mode of dress is too flamboyant."

She whirled around. "Aha! I *knew* you'd have something to say on that score. But I hope you don't think I'd take the word of someone who insists on wearing a ramshackle, seedy, ill-fitting coat like *that*! I'll have you know, Garvin Danforth, that I am considered to be *all the crack* in London!"

He turned around on the ladder again so that his back was to her. "Nothing at all the matter with my coat," he muttered, opening his book again. "Knew I shouldn't have started—"

"Well, what else?" she demanded.

"I have nothing else to say to you, ma'am," he said, trying to read.

"I might have known you'd lack the courage to speak your mind," she said disdainfully, crossing back to her chair and throwing herself into it. "You're nothing but a long-legged and bookish *jellyfish*!"

"Is that so?" he replied with a sneer. "I'd like to point out, my dear Miss Vickers, that the sea-creatures to whom you refer can not be long-legged or bookish, jellyfish having neither limbs nor libraries."

"*That* is just the sort of response I might have expected! I was convinced from our first meeting that you were a spineless mawworm!"

"And *I* knew from our first meeting," he retorted, stung to the quick, "from the way that you permitted yourself, in that horrendous and shockingly gaudy pink dress, to call at the apartment of a gentleman—and a married one at that—without escort, and the way that you flirted—and continue to flirt—with every male who comes your way, whatever his age, station or marital situation, that *you*, ma'am, are not a *lady*!''

"*Oh!*" she gasped. "Of all the insulting, degrading *calumnies*—!'' She jumped up and stalked over to the ladder.

"Now, Clio,'' he said, watching her fearfully, "you promised that you wouldn't—'' And he made a hurried attempt to scamper down.

But he was too late. She pushed against the ladder with all the strength that anger had stirred in her. It toppled over with a kind of slow certainty, sending Gar bumping against the bookshelves. It was only by grasping at them in his inexorable descent to the floor that he was able to break his fall. When he at last lay sprawled on the floor, a heap of books cascading down around him, he cried out in vexation, "You addle-brained *baggage*, you could have *killed* me!'' But she had already stormed out of the room.

Chapter Eighteen

Alec did not make an appearance until tea time, by which hour Priss and the entire party were wondering what had become of him. He gave only a terse explanation of his absence, saying he'd been riding in the rain. He was polite and attentive to all the guests, but Priss had the uneasy feeling that he was avoiding *her*. In addition, there was something in the set of his jaw that made her distinctly uneasy. But since he disappeared into his dressing room as soon as he could make an escape, she had no opportunity to learn what it was that had disturbed him . . . not, that is, until much later that evening.

When she knocked at his dressing room door to indicate that she was dressed and ready to be escorted down to dinner, she had almost forgotten that anything was amiss. She was wearing her favorite dress, a lilac crepe half-robe worn over a deeper purple round-gown trimmed with lace, and was feeling in a particularly hopeful mood. Each day had moved her into closer intimacy with Alec, and after the incident on the terrace the evening before, she felt some justification for permitting herself to dream that matters might yet work out between them. Ariadne's comments that afternoon had supported her own feelings and added to her cheerfulness. So it was with particular dismay that she noticed, when Alec emerged from his room, that his face was stiff with controlled fury. "Good heavens,

Alec,'' she couldn't help exclaiming, ''what has occurred to upset you?''

''Nothing at all, ma'am,'' he replied coldly. ''Shall we go down?''

''*Nothing*? You look as angry as if you'd been cheated of your last shilling.''

''And you, ma'am, look as merry as if *you'd done the cheating*! You seem to have made a remarkable recovery from your doldrums of last evening,'' he said, his voice exuding sarcasm.

She looked up at him bewilderedly. ''I sense some sort of accusation underneath those words. Have *I* done something to anger you?''

''Not at all. As I have told you several times, your behavior is of no interest to me. Of course, I *did* think that while we were engaged in this charade for my grandfather's benefit, you would exercise some *discretion*. A mere fortnight did not seem to me to be too long a time in which to expect you to refrain from . . . But never mind. It makes very little difference, after all.''

''Alec, I haven't the slightest notion of what you're *talking* about! Have I been indiscreet about something?''

''Well, if *I've* discovered his presence here, it is possible that others—''

''*Whose* presence? Alec, will you stop speaking in riddles and tell me what is on your mind?''

He looked down at her with eyes burning with revulsion. ''I *saw* him, you know. Almost ran over him on Cross Mill Road.''

''But *who*—?'' Then a flash of understanding broke through her mind like a searing bolt of lightning. ''Oh, my *God*! Not—?''

He smiled bitterly. ''What a performer you are, my dear. You'd make a worthy successor to Siddons. Yes, you're quite right. Your *friend*, Sir Blake Edmonds, rode right into my path.''

''But . . . what is he doing *here*?'' she asked, bemused.

He gave a short laugh. ''I admit to being a fool, my

dear, but don't take me for such a flat as that! He was very quick, I assure you, in his attempt to put me off. Said he and his wife were visiting her cousins, or some such story."

Priss's brow cleared in relief. "But of *course* that's it. The Beardsleys of Wirksworth. Her *maiden* name was Beardsley. I'd forgotten that."

"How very convenient," he remarked drily.

"What do you mean by *that*?" she asked, whitening. "You don't think he came here to see *me*, do you?"

"To see you?" His lips twisted into an ugly sneer. "Now, *how* could I entertain so wild a thought? It is mere *coincidence*, of course, that he had chosen this very fortnight to travel up from London. And mere coincidence that he had never before seen fit to oblige his wife to accompany her on a visit to her family. And mere coincidence, too, I suppose, that you have been disappearing from our midst every afternoon—"

"*Alec!*" she cried as if he'd struck her. "You *can't* believe such a thing of me!"

"No, of course I can't. You've been spending all your afternoons visiting your *mother*, haven't you?"

Frozen, she stared at him for a long moment. "You *are* a dastard!" she said, beginning to shake from head to foot. She turned, stumbled to the bed and sank down on it. "You'd better go. They will be wondering, downstairs . . ."

"There's no reason for a display of vapors, ma'am. If *I* can continue with this pretense, there's no reason why you can't."

"I . . . I'll continue with it," she said quietly, not looking at him, "but not tonight. I'm not . . . Please, make my excuses. Say I have the headache. Say anything you like, but just . . . go."

Without another word he left the room. For a long while she sat where she was, looking at the hands clenched in her lap. If she unclenched them, she knew they would tremble pathetically, and she would see the trembling and feel sorry for herself and begin to cry. And she didn't want to cry over him any more. Besides, a session of weeping always left her feeling exhausted and drained and didn't do a jot of good. So she kept her hands clenched and her back straight and didn't permit herself to slide limply to the floor and curl up in a little ball, which was another thing she had a yearning to do.

Her emotions were in a temporary state of shock, and therefore she was somewhat buffered from the pain she knew was bound to come later. But her mind was not benumbed—it was racing about, stirring up a whirl of questions and answers, accusations and defenses, schemes for revenge and abortive plots to salvage the rapidly crumbling framework of her dreams for the future. First her thoughts centered on the horrifying coincidence that had brought Blake into the vicinity. What a talent the blasted fellow had for turning up at the worst possible time! He was truly becoming the bane of her existence.

But on second thought, it was grossly unfair to blame Blake. He was—no matter what Alec believed—completely innocent, this time, of any intention to bother her. He was merely obliging his wife by coming to Derbyshire to visit her family. It was not *his* fault that Alec had come across him and had leaped to his disgusting conclusion!

When all was said and done, the entire blame had to be laid at Alec's door. It was his warped imagination that had devised this newest accusation. Whatever had happened, Priss wondered, her throat burning with unshed tears, to have changed the honest, clear-eyed, sweet-natured boy she'd once known into this bitter, suspicious, cynical and cruel man? No longer was she so foolish and lacking in self-esteem that she could believe *herself* responsible for this change in him. No, he had done this to *himself*, and only he was to blame for the wreckage he was making of his life. She could almost pity him.

But he was destroying *her* life, too, and for that reason she could feel no pity. How *dared* he deal so violently with her future! How dared he make assumptions about her character on the basis of the flimsiest of

circumstantial evidence! Had he seen nothing in her
behavior, her words, her appearance, her way of life to
make him question the soundness of his dastardly conclusions? Where were his eyes and ears? Where was his
judgment?

He deserved to be horsewhipped! If only she had a
brother who could call him out! If only there were
someone who could speak for her character and act for
her revenge. But there was no one. Her mother must
never be told this horrid tale; and of course the Earl
must never know. She had no one at all who could
defend her and restore her sense of honor.

It was this feeling that her honor—the pride in her
sense of herself—was being trampled in the muddied
swamp of her husband's imagination that undid her
control. Her shoulders began to shake and her chest to
heave in gasping breaths that were more like hiccoughs
than sobs. *Stop this*, she ordered herself, sitting up more
rigidly and clenching her fists more tightly. *You're not
going to give way!* But these hiccoughing gasps were
more painful than tears, and after a while she slid down
to the floor, let her head fall onto the bed and wept.

Kellam, who had been putting away Alec's discarded
clothing and setting the overcrowded dressing room to
rights, hadn't meant to overhear. When he first realized
that he was eavesdropping on the most private of
quarrels, he'd wanted desperately to steal from the
room. But he was afraid they'd hear him, and *that* was
certain to prove embarrassing to all concerned, so he
stood rooted to the spot and waited for them to leave.
But when it was over, her ladyship didn't leave. She was
there in the next room, crying her poor eyes out, and
Kellam was at a loss as to what to do about it.

When five minutes had elapsed, and there was no sign
of the sobs subsiding, Kellam opened the dressing room
door and peered inside. Lady Braeburn was sitting on
the floor, her head in her arms resting on the bed and
her shoulders heaving pathetically. Without attempting
to muffle his footsteps, he went back into the dressing

room, poured a glass of water from a decanter on the dresser and returned to the bedroom. Kneeling down beside the lady, he said quietly, " 'Ave a drink 'o water, m'lady. Do ye a world o' good."

She gave a stifled gurgle, caught her breath and looked up. "Wh-Who are y—? Oh, Alec's m'man, aren't you? G-Go away!"

"Yes, m'lady. Kellam's the name. But I'd be no better 'n a whopstraw if I left ye 'ere bawlin'. Take a tiny sip, now, like a good little poppet. Ye 'most bawled yerself dry!"

She gave a sniffling laugh and took the glass from him. When she'd finished and handed the glass back to him, she took a good look at him. "Did you . . . h-hear . . .?"

He nodded glumly. "I whiddled the 'ole scrap."

"I assume I n-needn't tell you, Kellam, that I would n-not like to have any of this repeated."

"You c'n trust me, m'lady. I knows 'ow to keep me clapper still. Ask the Cap'n. Been together through the 'ole campaign, we 'ave."

"Yes," she said, blinking away the last of her tears and wiping her cheeks, "Alec told m-me about you. His batman, he said."

"That's 'oo I am. Seed 'im through good days an' bad. I knows 'im better 'n most." He sat cross-legged on the floor beside her. "I 'opes ye won't think me too impudent, m' lady, if I tells ye 'e didn't mean it," he said confidentially. "Crazy jealous 'e is, y' know. 'As been fer years."

"You *are* impudent, young man," Priss declared, nevertheless looking the fellow over with interest. "Do you talk to his lordship in this sort of informal way?"

"Oh, we don't stand on points, the Cap'n an' me," Kellam said, unabashed.

"Then *we* needn't either, I suppose. What did you mean just now—when you said that 'the Captain' was 'crazy jealous.' "

"We used t' blab a good bit, y'know, durin' those long nights. I recall as 'ow the name Blake Edmonds used t' make 'im wild. And then, 'e'd dream . . . an' mutter in 'is sleep about it. It's a queer start, y'know, the way the 'ole business took 'old of 'im. 'E can't let it go, y'know what I mean?''

"An obsession?" she asked curiously.

He nodded eagerly. "Aye, m' lady. Ye've 'it it square on th' noddle.''

"Well," she sighed, "there isn't anything to be gained by talking about it. Help me up, please, Kellam. I must say that you're the strangest sort of valet I've ever seen.''

"That's cause I ain't no valet," he said, jumping up and assisting her to rise. "Mr. Smoot, now—that's Major Sellars' man—'e's a valet. I'm just a batman.''

"But worth your weight in gold, I would imagine," Priss said with a small smile.

Kellam grinned at her. "As t' that, m' lady, I won't pre-sume t' say. But I'd not argue wiv ye, neither. Is there anything I c'n do fer yer ladyship afore I takes meself off?''

"No, nothing. But thank you, Kellam. You've made me feel somewhat better, I admit.''

The man nodded and walked to the dressing room door. But before he went through it, he paused. "Ye'll try to forgive the Cap'n, won't ye, m' lady?" he asked hopefully.

"There's not much point in my doing that, is there? Not while he's in the grip of an obsession. Good evening, Kellam.''

"Good evenin', m' lady.''

"And, Kellam . . . you *will* keep all this a secret, won't you?''

"Don't ye go worryin' yerself about that. Me lips is sealed.''

The second course had already been laid when Priss appeared in the dining room doorway. "I'm feeling so much better," she announced cheerfully, "that I thought I'd join you for dinner after all.''

A chorus of voices welcomed her as she took her

place, and although her eyes glittered more brightly than usual and her lips were somewhat more red and full, none of the diners seemed to notice anything out of the way. Alec got up and held her chair for her as she sat down, but she did not even glance in his direction. Her bout of sobs had done her some good, for once. That, and her little talk with Kellam, had cleared her head and strengthened her self-confidence. Never would she permit Alec to make her cry again! She was a woman of some sense and of unimpeachable morals, and no man in the world would ever again make her feel degraded! With this resolve, she had determined to go down to her guests and behave in exactly the manner she ought— confident and guiltless, with nothing to hide and nothing to prove!

A footman served her a slice of beef, and as she cut into it she smiled warmly at the assembled faces. "How are the plans for Saturday's party progressing, Clio dear?" she asked.

"Quite well, I think," Clio answered, tossing a quick look at Gar to see if he had taken note that it was *she* who had been made the organizer of the fortnight's most important social event. But Gar was taking no notice of her at all. She turned back to Priss. "The room at the end of the gallery should serve for the dancing, I think, if you have no more than twenty couples on the floor."

"I don't think we'll have more than that," Priss assured her. Then, turning to Lady Vickers with a calculatedly casual smile, she added, "Speaking of invitations, Mama, you'll never *guess* whom Alec ran into today."

"Who was it, Alec?" Lady Vickers asked, puzzled.

"I . . . I don't know," Alec stammered awkwardly. "I mean . . . I must have forgotten."

Priss laughed merrily. "Oh, you men are the most absent-minded creatures! He met Sir Blake Edmonds on the road today!"

The name meant nothing to most of the diners, but Lady Vickers started, choked on a bite of meat and eyed her daughter in sudden alarm. "Sir *Blake*—?" she echoed hesitantly.

"A family friend from London, you know," Priss explained to the others blithely. "A *dear* old family friend, isn't he, Alec? May I have your permission, Grandfather, to add his name—and that of his wife, of course—to our list of guests for Saturday?"

Alec colored and bit his lip. "I scarcely think . . ." he began, and then thought better of it.

But Lady Vickers was horrified. "I don't think it necessary to invite them, my love. Not at all necessary."

"But why not?" the Earl said effusively. "The more the merrier, eh? Put 'em down, by all means."

"They aren't really *close* friends, you know," Lady Vickers persisted, glancing at her daughter in surprise and irritation. "We have only a nodding acquaintance. I see no reason to swell our ranks with mere—"

"Grandfather has agreed, Mama, so let that be the end of it," Priss said, throwing her mother a dagger-look. Then, with the brightest of bright smiles, she turned to Alec. "I shall *so* enjoy seeing Blake again, my dear. Won't you?"

Chapter Nineteen

The Saturday evening fête was to be the highlight of the holiday. Clio, with very little else to occupy her (since Ferdie seemed to be spending an inordinate amount of time in the company of Miss Courdepass, Gar wasn't speaking to her and Alec was remote and frozen-faced for much of the time), gladly took over the supervision of the details to prepare for it. With Clio's penchant for ostentation and the Earl's readiness to supply the girl with the wherewithal to indulge her every whim, the affair promised to be resplendent. The guest list, which included all the guests staying at Braeburn, Lady Vickers, and a number of the nearby gentry (who had not been invited to the Great House for years and were anticipating the event with mouth-watering excitement) numbered almost forty.

The large dining room had been opened up for the dinner, and the Blue Room (an oversized and seldom used upstairs sitting room) had been agreed upon as suitable for the dancing. The rugs had been rolled up, the furniture pushed back against the walls, and a small, railed platform had been erected for the musicians. Clio had also seen to it that huge vases of flowers and large numbers of candelabras decorated the room. Except for its smaller size, it was quite as elegant as the most admired of London ballrooms. Everyone who peeped into it that morning agreed that it looked marvelous.

Clio was delighted. The responsibility for the ball was the best thing that had happened to her during the entire fortnight. In the first place, it was a task she enjoyed and at which she excelled. In the second place, she needed something with which to occupy her mind. For if she weren't busy, she would only dwell on her growing discontent.

It was becoming increasingly clear to her that Alec was not concerned about her at all. He was obviously besotted over his wife. The strange thing about it was that Clio didn't feel as devastated as she would have supposed. It had occurred to her of late that Alec was a bit of a bore. His company was not at all stimulating, for he never seemed really to be paying attention to her. The truer source of her discontent seemed to be Garvin Danforth. *His* behavior was really fascinatingly disturbing. From the look in his eyes when they rested on her (which they seemed to do quite often) she would swear he was quite taken with her. But his manner in her presence was sullen and querulous. And now that he was not speaking to her at all, she was very much afraid that she'd not be able, ever, to solve the paradox of his behavior. It was all very frustrating, but, at least until the party was over, she had other matters to think about.

On Saturday afternoon, all the usual afternoon activities were suspended so that everyone could rest and prepare their toilettes for what they hoped would be an exciting occasion. Alec, unwilling to remain cooped up in his dressing room for hours, wandered about the empty downstairs rooms disconsolately. He alone, of all the people under this roof, anticipated the evening's fête with dread. How could he watch his wife dance with Edmonds (and he was certain she would find a way to do so) and still maintain a smiling, happy-host demeanor?

At a few minutes past one, when he had convinced himself that he could manage to concentrate on some reading, he picked up the *London Times* (which had come by post and was only a week late) and settled himself into an easy chair in the library. A movement out on the lawn caused him to glance at the window, and he caught sight of Priss running hurriedly across the lawn. He crushed the paper in his hand without realizing what he was doing. Was the incorrigible creature on her way to meet Edmonds *again*?

When he entered her room that evening to escort her downstairs, there was not a sign of guilt or misgiving in her expression. In fact, she looked quite lovely. She'd chosen to wear a white satin gown covered with an overdress of Copenhagen-blue gauze. She looked as ethereal and innocent as a child, her eyes clear and shining, and her bright curls bouncing over her forehead in careless disarray. Well, he, for one, would not be fooled by appearances. The careless-seeming arrangement of those curls was just as *calculated* as the innocent look in those eyes!

They said not a word as they went down the stairs. It was only when the Earl, who was already at his place in the front hall to greet his guests, turned to the stairs and smiled up at them, that they changed their frozen expressions for overbright smiles.

The Edmondses were among the first to arrive, Blake looking smug and jovial as he shook the hands of his hosts. Lady Edmonds, however, seemed reserved and distant, and it seemed to Alec that she studied Priss somewhat fearfully.

Alec offered his arm to Miss Courdepass for the parade in to dinner. Ariadne was in her best looks this evening in her dark-blue lustring gown (which made her seem taller) and with a becoming flush in her cheeks. Alec was quick to compliment her.

"Thank you, sir, for the kind words. I am blossoming in the radiance of the hospitality of this house," she answered contentedly.

Alec gave her a knowing smile. "Is *that* the cause for your bloom? I had supposed, from a remark or two that Ferdie let fall, that the color in your cheeks might have quite another source."

Any other girl would have blushed, but Ariadne's implacable calm remained unruffled. Only the slight upturn of her mouth gave indication of her inner glow. "Perhaps so, my dear, perhaps so. Time will tell," she murmured placidly.

"I hope, then, that I may soon wish you happy. There's not a man in the world for whom I have more affection than Ferdie."

Ariadne gave him a sidelong look. "I hope, Alec, that I may soon wish *you* happy, too. For there is not a *girl* in the world who more deserves happiness than your wife." And with that cryptic remark, she took her place at the table.

The dinner (a meal that included almost fifty different dishes and would become the yardstick for excellence against which the participants would measure all their future banquets) took more than two hours to consume, and after the ladies left the table, the men lingered for half-an-hour longer. Upstairs, meanwhile, the musicians began to play, and the assemblage made their way up the staircase and down the gallery to the resplendent "ballroom." Clio beamed with pleasure at the many compliments she received on her talent for decoration.

But her pleasure was not long lived. Although three gentlemen (all of the visiting gentry, all of them married and all of them middle-aged) asked her to stand up with them for the first dance, she refused them all. Couples began to take their places on the floor, but Clio stood on the sidelines, as if waiting for someone.

Everyone in the Braeburn party was absorbed in their own concerns, and no one but Ariadne took any notice of Clio's dilemma. But Ariadne was struck with the sudden awareness that there was something decidedly different about Clio this evening. Her magnificent red hair had not changed, but the girl herself was somewhat subdued. Her gown was a simple creation of pale green silk, with small puffed sleeves, a surprisingly modest neckline and a girlish bodice covered with tiny tucks. She wore no jewelry but a pair of small, pearl earrings. And, Ariadne noticed with particular amusement, the girl had not, this once, damped her petticoat.

Garvin Danforth, the cause of this reversion into modesty, stood forlornly near the doorway watching the dancers make up their sets. Ariadne walked up to him. "I see that Clio is not dancing," she said companionably. "That does seem unfair, doesn't it, after she's worked so hard to arrange everything? Although I quite agree with you, Garvin, that dancing can sometime be so improper that it's just as well to sit it out." Then she went off on Ferdie's arm to take her place in the set.

Gar looked after her for a moment and then went limping up to Clio just as the dance began. "I don't suppose," he said hesitantly, tugging at his neckcloth nervously, "that you'd care to stand up with me, would you? I'm not much of a dancer, and I have this . . . er . . . trouble with my knee—which of course is your fault anyway—but I think we can contrive if you don't expect me to make my turns too quickly . . ."

Clio smiled broadly and held out her arms. "Come on, you gudgeon! We're almost too late! And don't worry about your knee. Just lean on me."

Alec very properly asked his wife to stand up with him, and the pair took their places in the set with fixed smiles on their faces. They exchanged not a word during the first few figures, but after a few minutes, Priss hissed, "For God's sake, Alec, can't you even *talk* to me? I feel as if I'm dancing with a smiling *cadaver*."

His smile didn't waver as he responded coldly, "Be patient, my dear. I'm certain your *next* partner will be more satisfactory."

Priss was so infuriated that her smile faded, and she walked off the floor at the end of the dance with obvious annoyance. Alec was interested to note that she did *not* choose Edmonds as her next partner. But Edmonds *did* manage to secure her hand for two other dances. And later that evening, Priss and Edmonds were seen strolling around the edges of the ballroom arm in arm. When Alec saw them in so companiable a pose, his stomach turned over. He felt too sick to remain in the room staring at them. He went quickly into a small adjoining room that Clio had opened in the event that some of the party might wish to leave the dancing and play cards. There was a game of whist being played in the far corner—the Earl was, of course, one of the players—but the room was otherwise deserted except for one forlorn figure sitting alone, her back to the door. It was Lady Edmonds.

Feeling a strong rush of sympathy for her, Alec approached her and asked her to dance. "Oh! Lord Braeburn," she said, forcing a smile. "I . . . I'd prefer to stay here. Do join me, if you don't mind missing this dance."

Alec pulled a chair from one of the tables and sat down beside her. "Why do you not dance, ma'am?" he asked politely. "Are you worn down from the exertion?"

Her smile flickered bravely for a moment and then died. "I'm afraid that no one has asked me. My husband, who did his duty for the first dance, has been *otherwise* occupied for the rest of the evening."

Alec had not expected this frank and bitter response and was completely at a loss as to how to deal with it. "I'm certain it was an oversight, Lady Edmonds. Would you like me to find him and bring him to you?"

She shook her head and rummaged in her reticule for a handkerchief. "No, thank you. He would not care for that at all. He often . . . takes me to task for m-making demands on him . . ."

She was on the verge of tears. Alec looked about uncomfortably, but fortunately, none of the card players was taking the least notice of them. "I'm sure you exaggerate, ma'am," he said gently. "As a husband of some little experience, I can assure you that we are all guilty of sometimes making too much of little things."

"It is *n-not* a little thing when your husband constantly speaks of other women," she said in a rather unpleasant whine. "Where *did* I put that handkerchief . . .?"

"Take mine, ma'am, please."

She took it and blew her nose into it vigorously. "He's *always* admiring other women! Do *you* do that, sir?"

"What? I . . . I don't know what you mean," he answered awkwardly.

"I mean, do *you* tell your wife how lovely this one's neck is, or that one's ankles . . .?"

"Well, I—"

"No, of course you don't. It's quite a vulgar trait, and anyone can *see* that you're a perfect gentleman. But Blake is quite addicted to making such remarks. You'd be completely shocked, I know, if you could hear him prosing on about *your* wife, for instance. He thinks her quite a paragon, you know. He's been singing her praises for years! And now he's following her about like a pet p-poodle! It's enough to make one *sick*! I don't want you to think, my lord, that I'm in any way criticizing Lady Braeburn. Not a bit. I'm certain she's done nothing to encourage his excesses."

"No, of course not. I mean . . ."

"Although I did notice that she's given him two dances already . . . and the evening's not half over. It does seem to me to be a bit beyond the bounds of strict propriety. I hope I haven't said anything to offend you, my lord, but . . ."

Alec wanted very much to wring Priss's neck. It was bad enough that she'd been carrying on an affair with Edmonds for so long, but this sort of indiscretion (although he was not such a fool that he didn't realize she was doing it, at least in part, to spite *him*) was bound to cause unnecessary pain for a poor creature like this. "No, ma'am, I take no offense," he said kindly, "but it does no good to sit about by oneself and sulk, now does it? What do you say to our putting a good face on it and going out on the dance floor to enjoy ourselves. *May* I have the honor, ma'am?"

Lady Edmonds joylessly acquiesced, favoring him with her sour smile, and the two emerged from the card room and joined the dancers. It was, for Alec, just another ordeal in this awkward, dull and painful evening, and he passed the remaining hours of the party by imagining the satisfaction he would find in accosting the repulsive Sir Blake with a horsewhip.

With the fortnight coming to an end, Alec did not expect to have to lay eyes on Lady Edmonds or her husband ever again. To his intense surprise, however, he was informed by the butler, one windy afternoon two days later, that a Lady Edmonds was waiting to see him, having requested a "private interview." The butler had established her in the Earl's study, the Earl having gone upstairs to nap.

Alec went to the study at once. Lady Edmonds was pacing about the room and appeared to be in great distress. Her eyes were red-rimmed, and her hair—wispy and disorderly at best—was so carelessly pushed into her close-fitting and unflattering bonnet that a number of strands hung about her face and down her back. Alec urged her into a chair and, leaning on his grandfather's desk, asked her what he could do for her.

"I don't know how to tell you this, my lord, but I am convinced that my husband and your . . . w-wife are . . ." She wrung her hands miserably and looked down at the floor. ". . . *lovers*!"

Alec took a deep breath. "You are quite mistaken, ma'am. I don't mean to be unkind, and I can see that you're sincerely upset, but I think it ill-advised of you to go about maligning my wife. You must see that I cannot permit you to do so."

"I don't mean to malign anyone! Do you think me a complete fool? I have not breathed a word of this to another soul! I only want to put a *stop* to it, don't you understand?" She got up and began to pace about the room again. "I shall be frank with you, my lord. I'm not a pretty woman, and I know that Blake did not love me when we wed. I had the wealth he wanted . . . that was all. But I loved him, and I persuaded myself to . . . to . . . believe the promises he made to me . . . of loyalty and fidelity and devotion. It was not long, however, before I began to realize that his promises were worthless."

Alec found the tale unbearable. "If that's true, ma'am, why did you wait until now to speak out?"

"Because his earlier indiscretions were the sort I could put up with. I am not the first woman who has closed her eyes to her husband's . . . activities with servant girls and opera dancers and that sort." She turned and faced him squarely. "In this case, however, there is a difference. I have always known that Lady Braeburn had . . . how shall I describe it? . . . a special place in his heart. Such a liaison is fraught with danger. Doesn't it seem to you, my lord, that this can lead to the destruction of our marriages? What if they should decide to run away together?'' She sat down and put her hands up to cover her face. ''I simply couldn't . . . face it . . .''

Alec stood up and went to the window. Out on the lawn below, the dead leaves were blowing about in a mad dance. The whole world suddenly seemed mad to him. It was, all of it, a mad dance . . . a stupid, illogical whirl of unfulfilled desires, clashing wills, senseless accidents and unpredictable fortunes. This poor woman was sitting there behind him silently weeping for her hopeless future and her destroyed pride; and he was standing at the window engaging in pompous philosophical trivialities so that he could avoid facing the question she was about to ask.

As if she heard his thoughts, she asked it. ''What are you g-going to d-do about it, my lord?'' Her voice was choked with tears.

He didn't turn, but he answered in the only way he could. ''I don't believe a word of your accusation, ma'am. Therefore, I intend to do nothing at all.''

''But, Lord Braeburn, what if I t-told you I have proof?''

He turned around, sickened. ''Proof? What proof?''

''There is a gentleman staying under your roof by the name of Ferdinand Sellars, is there not?''

''Yes, but—''

''He has a valet named Smoot. Send for him.''

Alec stared at her and then shrugged. He went to the door, called the butler and gave him an order. Mr. Smoot appeared on the threshold in a very short time. ''You sent for me, my lord?''

''Are you Smoot, Mr. Sellars' man?''

''Yes, my lord.''

''Come in, then, and close the door. Are you acquainted with Lady Edmonds here?''

The man started at the sight of Lady Edmonds and licked his lips nervously. ''Yes, I am. Good afternoon, my lady.''

"Mr. Smoot," Lady Edmonds said, shading her reddened eyes with her hand so that Smoot should not see the state she was in, "tell his lordship what you told me."

"But . . . you said . . . I wouldn't never *have* to—"

"Never mind what I said! *Tell* him. I shall reimburse you properly, never fear."

Mr. Smoot looked decidedly uneasy. "I don't want no more payment. I never said nothing about telling anyone else."

"It's too late for qualms now, Mr. Smoot," Alec said coldly. "Either you should learn to keep such information to yourself, or you must be prepared for the consequences of telling it. Go ahead. I'm waiting."

There was something in Lord Braeburn's tone that quelled him. "It ain't nothing so terrible, you know. I have a female acquaintance, y' see, over at Three Oaks. Works in the kitchen there. I go over to see her when I have the chance. And the other day, when I was leaving, I saw . . . well, I saw yer . . . Lady Braeburn . . ."

"Yes? Go on."

The fellow shuffled his feet uncomfortably. "She was walking away from me through the grass with a man in a blue coat."

"What libelous rubbish is this?" Alec burst out. "You didn't see their faces, yet you make an accusation—! It could have been *anybody*. Another woman . . . or the man with the blue coat could have been *me*!"

"Yes, my lord . . . only the man was broader than you . . . and not as tall. And the blue coat . . . well, the color ain't one which a gentleman like you would usually choose."

"But Blake *does* have such a coat, my lord," Lady Edmonds put in quietly. "I showed it to Mr. Smoot, and he recognized it."

"And the lady?" Alec asked drily. "Are you equally sure of *her* identity?"

The man lowered his head. "Well, all those blond curls . . ." he mumbled.

"I see. So they were walking through the grass. Is

there anything more?" Alec asked, feeling sick with self-disgust at finding himself forced to discuss his wife with this repellent Peeping Tom.

"I saw her turn and . . . hug him."

There was a moment of silence. "Is that all?" Alec asked icily.

"Yes, my lord."

Alec walked around the desk and took a seat behind it. "Now, then, Smoot, how did you happen to feel it necessary to give this information to Lady Edmonds?"

"Well, sir, my female acquaintance . . . her cousin is an abigail at the Beardsleys. And she said Lady Edmonds might easily part with a hatful of yellow boys . . . I mean . . . might be interested—"

"I know what you mean. In other words, you told your 'female acquaintance' what you saw, and she, in turn, told her cousin . . . is that it?"

"Yes, my lord."

"And you all saw a way to extort a few guineas—"

"Well, I didn't *ask* Lady Edmonds for anything. She *gave* me—"

"No, of *course* you didn't ask. And, besides, your true motivation, no doubt, was your desire to be kind and helpful, isn't that it?"

There was no mistaking the scorn in his tone. Smoot was clever enough to hold his tongue.

"One thing more, Mr. Smoot, before you take yourself out of my sight. You are not in my employ, and therefore I cannot . . . er . . . *reward* you as I think you deserve. I shall, however, tell Mr. Sellars about your enterprising activities and leave it to *him* to act on the information. But if I learn that you, your 'female acquaintance' or her cousin ever breathe a word of this affair to anyone at all, I shall seek you out and with my bare fists teach you a lesson in the results of malicious gossip. Do you understand me, Smoot?"

"Yes, my lord."

When the fellow was gone, Lady Edmonds spoke up in a voice that indicated how deeply shamed she was by what had transpired. "I . . . I'm sorry about having used . . . these methods, my lord. You've made me see myself in . . . in a most unflattering light. I only wish to say that I didn't *intend* to spy on my husband, but . . .''

Her voice petered out, for she became aware that he was not attending. Alec, in fact, was listening only with half an ear. The rest of his mind was struggling to face the revolting fact that he now had to take some action. Here was yet another instance of the dire results of Priss's unforgivable interference with his solicitor's attempt to obtain an annulment six years ago. If she'd only permitted Newkirk to go ahead with it, this humiliating and degrading business would be none of his concern. Under *these* circumstances, however, he was still her husband and thus a proven cuckold. He was being *forced*, therefore, by custom, to take some action.

He ground his teeth in frustration and anger, frowning down at the unhappy woman who sat blinking up at him so pitifully. "I do not blame you, ma'am," he said shortly. "I can see you've not had an easy road in your marriage. You have my profound sympathy."

Lady Edmonds looked up at him tearfully. "Will you . . . can you tell me wh-what you intend to do?"

His jaw clenched, and he couldn't prevent his disgust from showing in his expression. "*Do*, ma'am? What do you *expect* me to do?"

"You'll not . . . kill him?" she cried in sudden alarm.

"I can't say. Anything is possible, I suppose," he answered curtly, crossing to the door and holding it open for her.

She jumped up, ran across the room to him and grasped his coat. "You must *promise* me you won't! There must be some other way—!"

"There is, Lady Edmonds, and I shall try my best to accomplish it. If I can possibly keep my temper in control, I shall merely blacken his eyes, bloody his nose and send him home to you. Good day to you, ma'am."

Chapter Twenty

Nevertheless, there was murder in his eyes as he stormed up the stairs to his dressing room. If he *did* find Priss and Edmonds together at Three Oaks, he knew that giving Edmonds a couple of blows to the face with his fists would never suffice to sate his fury. Even a horse-whipping might not be enough! He pulled his riding crop and a pair of riding boots from his wardrobe with hands that were not quite steady. A picture repeatedly flashed into his mind of those same hands choking the life out of a blue-coated Corinthian, and he was not at all certain that he could keep himself from making that vision a reality.

As he sat down on the cot and began to pull on his boots, the hall door to the dressing room unceremoniously opened and Kellam burst in. He closed the door behind him with ominous deliberation, put his back against it and spread out his arms. ''Y'ain't goin'!'' he declared.

''What?'' Alec eyed his batman as if the fellow had lost his mind. ''What are you going on about *now*?''

''Ye've no need t' play innocent wiv me. I knows all about it.''

''About what?''

''I seed ol' Smoot when 'e come downstairs. 'E'd been pitchin' gammon afore that 'e know'd somethin' t' do wiv Lady Braeburn. So when I seed 'is white face, I deducted that somethin' smoky wuz brewin', an' I got wind o' the lay.''

"Oh, you did, did you?" Alec muttered disgustedly. "And who asked you to pry into matters that are not your concern?"

"If you ain't my concern, I don't know 'oo is. Ye c'n climb down off them 'igh ropes, guv, 'cause y' ain't goin' nowheres."

"Since when, Harry Kellam, do I need your permission?"

"This c'n be the first time, then. I won't let ye go spyin' on 'er. It ain't fittin'."

"See *here*, man, I don't need *you* to tell me—!" He was interrupted by a violent knocking at the door. Kellam opened it a crack and found himself being inexorably pushed backward as Ferdinand Sellars forced himself in.

"Good heavens, Ferdie, what—?" Alec began.

"Getting ready to go somewhere, may I ask?" Ferdie demanded.

" 'E ain't goin' nowheres," Kellam told him firmly.

"Good!" Ferdie seated himself on the room's one chair and crossed his legs. "And I'm going to sit here and see that he doesn't."

Alec stared from one to the other in open-mouthed disbelief. "Is this some sort of joke?" What maggot's gotten into *your* brain, Ferdie?"

"I've just had an enlightening visit from my man Smoot. You can see him, by the way, if you look out of the window, making a hasty retreat down the road to Wirksworth, bag and baggage. But the important thing is that he has just revealed to me some details of an intersting bit of skulduggery in which he was involved. I suppose he hoped that, by confessing to me before *you* reported it, he might save his post, the dolt. I hope you weren't taken in by his stupid lies."

"If you thought they were lies, you wouldn't be here," Alec said bluntly.

"Of course they're lies. The only reason I'm here is because I was afraid *you* might believe them, knowing about your . . . your . . ."

"Ob-session," Kellam put in with a knowing nod of his head.

"Yes, obsession. Thank you, Kellam."

"No, permit *me* to thank him," Alec said witheringly. "Permit me to thank you *both*. It fills a man with pride to know that those nearest and dearest to him have such high regard for his judgment."

"My regard for your judgment, old fellow, is second to none in most matters. But on the subject of your wife—"

Alec's temper snapped. "I am *sick and tired* of being told how to regard my wife!" he bellowed, jumping to his feet and threateningly waving the one boot he hadn't yet put on. "What makes you—or even *you*, Kellam—so damned expert on—?"

Again a hammering at the door interrupted him. Alec's eyes sought the sky in disgusted and desperate appeal. "What *now*?" he asked of the heavens.

It was Gar. He put his head in the door somewhat diffidently, but when he saw all the others inside, he let himself in and closed the door. "*Thought* there was something brewing when I couldn't find anyone downstairs but Clio and Ariadne. May I join you? If something's the matter, Alec, you might want the advice of someone a little less . . . er . . . *dissolute* than Sellars, there."

Ferdie snorted, and Alec groaned and sat down on the cot again. "There's nothing I *need* advice about, Gar, so you may as well take yourself off . . . and take these . . . these *meddling fishwives* with you, too!"

"No, Alec, let the fellow stay," Ferdie said magnanimously. "Sit down, Garvin, old man, if you don't mind sharing the cot with our mutual friend. Give us the benefit of your very *un*dissolute opinion. Alec, you see, is about to seek out the notorious Sir Blake Edmonds for the purpose, if that riding crop is any indication, of giving him a memorable horsewhipping."

"But, why?" Gar asked, looking at each one in the room with a rather suspicious frown and seating himself gingerly on the cot.

"Because Alec has convinced himself that the fellow is playing fast and loose with his wife," Ferdie explained briefly.

"With *Priss*?" Gar rose in outrage. "I never *heard* anything so damnably scurrilous! Alec would *never* give credence to a story like that, would you, Alec?"

Alec, having put on his other boot, got up from the cot. With his eyes blazing, he looked deliberately at each one of the three other men in the room. "So . . . *these* are the three best friends I have in the world!" he said, a muscle in his tight jaw working angrily. "And all of you quick to impugn my judgment on a matter closer to me than any other and on which I've spent more than six years of anguished consideration. *Each* of you—on the basis of an acquaintance with my wife of so brief a time that you should have hesitated to recommend her as a *governess* if that had been asked of you!—has seen fit to put your judgment above mine. What do you really *know* of the matter, *any* of you? Do you have any awareness of the way in which the intimacy of marriage makes a man vulnerable? Do you have any idea of what it means to think of oneself as a *cuckold*? Yes, Ferdie, you may well wince. In life, you know, the word is far more humiliating than it is in a Covent Garden farce. I don't much relish the label, I can assure you, nor do I relish having to avenge my 'honor' by dealing with Edmonds. But you, my friends, have made it easier for me now. I see I am not the *only* cuckold! I can't blame Gar too much for permitting my wife to pull the wool over *his* eyes—he's so preoccupied with books, he's had even less experience with women than *I* had when I married. But *you*, Ferdie! You're past thirty, and the whole *world* is aware of the extent of your expertise! And *you*, Kellam, with your dozens of straw-hats—certainly *you* should have known better. Yet my sweet, good little wife has cozened all of you." He gave a sneering laugh, picked up his riding crop and strode to the door, unimpeded by the others who were staring at him aghast. "We're all cuckolds, *all four of us*. You ought to be thankful that it's only *I* who must wear the label!"

He knew just where he had to go. Priss had not denied it, and Smoot had confirmed it. The assignations had been held at Three Oaks. He could not believe that they had met *inside* the house, for he doubted that Lady Vickers would have sanctioned her daughter's transgression. Lady Vickers had been as easily duped by her daughter as all the others, he was certain of that. So Priss and Edmonds could not hold their meetings at the house. Somewhere in one of the numerous outbuildings . . . or even the stables, he surmised. Those were the sorts of places suitable for such . . . activities.

He decided against taking his horse. So short a distance—he could walk over in less than ten minutes, especially if he took the short cut through the woods . . .

He came out of the wood into the clearing behind the main house at Three Oaks and strode across the field. Since the death of her husband, Lady Vickers had not been able to afford to keep up all the grounds around the house, and this field was one that had been returned to nature's own care. The grasses, now brown and dry, were as tall as his waist, and, waving in the November wind, they took on a motion like that of the swells of the ocean. As he made his way through, he felt a bit as if he were swimming through a choppy sea. He ignored the sharpness of the wind, but when it ruffled his hair he realized that he'd forgotten his hat. Well, he wouldn't need it. There were no rules of dress nor special etiquette required for a horsewhipping, as far as he knew.

Suddenly his pulse began to throb in his temples. There, across the field, he saw a man leaving the stable. The fellow's coat was not blue—it looked quite black from this distance—but the identity of the man was unmistakable. He'd been foolish to expect to see a blue coat anyway—a Corinthian of Edmonds' stripe would never wear the same coat twice in one week!

He quickened his pace and caught up with Edmonds just as he was about to turn the corner of the main house and make his way round to the front. "Damn you, Edmonds," he muttered, grasping the fellow's coat collar roughly, "I have you *now!*" And he pulled the man around and raised his whip.

"Captain *T-Tyrrell!* *What*—?" the man stammered in surprise.

Alec staggered backward, completely confounded. "*Hornbeck*!" he gasped.

It was indeed Mr. Hornbeck who stood before him. The older man was looking at Alec with an expression of puzzled embarrassment while he rubbed at his bruised neck with one hand and clutched a small but artful bouquet of flowers to his breast with the other. "I didn't expect . . . I didn't realize ye'd have so strong an objection, Captain," he mumbled awkwardly.

"Objection?" Alec echoed, feeling as if he'd stumbled into some sort of incoherent dream.

"To the weddin'. That *is* what's troublin' you, isn't it?"

"No . . . I don't know what you're *talking* about. I'm sorry I handled you so . . . unkindly, sir. I thought you were someone else."

Hornbeck blinked. "Then ye *didn't* know about the weddin'?" He made a grimace of self-disgust. "Dash it all! I've given it away!"

Alec's eyebrows drew together in his attempt to make sense of a most confusing state of affairs. "You haven't given *anything* away, sir. I can't make head or tail of this. Are you here to attend a *wedding*?"

"Well," Hornbeck grinned sheepishly, "ye might say that."

"But are you sure you've come to the right place. This is Three Oaks, you know."

"Oh, yes, I've come to the right place," Hornbeck assured him with a chuckle. "Been comin' here every afternoon fer almost three weeks. Been lodgin' at Wirksworth and comin' out here each day. I ought to know my way by now."

Alec's head was swimming. "Every afternoon for *three weeks*? Do you mean *you've* been coming to see Priss?"

"Well, she's been here, of course . . . as a chaperon, ye might say. But it's Lady Vickers I've been visi—"

"Isaiah?" came a voice from round the corner. "Is that you?" Priss came running into view with an eager smile, but she stopped short at the sight of Alec. "Good heavens!'' she exclaimed, her smile fading. ''What are *you* doing here? Who *told* you?''

''Nobody has told me *anything*!'' Alec muttered, putting a hand to his bemused head. ''I only know that Mr. Hornbeck says he's to be a guest at a *wedding*—''

''Not a guest, my boy. The *groom*!'' Hornbeck chuckled. ''I hope it won't upset ye too much—I'm goin' to be yer *father-in-law*!''

While Alec gaped and looked from one to the other speechlessly, Priss took Mr. Hornbeck's arm. ''There won't *be* any wedding if we don't hurry, Isaiah. The vicar has been waiting this past hour! What's kept you?''

''Well, first, I didn't like the nosegay they made up fer me, and I had 'em do it over. Then I'd ridden more than half way here before I realized I'd forgotten the special license. And *then* I was accosted by yer wild husband, here, who looked for all the world as if he was goin' to *horsewhip* me. Gave me quite a turn, I can tell ye.''

Priss shook her head. ''I'm not sure I understand what's going on, Alec, but now that you're here, you may as well come in for the ceremony. Mama will enjoy having you, I think.''

Alec's head was whirling. ''Your mother is marrying Mr. *Hornbeck*? *Today*? But why didn't she *tell* us?''

''I told her she was being silly, but she insisted on keeping it secret until the knot was tied. She wished to avoid any comments on . . . on . . .''

''On the impropriety of weddin' a fellow in trade,'' Mr. Hornbeck finished cheerfully. ''I don't blame her fer it. I've told her time and again that she's stoopin' too low.''

''Nonsense, Isaiah. I've never *seen* Mama so happy. But come along, both of you, or the vicar will have an attack of apoplexy.''

Alec stood beside his wife in the sunny drawing room of Three Oaks and listened to the vicar read the marriage vows. But his mind was wrestling with far different matters. He had to reconstruct his entire view of his wife. He glanced surreptitiously at the face of the girl beside him. The dappled November sunlight lit her hair and face as she watched in rapt joy the proceedings before her. There was nothing devious in Priss's clear eyes, nothing sly in the curve of her smiling mouth. His friends had been completely right . . . and he was the very worst kind of a fool! There had been no assignations, no liaisons. She had spent her afternoons *chaperoning Hornbeck's courtship of her mother*, that was all! If Blake Edmonds was dallying with a local temptress, she was *not* his wife. The truth was as blindingly clear and as brightly warming as the sunlight on her hair.

As if she felt his eyes on her, Priss turned her head and looked up at him. Whatever she saw in his eyes made her catch her breath and blush. She quickly looked away, but after a moment, he felt her fingers touch his hand. He grasped them tightly and held on for the duration of the ceremony.

After the words were said and the license signed, Mr. Hornbeck kissed his lady with touching affection. Priss, with the help of the butler, passed out the glasses of sherry to the wedding party of five and to the half-dozen servants who stood in the room beaming. Then the entire group went out to the front steps where Mr. Hornbeck's shiny new carriage had been brought and now stood waiting. While Mrs. Hornbeck's bags were loaded aboard (the wedding trip was to start with a fortnight at Bath, to be followed by a trip to Birmingham so that Mrs. Hornbeck might inspect the source of her new riches—her husband's rapidly expanding cotton mill), Alec took the opportunity to shake his father-in-law's hand and offer him the most sincere good wishes. Priss, in the meantime, gave her mother a tearfully joyful embrace. "You *will* be happy, I know!" she whispered.

Her mother held her off and looked at her keenly. "And *so*, my dear," she said with a wide smile, "will *you*."

Chapter Twenty-one

Alec suggested that they walk back to Braeburn along the road rather than through the woods. He had so much to say to her that he wanted to take the long way round. For a while they walked silently along. The only sounds were the soughing of the wind in the trees and the rustle and crunch of the fallen leaves that covered the road. "Priss, I . . . I've been unforgivably wrong, and I don't know how to apologize," he said at last. "I thought—"

"I know what you thought," she said, keeping her eyes on the leaves she was kicking up with each step.

"I was the greatest fool. Everybody tried to tell me so—your mother, Gar, Kellam . . . even Ferdie. I've been so *stupid*!"

"Yes, you have."

"I suppose I've been wrong as well about . . . about all those things I said to you in London . . . about *everything*!"

She looked up at him levelly. "I had not seen nor spoken to Blake Edmonds from that day you left six years ago until Saturday's ball," she said.

He stopped walking and stared at her for a moment, his brow furrowed in an agony of indecision. Abruptly, he grasped her arms and made her face him. "Priss, it's all such a muddle! If only you'd told me at *first* that you loved Edmonds . . . I would have tried to understand. We could have worked things out somehow . . ."

"Hang it, Alec," she cried in disgust, flinging his hands from her arms, "don't you ever *listen*? I've been trying for six years to make you understand! I did *not* love Blake when I married you. I had a girlish infatuation for him long before. It lasted three weeks. *Three weeks*! My only mistake was that I didn't have the courage to tell him *then and there* that I no longer cared for him. I don't care whether your obsessed brain will permit you to believe me or not, but in either case, I don't *ever* want to hear *another word* about Blake Edmonds! Do you hear me, Alec? Not ever again!" And she turned and walked rapidly down the road away from him.

"Priss, *wait*!" He sped down the road after her, but the leaves clung to the bottoms of his boots, and he'd not gone a dozen steps before his feet slipped from under him, and he crashed down on the ground.

Priss heard the fall and flew to his side. "Alec!" she cried in alarm, kneeling down beside him.

He sat up and grinned diffidently up at her. "I'm all right. You needn't look so stricken." The familiar words stirred both their memories. He reached up and pulled her down beside him on the bed of leaves. "Oh, God, Priss," he whispered, bending over her, "I *do* love you so!"

They were quite dizzy when at last they got up again to make their way home. The sun was setting, and the wind had grown chill, but they walked unheeding through the darkening shadows. "I don't deserve that you should be so forgiving," he said quietly, putting an arm about her waist.

"That's true," she said with happy complacency. "But you were obsessed. It's like an illness, you know. You couldn't help it. Fortunately, you still possess a loving and faithful wife to make you well again." She giggled as she slipped her arm around him. "I never would have believed, yesterday, that I could feel again as young and happy as I did the day before you went away. It's almost as if none of the last six years had even happened."

"But they did happen." He sighed, a long, drawn-out expulsion of breath. "Do you remember the other night, when I found you crying on the terrace? You said it was for the summer that was gone. Well, I've made us lose six years . . . the . . . the summer of our marriage."

But she was too full of joy to be daunted. "I wasn't really crying for the summer, you know. It was for *you*." She bent down and scooped up a handful of brightly colored leaves and tossed them whirling into the wind above them. As they floated down like festive confetti, she turned a glowing face to him. "See what I've discovered, my love? The other seasons have their beauty too."

During the remaining two days of the Earl's house party, everyone was singularly hilarious. It was obvious to all that Priss and Alec were the happiest of mortals; Ariadne and Ferdie announced their intention of becoming betrothed by Christmas time; Clio and Gar were discovered kissing in the library—all of these occurrences occasioned unrestrained mirth. But the highest point of merriment occurred when Gar found a recipe for "Humble Pie" in an old book (it was, he discovered, a true edible, being made of the "umbles" or entrails of deer), Kellam coaxed the cook to make one, and Ferdie, Gar and Kellam trapped Alec in his dressing room and made him eat every morsel of the evil-tasting concoction, to the accompaniment of their very rude and raucous laughter.

About a week after they all had gone, Priss awoke one morning in the huge gilt bed of the "love nest" and looked over at her sleeping spouse. He was snoring ever so slightly, and his lips were curved in a small smile as if over a private but very enjoyable dream. She let her fingers drift over the lines of his cheek, the scar under his eye and the bridge of his nose. But since her touch failed to rouse him from his dream, she sighed and slipped out of bed. She put on a loose morning robe and went downstairs.

The Earl was already at the breakfast table, just finishing a second cup of tea. "Sit down, my dear, sit down," he urged. "Shall I butter a biscuit for you?"

"No, thank you, Grandfather. I'll wait for Alec. You are in fine looks this morning, my dear. Evidently the illness which troubled you before we came has not recurred."

"What illness?" the Earl said, sipping his tea innocently.

"The illness you wrote about when you invited us for the house party," she said, looking at him curiously.

He chuckled. "Oh, that. Nothing but a slight attack of gout, that's all."

"Gout? Why you . . . you made it sound so . . . so ominous. As if you'd had a heart seizure or something equally frightening."

"Did I?"

She looked at him suspiciously. "You *know* you did!"

"Well, if I hadn't," he said, pushing himself out of his seat with the help of his cane, but moving quite vigorously to the door, "you two would never have come here to play that little charade of yours. And you might still be crying yourself to sleep in Hanover Square and Alec might be entangling himself with your little minx of a cousin."

"Grandfather!" Priss gasped. "You *knew*!"

"Of course I knew," he said as he made a hasty escape from her flashing eyes. "Know just as much about people as I do about decorating bedrooms," he chortled as he retreated down the hall, "and you can lay odds on *that*!"

While this exchange was taking place in the breakfast room, a caller was being ushered into the study. He had arrived in Derbyshire the night before but had put up at lodgings in Wirksworth so that he wouldn't disturb the family so late at night. However, feeling that he had to deal with the business that had brought him as soon as possible, he'd risen at dawn and hired a conveyance to take him to Braeburn. The butler installed him in the study and gave Kellam the unpleasant task of waking his lordship.

Kellam tapped at Alec's door several times before he received a sleepy "Come in." He entered briskly and drew back the drapes. Alec blinked at the light. "Have I overslept? Where's Priss?"

"Waitin' fer you at breakfast. But ye'd best see Mr. Newkirk first, I think."

"*Newkirk*? Is *he* here? Whatever for?"

"Queers me. But 'e looks mighty worried, wringin' 'is 'ands an' pacin' about. Lost yer fortune on the 'change, more 'n likely."

Alec laughed and tumbled out of bed. "Well, that wouldn't be so bad, would it? All we'd have to do is sign up again. It wouldn't be a tragedy to take the King's shilling again, would it?"

Kellam looked at him disgustedly as he helped him into an ostentatious green satin robe with enormous frogs that Priss had bestowed on him after a recent shopping spree. "An' what would we do with the Missus, might I ask? Ye can't expect *'er* to follow the drum."

"Well, then, I suppose we can always sell the family silver. But before we despair, let's see what Newkirk wants, shall we?"

The solicitor was indeed in a state. Alec found him chewing his underlip as he paced about the study nervously. "We hardly know how to tell you, my lord," Newkirk said despairingly after the greeting had been exchanged. "It's the most unexpected and disturbing news."

"Well, don't take on so, Mr. Newkirk. Whatever it is, I'm certain we shall manage to survive it. Please sit down."

"Very well, my lord," the solicitor said, perching on the edge of a wing chair and opening his black case, "but we wish you to understand that we did our very best. We presented what we truly considered our *strongest* arguments, but all to no avail."

"Yes, I'm sure you did. But what arguments? What is it you're babbling about, Newkirk?"

Mr. Newkirk looked at Alec in considerable surprise. "We're speaking of the decree of nullity, of course, my lord. What else?"

Alec paled. He'd completely forgotten! "Good lord!" he croaked. "You're not trying to tell me that I'm—"

"Yes, my lord, that's *just* what we're trying to tell you. The petition has been rejected." He removed a thick sheaf of papers from his case as if to substantiate his statement.

"*Rejected*?"

Newkirk held up a trembling hand. "Now, let us not lose our heads. It will not do to fall into a rage, my lord. The grounds we presented were simply not sufficiently strong for the courts to grant it. It was the matter of coercion. We couldn't prove coercion, you see. We had hoped that this case might mark a giant step forward in divorce legislation . . . forge new *grounds*, if you'll forgive a little pun. At the very least, a new precedent. But it was not to be."

"Let me make sure I understand you properly," Alec said firmly. "I want no possible misunderstanding in this matter. You say I am *still married*?"

The lawyer threw him a fearful look. "We're afraid, my lord, that that is the case. You are still married."

"Just as if none of this . . . er . . . legal business had ever been executed? Just as married as the day I first came to you six years ago?"

Mr. Newkirk shivered in the expectation of a monumental explosion of wrath. Tightening himself into a tense knot and wincing so that every muscle of his face clenched, he nodded. "Yes, my lord. Exactly so."

Instead of an explosion, the door opened. "Alec, love, what's keeping you? The biscuits will be quite cold and the—Oh! Mr. *Newkirk*!"

Newkirk jumped out of his chair. "L-Lady Braeburn! I didn't know you were . . ."

"And I didn't know you were here either," she

laughed. "Please excuse me. I'll let you get on with your business."

Alec got out of his chair and brazenly pulled her into his arms. "Never mind business. You haven't yet kissed me this morning." And with a wink at Newkirk over her shoulder, he proceeded to kiss her with unmistakable fervor.

Newkirk's eyes widened until they almost popped from his head. His mouth dropped open in a disbelieving "O", but soon spread into a beatific smile.

"Alec, are you *mad*?" his wife hissed in embarrassment as she struggled to free herself. "What will Mr. Newkirk *think* of us!"

"I suspect, my love, that he will not mind. Will you, Mr. Newkirk?"

"Oh, no! I assure you, my lady, that I . . . we . . . don't mind *at all*!"

She nevertheless extricated herself from Alec's embrace and glared at him, blushing most becomingly all the while. "I'm certain, Mr. Newkirk, that you would not have come all this way unless you had some important business to discuss. Therefore, I'll leave you to complete it. But I shall expect both of you to join me in the breakfast room when you are finished."

"But, my dear, we'll join you right now," Alec said, putting an arm around her and leading her to the door.

"But . . . what about your business?" she asked, looking from her husband to the solicitor in bewilderment.

Mr. Newkirk and Alec exchanged grins. "Well, it seems, my lady," Mr. Newkirk said with a chuckle, ripping his papers in half and tossing them into the wastebasket, "that we have no business to discuss after all."